The Weldons of Tibradden

By
ANNIE M.P. SMITHSON

THE MERCIER PRESS
CORK

THE MERCIER PRESS, Cork.

First Published by The Talbot Press
This edition © The Mercier Press 1988
British Library Cataloguing in Publication Data
Smithson, Annie M.P. 1873 - 1948
  The Weldons of Tibradden
  I. Title
  823'.912[F]

  ISBN 978 1 78117 924 6

TO THREE MEMORIES —
That of an honest man; an old house;
and the boy cousin who taught me to
fish in the streams at Tibradden
many a year ago —
I DEDICATE THIS STORY

Transferred to Digital Print-on-Demand in 2024

Contents

I	Clodagh Cottage: 1870	7
II	Father and Son	16
III	George Harvey gets a Surprise	27
IV	Hubert L'Estrange	36
V	Kathleen	47
VI	A Christmas Gift	57
VII	The Passing Years	66
VIII	Clodagh: 1916	72
IX	The Other Ursula	82
X	Three Girls in a Flat	91
XI	The Shadow over Clodagh	101
XII	Love — or Friendship?	110
XIII	At the River House	119
XIV	The Passing of a Dream	127
XV	'Our Lady of Dublin — Pray for Us'	135
XVI	The Soul of Ursula	143
XVII	Desolation	151
XVIII	In City Pent	160
XIX	The Auction at Clodagh	168
XX	Exit	175
XXI	Clodagh: 1935	180

'The moving finger writes, and, having writ,
Moves on, nor all your piety nor wit
Shall lure it back to cancel half a line,
Nor all your tears wash out a word of it.'

— OMAR KHAYYAM

CHAPTER I

CLODAGH COTTAGE: 1870

Clodagh Cottage—built during the close of the eighteenth century—stood at the foot of Tibradden mountain, beyond Whitechurch, in the county of Dublin. A one-storeyed house, but of fair size, containing seven rooms besides a large kitchen with pantry, scullery, and other outdoor offices.

Behind the house was a fruit and vegetable garden in which flowers could also be found—as, indeed, they could be found all over the place. There were flower-beds in front of the house and around it; they seemed to grow everywhere. Old-fashioned and fragrant, they filled the air with their perfumed sweetness.

The gable end of the house was to the road, where a high wall ran the length of the garden. At the rear were the stables, and from a field beyond, could be heard the cackle of poultry, and the soft lowing of the Kerry cow, as she grazed there peacefully and happily.

But both the cow and hens had gone to bed and all was quiet at Clodagh Cottage on a certain June evening in the year of Our Lord, 1870. It was nearly nine o'clock and growing dark, but the two people pacing back and forth in the garden were too absorbed in each other to mind what hour it was. And after all, was it not but natural? They had only arrived back from their honeymoon that afternoon and this was their first night at home.

'So you like Clodagh, my dearest?' asked John Weldon. He was a man in the forties, with side whiskers which made him look fully ten years older than a modern man of the same age. Rather pompous and self-opinionated, there was a shade of condescension in his tender tones. Not that John Weldon meant to be condescending in the slightest. His attitude was simply typical of the 'superior male' of the Victorian days.

The girl—she was no more—looked up at him with shining eyes.

'Oh, it is a lovely spot, John! I shall be so happy here.'

'God grant it, my love,' was the reply, as John Weldon stooped to kiss his wife.

He was a successful business man, and up to his marriage had lived in the city, over his place of business, as was then quite customary. A few months ago he had purchased Clodagh Cottage from the widow of its late owner, thinking what a charming setting it would make for his pretty young bride. At that very moment he was thinking how lovely she looked. And this was true—a fairer sight than Faith Weldon it would have been hard to find.

But John Weldon—honest man—would have been more than a little surprised if he could have read the mind of the girl at his side. Faith Stone had been the daughter of a poor country doctor, and when she had met Mr Weldon while on a visit to some Dublin cousins, she had determined that he would marry her. She was quite penniless and there was no prospect before her except the rôle of either nursery governess or companion to some old lady, and Faith Stone was resolute that no drudgery of that sort should be her fate. Young as she was, she realised the misery endured by so many penniless spinsters in such positions.

But John Weldon thought his wife the most innocent girl in the world—so shy, so modest. Her blushes and confusion when he asked her to marry him were proof of that. At least, so he thought. They were married after an engagement which was very short for those days, and she was to rule him for the next twenty years, until the day of his death. Rule him absolutely, but yet so unobtrusively, that he was never to know that he had been ruled at all.

Meanwhile as Mr and Mrs Weldon strolled in the garden, they were being discussed in the kitchen. The domestic staff consisted of the cook, Mary Molloy, and the housemaid, Ellen Maguire. There was a gardener, Pat Doyle, who had his nephew Joe, a boy of sixteen, to help him. They had been the servants of Mrs Owens, from whom John Weldon had purchased Clodagh Cottage. As she was going to America and Mr Weldon wanted servants for his new home, and they had been well recommended by their former mistress, he had engaged them to remain on in his employment. He also bought most of the furniture belonging to Mrs Owens, and with some new purchases, he had made the house very comfortable.

'Well, what do you think of her? Isn't she lovely?'

It was Ellen Maguire who asked the question. She was a fresh-faced girl of twenty, while the cook was stout and middle-aged. Pat Doyle was also present, having dropped in for a chat before going home to his cottage where he lived with his old mother and his orphan nephew.

Mary pursed her lips. 'Well—that's as it may be,' she replied. 'Handsome is as handsome does, is my motto.'

'All the same, she's a sweet little cratur and no mistake,' remarked Pat, who was always prone to fall for feminine charms, in spite of the fact that he had escaped matrimony and was now nearing fifty. 'I expect she won't trouble you much Mary. She's not like them wans that do be nosing round the kitchen, asking how much meat was cooked for dinner and counting the vegetables and such like.'

'Well, that's true,' agreed the cook. 'I expect she will be easy enough to manage that way. But the master is a different kettle of fish. Not that he's close-fisted or the like, but I wouldn't like to cross him in any way.'

'I'd be afeared of me life of him—so I would!' declared Ellen. 'But the mistress—sure she's only a bit of a girl. Not as old as meself, I heard tell.'

'Well, it's to be hoped she has more sense, for it's not much you have, Ellen Maguire,' replied Mary. 'But as you say, Pat, I expect I'll have things me own way as regards the housekeeping. Not that Mrs Owens interfered much—at least not since the trouble kem on her.'

She had lowered her voice instinctively at the last words.

'God help her!' said Ellen, and Pat Doyle murmured an 'Amen!' Then he added: 'I suppose, Mary, that it was to him she went? They say that it was to Ameriky he was bound?'

The cook nodded. 'Yes, it was,' she said, 'but she would leave no address where to send a letter. She said she would write to me when she got there safe.'

'Well, may God protect her!' said Ellen. 'It's the dear lady she was, and as to the young master——'

'Hold your tongue!' cried Mary, sharply. ''Tis the foolish girl you are, Ellen, to be mentioning any names. All is over now, but all the same, let ye keep a silent tongue in your head.'

'Aye—that's right,' agreed Pat, 'for I hear tell that Mr Weldon is very strict the other way round.'

'That's true,' said Ellen. 'I heard me brother sayin' that Mr Weldon is terrible hard entirely agin the boys—rebels, he calls them.'

'Well, we needn't be mindin' them things,' said the cook. 'We have a good place here and the wages are not bad, so let us be mindin' ourselves. And, as I was sayin' before, 'tis little trouble the new mistress will be givin' us. Sure what is she but a bit of a girl?'

But Mary Molloy was to receive one of the biggest surprises of her life on the following morning.

John Weldon had greatly enjoyed his substantial breakfast taken in the company of his pretty wife. It was a beautiful morning, the sun shining on the silver and china of the breakfast table, the roses tapping at the old-fashioned diamond-shaped windows.

John felt almost sorry for himself at having to spend the day in the dusty city, and he said as much to Faith. She smiled charmingly as she replied: 'Never mind, John, dear, the evening will soon come and you will be home again.'

'Will you miss me?'

'You know that I will. But I will be busy, too.'

'Why, what have you to do, except sit in the garden or go for a walk? But I suppose you are not quite unpacked yet?'

'No—not quite. Besides, I must see about the housekeeping—'

'Oh, don't bother your pretty little head about that sort of thing! I understood from Mrs Owens that the cook—what's this her name is? Oh, yes, Mary Molloy—was quite capable. She will take all the worry off your shoulders in that respect.'

His wife smiled pleasantly, but shook her head. .

'That would never do, dear,' she replied; 'now that I am your wife and the mistress of your house, I must perform my duties conscientiously.'

Mr Weldon laughed as he kissed her goodbye—she made him think of a little girl playing at keeping house. But his carriage was at the door and he could see that the coachman and horses were both getting impatient. From that day, every morning, at eight-thirty to the minute, John Weldon was driven to his house of business in Capel Street, and every evening at six precisely, he would leave there for home. Dan Brophy, the coachman, was a queer character, taciturn and silent. Mr Weldon had known him for years as the coachman of a business friend who had died recently and had been happy to employ him as a coachman at Clodagh Cottage. Besides looking after the fine pair of carriage horses and being ready to drive his master in and out to the city, Brophy was to attend to the pony and trap in which he was to drive his young mistress whenever she wished, provided, of course, that she was back in time for Brophy to start for the city to bring Mr Weldon home from business.

Now, on this first morning, Faith Weldon stood on the steps, waving to her husband as he drove away. He thought what a lovely girl she was, little more than a child. How careful he would be to see that her life would be smooth and easy and that she would not need to worry about anything. How astonished the honest man would have felt had he been present at Mrs Weldon's interview with the cook a short while after his departure.

She had entered the kitchen to find Mary and Ellen talking to Pat Doyle who was standing at the back door. They did not notice her entrance, and Mary was just saying: 'Yes—that will do for today. Potatoes and peas—I am having duck for dinner this evening.'

She turned quickly as she saw Pat gazing over her shoulder. 'Good morning, ma'am,' she said, 'I did not hear you come in. Would you be wanting to speak to me?'

'Yes, cook, I do. But first, did I hear you saying that you had ordered duck for dinner?'

'Yes, ma'am. Do you not care for it?'

'As it is ordered it will do all right,' was the quiet reply, 'but for the future, cook, please understand that I will order the dinners. And now I will see the pantry and go through the stores with you.'

The following hour was not a pleasant one for Mary Molloy. Every detail of the household management was investigated by the new mistress, who, far from being the ignorant, easy-going girl imagined by Mary, proved herself to be a capable and shrewd housekeeper. Not for nothing had Faith Stone been born, the eldest girl of a family of seven, where every penny had counted.

'I will have keys made for this larger pantry,' she announced to a silent Mary, 'and it can then be used as a store room. I will arrange the meals with you each morning and order what is required. I will now see the gardener.'

She went through the back door on her way to the garden, leaving an astonished and far from happy woman behind. Ellen had long since vanished to the upper regions, feeling, as she afterwards said, 'as if you could knock me down with a feather!' Pat also had faded towards his own regions, and there Mrs Weldon now discovered him digging industriously.

She went over through the garden and glass-houses, noting the vegetables and fruit with a keen eye. It was a fine garden, everything in abundance, ordinary vegetables flourishing in the open, and under glass were tomatoes, cucumbers, and grapes.

'And what is done with the surplus after the house is supplied?'

'Is it the surplus, ma'am?'

'Yes—all that is left after the house has been supplied. There must be quite a lot. Has it been customary to sell it?'

'Well, Mrs Owens did sell some of it but of course she was not a rich lady. But since Mr Weldon bought the place nothing has been settled, and——'

'Oh, well—I shall arrange about it,' was the brisk reply; 'I know that the Dublin shops will be only too glad to take all we can send them. I will let you know later what arrangements I have made.'

'Very good, ma'am.'

But Pat thought it very bad. He had had rosy visions of making a little bit himself that way from the garden now that the master would be away all day at business and the mistress of Clodagh Cottage only a bit of a girl. He stood now, staring after her, as she daintily stepped down the paths, small head held high, tiny feet peeping from beneath her wide full skirts. 'Well—if that doesn't beat Banagher!' he said softly to himself, and returned to his work a sadder and wiser man.

The awakening for the servants had been a rude one and quite unexpected. However, after a short time they became used to the new routine. Mrs Weldon, if a strict mistress, was a just one, and her household management was excellent. No older woman could have made a better mistress. Never a penny or a crust went to waste; the garden and the poultry paid well; the meals were well cooked and served; the whole household arrangements went on oiled wheels. Very soon Mr Weldon, who had at first been rather amused to think of his young wife in the rôle of housekeeper, had to admire her administrative powers. These were really good, and had Faith Weldon lived in the present day, it is probable that she would never have married, but have carved out a fine career for herself. As a hospital matron, inspector of factories, head of any big business concern—even as a cabinet minister—Faith would have made her mark. But she lived in an age when women did none of these things. Even the hospital matrons in those days were very different from what they are today. In the 'seventies, a penniless girl married or went out to earn her living as a nursery governess or companion. And Faith, as we have seen, would have no life of that sort. So she married John Weldon, more than twenty years older than herself, and settled down to do her duty in that state of life to which she believed God had called her.

And her husband never repented the fact that he had married a penniless girl, young enough to be his daughter. He never realised that she was the real ruler of Clodagh Cottage, and of everyone within its walls, so well and tactfully did she manage him.

To a modern woman, the life that Faith led would have seemed monotonous and dull, but she did not find it so. When she was an old woman she would often look back at those early years of her married life, and they seemed like a vision of happiness and peace.

They were early risers at Clodagh, as Mr Weldon had to leave for the city at half-past eight, and he liked a good breakfast and time in which to eat and enjoy it. It pleased him that at this first meal of the day his wife was always there to pour out his tea and see that the bacon and eggs were to his liking. She would wave him good-bye each morning as he stepped into his carriage, and stand to watch while he drove through the gate and out to the road beyond, turning steeply to the right on the way to the city. A long drive for the horses twice daily—by Whitechurch, Rathfarnham, Terenure, Harold's Cross, Clanbrassil Street and across the river to Capel Street. But they were fine horses, well fed and cared, and on Sundays they had a complete rest. John Weldon would allow neither man nor beast to work on that day. Only the minimum of housework was done, and winter and summer there was a cold midday meal, after which the maids were allowed out until ten o'clock. Pat Doyle was free for the day and never came to the Cottage on Sundays, while the same could be said of Dan Brophy. Dan lived over the stables in what Ellen called a 'gazebo' of his own, and it was his custom to leave Clodagh early on Sunday morning and not return until night. He did not even return for his meals, which on weekdays he always took with the other servants. He was a silent, secretive man, and although it was presumed that he had friends with whom he spent the day, who they were, or where they lived, the others did not know.

Faith liked Sunday. On that day she would walk to church with her husband, leaning upon his arm, her Sunday bonnet framing a face which she well knew to be one of the fairest in the congregation. It was a long walk, and on very wet or stormy days, Faith did not go. But her husband enjoyed the walk; he got little exercise through the week, and regarded his attendance at church as good for both soul and body. After the midday meal, husband and wife would spend the afternoon together; in the garden in summer, by the fire in winter.

On the Monday morning, the weekly round began again. As soon as Faith had seen her husband off to the city, she would go along the short passage leading to the kitchen, her little household basket on her arm, the keys of the store room jangling as she stepped briskly through the kitchen door, her full skirts billowing around her slight figure and accentuating the tiny waist. She wore a diminutive piece of lace on her soft hair, called by courtesy a cap, and then the fashion amongst married women, no matter how young they might be. Faith knew that in her case it was a most becoming fashion.

Mary was interviewed, meals ordered, and the work for the day arranged. And it was work in those days. No labour-saving devices were then in fashion, they were as yet unknown. The servants worked hard and for wages which no maid today would accept, yet they stayed for years in one situation and seem to have been much more contented than the modern type.

When she had finished indoors, Faith went to the garden. The young mistress of Clodagh loved her garden, and it was surely a thing of fragrant beauty, a delight to the eyes, and to Faith one of the greatest pleasures in life. By now, she and Pat were quite friendly, understanding each other perfectly. He knew that he had to work for his wages as he had never worked before, and also had to account for all the produce of the garden. Faith sold what fruit and vegetables she did not need to the Dublin shops, and made a good profit. From this she allowed Pat a small percentage with which he was quite satisfied. She also told her husband about her own profits, but he only laughed and told her to keep it for pocket money. John Weldon had really no idea of the money which his thrifty wife was able to make from the garden. Not that he would have cared; he was generous to a fault where she was concerned, although in business matters shrewd and keen, able to make a better bargain than most men. He was as honest as the day, God-fearing and just according to his lights, and they were those of the majority of his class and creed in that day. Intensely loyal to England, hating the name of rebel and papist, he was yet kind and just to those of his workers who were Catholics. He was of the opinion that they were brought up in ignorance and knew no better. But if one of his employees had been known to be 'disloyal' he would have been dismissed at a moment's notice.

Faith took no interest in politics or any national question. Like most women of that time, she was content to leave such matters to the other sex. Queer old Victorian days! Not far off, as we count time, but in regard to the status of women, they might be centuries away. Yet how strange, too, to think how many women ruled their husbands and their households then as few women can do today. Women may have greater freedom now, but with that freedom it seems as if much of their real power has vanished.

Faith Weldon was quite content with her quiet life. She was a perfect housewife, and young though she was, ruled her house justly and well. It never entered her head that she was wasting her talents, or that she was fitted for a wider sphere of activity. She was intensely grateful to her husband; if he had not married her, it was probable that she would now be getting a miserable livelihood by acting as nursery governess or companion to some horrid old lady. She might have married some other man—or she might not. In any case few would have been so kind to her, or have given her such a delightful home.

She had been married a little over a year when her son was born, and a year later came a daughter. These were the only children born to John Weldon and Faith, his wife.

Mr Weldon was delighted and very proud to be a father. His son was not a week old before he was planning out his future as partner in the business. Already he could see the magic words— 'John Weldon and Son', over his business in Capel Street. But as the children grew older, although still proud of his son the greater love of the father went to his little daughter, Ursula. And she loved him with a love that she could never give to her colder and more reserved mother.

So the years rolled on, until twenty had passed since that June evening in 1870, when Faith Weldon had first come as mistress to Clodagh Cottage at the foot of Tibradden.

CHAPTER II

FATHER AND SON

'Then your mind is made up? You are quite sure that you do not wish to enter the business?'

'Well—as I have told you, sir, it is my earnest desire to read for the bar. But, naturally, it rests with you.'

'I would never force you to enter the business against your own wishes,' was the reply; 'but I need not tell you, William, that your decision is a great—very great—disappointment to me.'

'I know that, father, and I am sorry—more sorry than I can say. But I simply feel that I would be no good at business, I am not suited for it. Perhaps if you had not sent me to college—'

'Yes, I was wrong when I sent you to Trinity. A business man does not need a university education. Still I did it for the best, and your mother thought—. However, we will not discuss the matter further. I have decided to allow you to remain at college and continue your studies for the bar.'

'Thank you, sir—oh, thank you! I am ever so grateful, and I will try to do well, indeed I will.'

His father cut him short. 'Yes—yes, I am sure you will. But leave me now—I am busy.'

William Weldon left the room without saying any more. He knew well that this had been a bitter blow to his father, but for some time now he had felt that he could not enter the business.

He hated the very thought of it. Wholesale manufacturers of soap and candles! No, he could never have stuck it. Besides, he would be wasted at business—he felt convinced of that. He knew that he had a certain gift for oratory, as shown in some of the debates at college, and he had always had a great wish for the legal profession. Many a time he had seen himself arrayed in wig and gown, with the letters 'Q.C.' after his name, making a brilliant speech during the hearing of some celebrated trial! Soap and candles, indeed!

Yet only for his mother's advice, it is unlikely that he would ever have taken his courage in both hands and spoken to his father about the matter. And when he had done so, he did not know that Faith had already prepared her husband for the interview, although he had been surprised that his father had taken the matter so quietly. But it was the quietness of a broken spirit, of hopes withered by a blow that was as unexpected as terrible.

Left alone, John Weldon stood motionless, staring out of the window with eyes that saw nothing of the beauty without. And it was a lovely scene upon which his unseeing glance fell. The garden at Clodagh, always beautiful, was in its summer glory now, and beyond were green fields and in the near distance the blue of the Dublin hills. The heather was beginning to bloom on Tibradden, showing amongst the gorse and bracken on the slopes above Clodagh.

But John Weldon saw none of these things. He saw only the ruin of all of his hopes and ambitions, falling, falling, like a house of cards, at his feet. Only his wife knew how he had planned for the future, what high hopes he had for the business when the name over the doorway would have the words 'And Son', added to it. He had never dreamt that the boy would wish for anything else in life save only a partnership in the firm, which had been founded by his father and built up by him to become the good business it was today. Mr Weldon had been so proud of his work, so sure that his son would carry on the business and make it even bigger and better. And now all his plans were gone—blown away, like straws in the wind. He smiled grimly as he found himself repeating—'The best laid schemes of mice and men—' Yes, so it had been with him.

If only Ursula had been a boy she would surely have fallen in with his wishes, done as he desired. And yet, would she? In some ways she was more self-willed than her brother, more determined to get her own way. Her mother did not like it, and often asked him to exert his authority with the girl, but he could never speak harshly to his young daughter—she was the very apple of his eye. Besides, girls were different nowadays from what they were when Faith was one herself. The modern young lady was getting quite a problem. Thinking of his daughter and her independent attitude which so shocked her mother, John Weldon smiled in spite of his trouble.

He was now a man of sixty-five, and although to the lay eye he looked strong and healthy, his colour was too high, and his doctor had lately warned him against too much work and too little rest and amusement.

'I should advise a long holiday,' he had said. 'Go away with your charming wife and leave the business for a while. Travel where you like, the more changes of scene the better, but take life easy, plenty of rest, and occupy your mind with something else besides business. I promise that you will come back a different man.'

'Later on, doctor, later on! You must wait until my son is able to look after the business for me—he will soon be coming in as my partner and it won't be long until he masters it all. A clever boy, my son, although I say it myself. At present I cannot leave.'

Yet he knew that if real necessity arose, he had in his head clerk a man who knew as much about the business as he did himself. But he was determined not to go away until William was ready to take over from him. And after all, he did not feel really ill. A trifle giddy at times, short of breath, not able for the hills now. Yes, he would be glad of the holiday when he could take it. Just he and Faith together—delightful! He had been looking forward to it for quite a while now, and then this blow had fallen, and he suddenly felt like an old, old man. He groped for a chair and sat down, trying to pull himself together. It was thus that Faith found him a little later.

'Why, John!' she exclaimed. 'Are you not well?'

She knelt beside him and he put out his hand and laid it on her head. There was no little cap there now, her hair was piled high in the prevailing fashion. There was not a grey hair in it; her figure, too was as slight as if she had still been a girl, and any stranger seeing these two together would have taken them for father and daughter instead of husband and wife. After all Faith was only thirty-nine, and nowadays would have been considered a young woman.

'I am all right, my dear—all right.'

But the reply was so weary, so hopeless, that she knew at once how much John was feeling the decision of his son not to enter the business.

Kneeling, she leant her head against him.

'Do not take it too much to heart, John,' she said 'These things have to be—they cannot be helped. After all, if Willie has a real wish for the legal profession and does well at the Bar—will you not be proud of him?'

'Not as proud as if he had been my partner and we had been

John Weldon and Son. Oh, Faith, my dear,' he suddenly cried, 'it is a bitter grief to me—bitter! The business which I built up myself, which I have been extending, and for which I have worked so hard—for the sake of my son. You know the struggle I had when I was young.'

'Yes—I know, dear, but tell me again—it will ease you to talk a little.'

'Ah, well—it's an old tale now! I was left at the age of fourteen with a mother and two sisters to provide for. My father had been an architect with a good connection, I believe he was quite well off. My mother, however, was not fit for any business matters whatever. She always made me think of a little china doll, so fragile and pretty was she. My father was not strong, and had appointed in his will his great friend, one Charles Dart, to be sole executor for his widow and family. He trusted this man absolutely, and impressed upon my mother to do so also when he himself should be no longer by her side. It seemed as if my father had a premonition of his early death, for this took place a few months after his will was made. Dart was a rogue, he made my poor mother sign any papers he wished, and before she knew what she had done, she had made over to him all the house property left her by my father, and she herself was penniless. The only thing he did not take from her was the house in which we were living— that remained so that we were rent free. As for Dart, he left the country and we have never heard a word about him to this day. By now no doubt he is dead and buried.'

He paused, and his wife prompted gently, 'Yes, dear?'

She wished him to talk about his early days—anything which might take his mind off William for the moment.

'Well, there I was—a boy of fourteen, and I had to put my shoulder to the wheel. I had to get work of some sort. I had never cared for study or books, as you know, but I was willing to do any kind of honest work. I went to several of my father's friends asking if they could employ me. Some refused unkindly, others were decent enough but had no work to give me. But at last I went to Mr Halliday—you have often heard me speak of my dear friend, Charles Halliday. He it was who got me employment with a business man whom he knew. And I did well—got on step by step, until I was able to start on my own soon after I was twenty-five. Perhaps I became rather hard and self-opinionated, I know that I have been

thought so by many people, but it is difficult to make your way in
the world and not become hardened. My poor mother died when
I was still young and my sisters married and went to England. I
had a lonely life until I met you, my dear, but you have made me
very happy. Maybe too happy, and that is why God has sent me
this trial.'

'Try and not grieve too much, John. After all, how much worse
it might have been. Suppose we had lost our son.'

'You are right, Faith, as usual,' he replied, 'and you comfort
me now as you have always done. God bless you, my dear wife.'

'And you too, dear. Now, do not let this thing embitter your
life. Think how often you have won through. Remember Mr
Carleton!'

They both laughed. The name recalled an incident in the past
which had taken place soon after John Weldon had set up his
establishment at Clodagh. Driving home from the city one evening,
he had been hailed by a gentleman, who, walking in the same
direction, put up his hand to stop the carriage. Dan drew up and
the gentleman came to the carriage window, with hand-out-
stretched, while he exclaimed effusively:

'Mr Weldon, I believe? I have only just heard that you have
taken Clodagh Cottage and will be a near neighbour of ours. I am
delighted to welcome you among us.'

John Weldon had stared back in stony silence, apparently not
seeing the extended hand. He was seeing, instead, a vision of
himself as a boy of fourteen, standing in front of this man in his
office, and asking for work— 'any kind of work, sir, just to give
me a start!' He remembered the angry, rude refusal, ending with
the words. 'Get out now, quickly—or I will have you put out!'
That was many years ago and circumstances were different. The
man standing in the road was an old man now, and it was reported
in the city that things were not going well with him. No doubt he
thought that the wealthy Mr Weldon—now his near neighbour—
might be of use to him. But John Weldon was not one to forget.

'Mr Carleton,' he said, in icy tones, 'when I wanted your help
you did not give it. I do not want your acquaintance now. Drive
on, Dan!'

He had told Faith about it when he got home, and although
she had told him that he had not acted like a Christian, still in
her heart she did not blame him. Mr Carleton was dead now

these many years, and Faith hardly knew what had made her remember the incident of the past.

'Here is Ursula,' she said, as quick footsteps were heard in the hall, 'take a turn in the garden with her, dear—it will do you good.'

Ursula Weldon was just eighteen, tall and slight, with dark hair and grey eyes. She resembled her father's people, not being in the least like her mother. William was fair-haired and had his mother's blue eyes, of which Faith was very proud. He was her favourite, she and Ursula having little in common and often getting on one another's nerves. Seeing them together, one would not have thought that they were mother and daughter; Ursula so tall and dark, graceful, rather dreamy-looking, of a definite Celtic type; while Faith, short, fair, and practical in every way, was a direct contrast. John Weldon loved his daughter very deeply, and the love was returned.

'Father,' she said now, 'you don't look well. Is anything the matter?'

Faith answered quickly: 'No—of course not. Your father is tired and would like a stroll in the garden.'

'Come along then, father—it's a lovely evening.'

Walking arm in arm along the garden paths, father and daughter talked together in low tones. They were always in perfect harmony, except on those occasions when Ursula was inclined to criticise her mother, and this her father would not allow. He could not understand how it was that those two did not agree better.

'Are you really all right, father?' the girl asked. 'You look as if something has upset you.'

He could not withhold his confidence from her.

'Did you know about William?' he asked.

'What about him? Do you mean that he wants to be a barrister?'

'Then he has told you?'

'Of course. He is always talking about it and the great name he will make at the Bar! He hates business—always did.'

Mr Weldon sighed.

'Strange that a son of mine should be like that,' he said.

'Oh, but Willie is not a bit like you, father—he is quite different. I wish I were a boy!'

'But, my darling—why? *I* much prefer you as a girl.'

'But there are so many things a boy can do that a girl cannot.'

'For instance?'

'Oh, a boy could be a doctor or a barrister, or I could have entered the business instead of Willie.'

Her father sighed again. 'Ah, yes—that is true. I should have liked that. But you see, my dear, you *are* a girl, so it is no use talking about it.'

'Do you know, father, I was talking yesterday to Enid Brown. She is just back from England, and she says that there are women doctors there, and that plenty of girls are going in for typing and shorthand so that they can take positions in business houses or offices. What do you think of that, father? And would you let me try to fit myself for office work?'

John Weldon laughed, the first real laugh Ursula had heard from him that evening.

'I never heard such nonsense!' he exclaimed. 'Women doctors are disgusting to even think about; and as for business, my dear little girl, women have no head for business—and never will.'

'But, father, think of the great women in the past. Queens and rulers. And then our own Queen Victoria—you know how much you think of her. She must have a business head, as you call it, and the other women rulers, too.'

'Not at all—not at all! Their ministers guide them and advise them what to do. Those who really rule the state are men—and always have been men.'

'But I don't think Queen Elizabeth would have allowed any man to dictate to her?'

'You may be sure she took advice when she needed it, although I admit she was a remarkable woman. But now, Ursula, my dear, do not get any of these absurd notions into *your* head. New women and all that kind of thing. Why'—and he laughed again with real amusement—'I believe that they are actually asking for *votes for women!*'

'That's all right, father. I don't care one way or another about such things—I just talk to shock mother sometimes. I know I should not do it, but it's only for fun.' Then, rather timidly, she said: 'I do wish you could have a change and a real holiday, father. It would do you so much good, and you know that Dr Merville has recommended it for you.'

'I know—I know. But I cannot take a holiday just yet. Perhaps later on. I am not ill, Ursula, only sometimes a little giddy—'

Even as he was speaking John Weldon reeled slightly, and Ursula steadied him with her strong young arm.

'There—you see, father—you do need a rest. Are you all right now?'

'Yes—yes—all right, my dear. But I am rather tired and we will go indoors now.'

It was later that same evening that a scene took place between Mr Weldon and his son which upset the elder man very much, and was never forgotten by any member of the household.

John Weldon had been alluding in a jocular manner to part of the conversation which he had had with his daughter in the garden and her remarks about the women rulers, and Queen Victoria in particular.

'I told her, however,' he said, 'that our good Queen is guided in all important matters by her ministers—she does not trust to her own feminine judgement in affairs of state.'

'*Good* Queen, did you say, sir?' asked William.

His father stared at him.

'Of course! I was speaking of her Majesty—our present Queen.'

'I know that, father, but I cannot see how anyone in this country can call her "good".'

'What do you mean?'

Faith flung a warning glance at her son of which he took no heed. It seemed as if some perverse spirit had entered into the boy that evening, which was all the more strange, considering that his father had been remarkably kind to him that very day, saying little of the terrible disappointment and sorrow which he had suffered through him.

'Well, she may mean to be good in her own way,' replied William, 'and for England, her reign *has* been good. But for Ireland, quite the reverse, I should say.'

'And how, sir?' John Weldon thundered.

'The population of this country has fallen to one-half of what it was when Victoria ascended to the English throne; the people died in thousands from a "famine" so-called, when ships were leaving our ports loaded with wheat grown on Irish soil; the landlords were mostly absentees, and their agents rackrented the unfortunate tenants who could not call their soul their own—'

'Hold your tongue! How dare you speak in this manner! Where

did you imbibe such disloyal sentiments?'

   'At Trinity, sir. There are quite a number of fellows there who think as I do in these matters.'

'Think as you do! Brainless boys who know no better. Yet, I never thought to hear a son of mine give vent to such opinions.' His hand shook as he raised a glass of wine to his lips. He had been warned by his doctor to take little alcohol, and it was seldom now that he drank wine or spirits. His wife watched him anxiously as he stood by the sideboard, noting that the dull flush which had appeared on face and neck was disappearing, giving place to a deathly pallor. How she wished that Willie had kept silent. What on earth had possessed him?

She rose now from her seat and went towards her husband.

'You are over-tired, John,' she said, in the quiet tones which never failed to influence him. 'Come to your room and rest for a little while.'

She slipped her arm through his, and he followed her without a word. Ursula, watching him, thought that he seemed like one who was dazed. She turned furiously upon her brother.

'What do you mean annoying father like that?' she exclaimed. 'Don't you know he is not well? You upset him before today when he knew that you would not enter the business, and now you must go and vex him again by talking a lot of rebel nonsense—'

He interrupted her angrily, 'It's not nonsense—let me tell you that! I only wish I had lived in the time of the Fenian Rising and I would have been out with the boys in the hills around here. Do you not know that Terence Owens, the son of that Mrs Owens who lived here before us, was one of them? He was at Trinity, too, and he and some of the other students joined up and took to the hills here.'

'And much good they did!'

'They did their best, but the weather was against them and they were nearly frozen in a terrible snowstorm. Here, in this very house, several of them were hidden for days. Mary could tell you all about it—she was here then with Mrs Owens. Terence escaped arrest and got away to America, and his mother followed him when father bought the place. It is also said the Robert Emmet was hidden here for some days on his way to Wicklow.'

'Why on earth you admire those silly rebels, I do not know! I am surprised at you, Willie. And then to upset father the way you did. Why, no rebel is worth that!'

'That is what you think, Ursula, but it's not my opinion—nor the opinion of many others in the country.'

'Oh, don't be bothering me! You ought to be ashamed of yourself! Anyway, I'm tired and going to bed.'

It was in the small hours of the morning that the sound of hurrying feet was heard through the house. Mary Molloy—an old woman now, but still at Clodagh—knocked loudly at William's door. Stupid with sleep he opened it.

'Ye are to go at once to the master's room—he's took mortal bad!'

'My mother—the doctor—'

'The mistress is with him, and Dan is goin' for the doctor. Let ye hurry now, Master Willie—like a good boy!'

Poor Mary was speaking as if he were a little boy again, and as she turned away, he saw the tears running down her cheeks. At the same moment he heard the carriage thundering down the road on its way to Rathfarnham.

Hastily pulling on some clothes, William Weldon went along the corridor to his father's room. His mother was kneeling by the bed, holding her husband's hand, while Ursula, standing at the foot, was crying bitterly. She threw a glance at her brother as he entered the room, a glance which said as plainly as words could have done—'This is your doing'.

His father was quite unconscious. He just lay there, motionless, breathing heavily, staring in front of him with open eyes that could see nothing. That stertorous breathing was the only sound within the room, but from without there came the sleepy twitterings of birds awaking in the garden.

Dr Merville was not long in coming, but one glance at his patient was enough.

'I fear he will not regain consciousness before the end,' he said. 'I have been afraid of this happening for some time past. Only a few days ago I warned him against any excitement or undue worry. May I ask if he has been more worried than usual—if there has been any cause to account for this sudden seizure?'

Faith lifted her eyes for a moment from her husband's face.

'He was rather worried about a certain matter today,' she replied, 'but I do not think that it can have been the cause of this illness.'

She looked at her son as she spoke as if to assure him of her forgiveness. But there was another there who would not forgive him.

'It was the cause of his illness—and you know it was, mother! Dr Merville, my brother behaved very rudely to father tonight, and before that—earlier in the evening—he had annoyed him terribly by telling him that he would not enter the business—' She stopped as her mother rose to her feet and came towards her.

'Ursula, you will either keep silent or leave the room.'

Faith had spoken in her usual quiet, unemotional tones, but the effect on her daughter was instantaneous. She turned away and stood looking out of the window, watching the dawn as it crept over the countryside.

But before the morning had fully come, John Weldon had left this world, and his soul had gone forth to meet the Great Judge of us all.

CHAPTER III

GEORGE HARVEY GETS A SURPRISE

The newspapers of that day described the funeral of John Weldon in detail, stating that the attendance was 'representative of the commercial and professional world of Dublin'. And this was true. The funeral was a large one, for he whose body they were following to the grave had been held in universal respect by all who knew him.

As was customary, Faith and her daughter remained at home, while William, as chief mourner, shared his carriage with the Rector who was to conduct the service in the little chuchyard on the hillside.

Poor boy, he was unhappy and wretched. Since the hour of his father's death, he had been reproaching himself, wondering if his conduct could have been the cause of the sudden illness. He had not realised the state of his father's health; had he done so, he would have been more careful. He had not meant to distress his father, he would have done anything to save him pain, but like most young people, he was thoughtless. If only his father were alive again how differently he would behave towards him. How many of us feel like this when someone we love has gone from us.

His mother was William's only comfort at this time. She understood him, she knew that he had really loved his father and guessed how he was suffering now. As for Ursula, she had not spoken to him since their father's death.The girl was simply heartbroken, she felt as if she were now alone in the world, and her mother and she might have been strangers, so little had they in common. This was especially noticeable at a time of sorrow like the present.

William had to listen to the sympathetic remarks of friends and neighbours and return the respectful salutations of the poorer folk who stood on the road, outside the church gates. He kept a stiff upper lip before all these people, trying to act as a man, yet he could have cried like any girl . . .

It was soon over, his father was laid to rest in the quiet churchyard, where in summer and spring the flowers would grow over his grave, and in winter, there would fall a mantle of snow, and a little robin would sit and sing to all those quiet folk sleeping so soundly on the slope of the Dublin mountains.

Luncheon was prepared at Clodagh Cotttage for those intimate friends who had come a distance. No one stayed long, and when they had gone, the family assembled to hear the will read.

Mr Manton, the solicitor, was a dried up little man, brisk, businesslike. To him the reading of wills was part and parcel of his work. In some cases these wills would cause heartburning and jealousy amongst the bereaved families—even litigation at times. But he did not foresee any such result from this will.

Clearing his throat he began at once, and his task was soon finished. John Weldon's will was short and to the point. After a few bequests to the servants and some charities, he left the business to his son, William; a thousand pounds to Ursula, and the residue of his personal property to his wife, together with Clodagh Cottage and furniture. He appointed her as guardian and trustee to his son and daughter. William was to take charge of the business when he became of age, and until then he advised that the chief control should be in the hands of 'my valued confidential clerk, George Harvey, whom I trust absolutely, and who, I feel sure, will serve my family as faithfully as he has served me.' Harvey was not forgotten, being left a legacy of one hundred pounds.

The will had been drawn up a few years before his death, when John Weldon had thought that his son would be sure to succeed him in the business. There was a certain clause in connection with the legacy to Ursula, and this was to the effect that if she married before she was of age, without her mother's consent, she was to only receive five hundred. John Weldon expressed the hope that his daughter would allow herself to be guided by her mother 'in this, the most important event in a woman's life.'

Ursula, sitting there dry-eyed and miserable, hardly understood the meaning of what the lawyer was reading, and did not care. Her grief was too terrible, too devastating, and she was incapable of taking an interest in anything else.

Mr Manton had a private conversation with the widow before he left. On asking her what arrangements she would make with George Harvey, she stated that she would see him in a few days. He had been unwell and not able to attend the funeral—to his deep regret—but had written to say that he would be back at business on the following Monday—this was Thursday. He offered to come and see her at Clodagh, but she told Mr Manton that she preferred to call at the place of business in Capel Street herself.

'And if I can help you in any way, my dear Mrs Weldon—'

'Thank you, Mr Manton, you have been most kind. If I should require any legal advice at any time, I shall be sure to let you know.'

'A cold woman,' thought the lawyer, as he left Clodagh, 'very reserved. Self-centred, too, I should say. I would not care to be her husband.'

Yet in that estimate of the widow's character, he was wrong. Faith Weldon had been a good wife, and her husband, like the one in the Book of Proverbs, would have said that her price was above gold and precious stones. She had been attached to her husband, he had taken her from poverty, given her a lovely home, surrounded her with comfort, and she never forgot all this, and in return had done her best to repay him. But she always got her own way, while never allowing John Weldon to suspect that she was the real ruler of their lives—and not he.

Faith was one of those women who are almost sexless in character. True, she never met any man who awakened her love: had she done so, she might have been a different woman. As things were, she had little patience with either lovers or their lasses. She was wont to describe all that kind of thing as 'rubbish'. She believed that a girl should endeavour to make a good match for herself, and in return, should be a good wife—as she had been herself. It was due to her advice that the clause relating to Ursula's marriage had been inserted in her husband's will. Indeed, Faith had wished that the clause should relate to the girl's marriage, whatever her age, but there she found her husband unexpectedly determined. He said that a girl over twenty-one should be able to know her own mind, and he was sure that Ursula would, anyway! So Faith had perforce to give way on that matter.

Now that John had left her she felt very strange. Not that she feared she would not be able to manage alone; she had always had plenty of self-confidence, and was not afraid of the future and her ability to do what was best. As for William and Ursula, she regarded them as little more than children. She sorrowed for her husband, if not with any very deep feelings, yet sincerely, and for some time after his death missed him greatly. She had been perfectly happy all those years of her quiet married life. The one flaw in that perfect happiness had been her daughter. Ursula had always been a thorn in her side. Why this was so, she could not have said, but the fact remained.

William was quite different; mother and son were devoted to each other, and she shared all his confidence. It was really through her influence that John Weldon had consented to allow the boy to remain at college and continue his studies. She knew that William was now anxious, fearing that his father's death might alter his prospects, that he might be compelled to take his place in the business.

On the night of the funeral, mother and son had a long talk together, and although at first the boy had been amazed and rather dismayed by this conversation, before it was finished he was perfectly satisfied, and much relieved. He was content to leave everything in his mother's hands; her quiet common-sense, her serenity of manner even at this time, were as balm to his troubled spirit. She soothed him, too, with the assurance that he must not blame himself for the stroke which had caused his father's death; such a thing might have happened at any moment for some time past now. 'Indeed, it was bound to come, sooner or later. So do not let it worry you my son. You have your studies now to think about, you will have to work hard when the vacation is over. I want to be proud of you yet!'

'I will do my best, mother—you have been so good to me.'

Neither of them spoke of Ursula, sobbing her heart out on her bed in her little room at the end of the passage. They probably never even thought about her.

On the following Monday morning, work was commencing in the place of business of the late John Weldon, Capel Street. It was an old-fashioned shop with house attached, and at the rear a large yard. In the shop, retail business was carried on, in the offices above—once the private dwelling-house—the wholesale business was transacted. There were four shop assistants and a staff of clerks for office work.

As a rule, especially on Mondays, the whole place hummed with activity as each took up his job. This morning, however, there was an air of expectation, a good amount of gossip—a sort of 'take it easy' feeling all round.

In the shop the four assistants were grouped behind the counter discussing the future of the business, wondering if any changes would follow the death of Mr Weldon. They were all sincerely sorry that he had died, for if he had been a strict employer, John Weldon had been a just one. All the staff had been to the funeral and were now talking of William, and saying amongst themselves that as he was only a boy still, it was likely that 'old Harvey' would carry on, and so little change would follow in the working of the establishment.

Peter Mead, a dapper youth with a collar that looked as if it must surely choke him, and a straggly moustache in the fashion of that day, was airing his views to his fellows.

'I declare if old Harvey isn't two minutes late,' he said. 'What can have happened to him? Unless he is worse, I know he will be in today. He hates being off work for an hour. By Jove! I wish I were in his shoes, and I would take more than a few days off in the year! But I bet he won't do it—even now when I suppose he will be more or less his own boss.'

'Oh, sure he is such a dry old stick he will only be worrying on the double now—so conscientious, you know.' This from Jimmy Halligan, the youngest there.

'I suppose the young fellow will be taking over when he comes of age,' remarked Joe Martin. 'I hope he's as decent as the old man was.'

'Amen to that,' said Mead, adding: 'I hear the daughter is a fine, good-looking girl, and she must have a tidy bit, too. She will be a great match for some lucky fellow.'

'Maybe yourself would like to do the Dick Whittington stunt and marry the girl?' This from Jimmy, the wit of the staff. As Peter was a pimply youth, and far from prepossessing, this remark was greeted with loud laughter. But it ceased as suddenly as does a modern wireless when switched off. The silence was absolute as they turned to gaze at what almost seemed an apparition which had entered the shop unheard by any.

No apparition, as they soon realised, but all the same they were dismayed and astonished. Although Faith Weldon had seldom come to see her husband at his place of business, she was yet well known by sight to the young men. She stood there, a slight figure enveloped in her deep mourning—the cumbersome 'widow's weeds' of the period—and as she threw back her veil not one of the four but wished that the earth might open and swallow him. Her tones were of ice as she said: 'When you gentlemen have quite finished discussing the affairs of your late employer, perhaps you would be so good as to show me to Mr Harvey's office?'

'Yes, Mrs Weldon, certainly—he is not in yet, but we expect him any moment—'

It was Peter Mead who spoke, rushing forward to show the way.

But before he could take her to the office, Harvey entered the shop. He was amazed to see Faith.

'Mrs Weldon—so early! I did not expect you.'

'I suppose not, Mr Harvey. I trust that you are feeling better?'

'Oh, yes—much better! But come this way, please, Mrs Weldon—this way.'

He led the way to his office. It was next to the one which had been Mr Weldon's.

'Sit down, Mrs Weldon, if you will, please. I do not need to tell you how much I feel for you in this great trouble. Such a loss. And to us also, if I may say so. To me, indeed, he was more than my employer—a dear friend. You will not mind my speaking like this, I hope?'

'No, indeed I will not. I know how much my dear husband thought of you—how he trusted you.'

She was taking stock of him, as it were, while she spoke. A little man, below average height, stooped and thin, and now, after his recent illness, looking pale and worn. Never very strong, he seemed much worse than Faith had ever seen him look before.

'I am afraid that you are not properly recovered yet, Mr Harvey,' she said.

'Oh—but I am really all right now, Mrs Weldon. It was just the shock of Mr Weldon's sudden death coming so soon after my illness. You will forgive me for alluding to it but—'

'I quite understand, Mr Harvey—do not distress yourself. But now, if you really feel able for it, I should like to see the books and go thoroughly into everything connected with the business. Will you feel equal to it today?'

He stared at her in bewilderment. What did she mean? Did she think that he was not to be trusted?

She was speaking again.

'You see, Mr Harvey, I wish to be able to take my husband's place in the business as soon as possible. I intend to come here each day just as he did, to keep the same hours. My son does not wish to enter the business, he is to read for the Bar. I discussed the matter fully with him last night. I felt that although he is not yet of age and I am appointed his guardian, still I should wish to let him know my intentions regarding the future of the business. I need hardly say that he quite approved of all my plans. I wish to say now, Mr Harvey, how much I appreciate your work in the past, and I sincerely hope that you will stay on, and be to me what you were to my dear husband—one who could be trusted in all things.'

George Harvey was almost incapable of speech for the moment. The surprise was great, so unexpected. That a woman should talk of taking over the business, taking the place of a man!

Presently he heard himself murmuring: 'But, of course, Mrs Weldon—of course. Surely you know that anything in my power— I did not think, however—in fact I never thought for an instant— that you would take an active interest in the business. It is not usual—if I may say so—for ladies to do so, even now, when I understand that they are considered very advanced in many ways.'

'I intend to take my husband's place in the business, Mr Harvey. If you agree to remain in my employment—as I hope you will—it must be solely on that understanding. My son, as I told you, does not intend to succeed his father, so therefore I wish to see to things myself.'

George Harvey bowed, stammered some words of assent, feeling as if he were in a dream. He had always known that his late employer's wife was a woman who liked to rule. But that she should want to enter the business—those premises hitherto sacred to masculine authority—that seemed to him—simple, old-fashioned man—almost beyond belief. However, there was no more to be said now. He must only wait and see how things went on. For the moment he must take his orders from her.

He was amazed at the evidence of her quick intellect when presently they went into the affairs of the business. The book-keeping was incomprehensible to her at first, but after a few lessons, she was able to understand the methods then in vogue. That she was determined to make herself complete mistress of the business was evident.

It had been Mr Weldon's custom to have a light lunch at one o'clock, which was supplied by a nearby restaurant. His widow now followed his example.

At six o'clock the carriage arrived to take her home, but before leaving her office — she had installed herself in the one used by

John Weldon—Faith asked George Harvey to request the staff to come and see her. When they were assembled—both from the office and shop—she informed them that from henceforth she would be in absolute control of the business. They would be in her employment exactly as they had been in that of her husband.

'And I feel sure that I can rely upon you serving me as well as you served my dear husband. The business will be conducted on the same lines, and Mr Harvey is remaining as my head clerk. If, however, there should be any among you who do not care to work under the control of a woman—then he can hand in his resignation immediately. But this, I hope, will not be the case. It is my wish that things should go on as well and as smoothly as they have done in the past. I do not think that there is one among you who had ever cause to complain during my husband's lifetime, and I can assure you, one and all, that you will receive the same treatment from his widow now, as you have done for many years under John Weldon himself.'

There was silence for a moment when Faith had finished speaking. News of the extraordinary position had filtered through the place, so that her words were not wholly unexpected. Still, just for an instant, they felt at a loss, hardly knew what to say. Then Roger Mildmay, the clerk second to Harvey, speaking for his fellow-clerks, said how gladly they would serve her, expressing their hope that she would be satisfied with them. Then came Peter Mead, perspiring with nervousness, as he spoke on behalf of his fellow shop assistants.

Mrs Weldon replied in cold but gracious tones, and they withdrew to discuss this queer matter amongst themselves before leaving work. Faith, after a few words to George Harvey, telling him that she would be in her office at nine o'clock on the following morning, went down to her carriage and was driven towards Clodagh. She cared little for the dismay which she had left behind her. It is impossible to say whether she was then able to visualise, even in a small way, those coming days when women would be taking their place in the business world as heads of large firms, and when it would be as usual for the daughters to have a career, to be able to earn their own living, as it was for the sons in her day.

Be that as it may, Faith Weldon was a proud woman as she drove home through the city streets, out to the suburbs, and so on to the scented lanes beyond Rathfarnham. She felt as if her real life work was but beginning. She would control the affairs of that business of which her husband had been so proud. And she knew that she was well able to take his place. For the future she would be, not a mistress, but a master of men.

CHAPTER IV

HUBERT L'ESTRANGE

Just across the road from the churchyard at Whitechurch was a coppice with a stream running through it, on the banks of which grew wild forget-me-nots. And on the banks of this stream, one lovely day in mid-June, stood Ursula Weldon.

Over two years have passed since the death of John Weldon, and his daughter is now nearly twenty-one. Two long, dreary years they had been for the girl. All day she was alone at Clodagh. Her mother was at her office in the city and William engaged with his studies or his own circle of friends. Neither of them seemed to be anxious for her society, each had their own particular interests, and if they thought at all about Ursula, they probably considered that she was very fortunate and should be perfectly happy at Clodagh. Yet there was literally nothing with which the girl could fill in the time which hung so heavily upon her hands. The Weldons had a circle of acquaintances scattered in the country houses of the neighbourhood, but there was no girl amongst these families of whom Ursula had made a real friend. She could visit them, driving in the pony trap; she could sew or do crewel work or a little amateur gardening, or help with the dusting and arrangement of the flowers for the house.

But Ursula hated sewing and dusting and paying calls to dull houses, and there was nothing for her to do in the garden where now two men were employed and a good yearly profit made by sale of the produce. So that time hung heavily indeed and a day seemed a year to this young girl of 'sweet and twenty', now gathering forget-me-nots by the stream.

She was going to lay them on her father's grave. Not that the grave was neglected or needed flowers of any sort, it was attended to by the gardeners at Clodagh. But Ursula liked to place her bunch of forget-me-nots there whenever she came that way. She wanted her father to know that he was not forgotten—that he never would be forgotten by his daughter. How she missed him!

Sitting now idly by the stream, she was thinking of him, wishing that he were alive once more. She would not be so lonely then. As it was, her mother almost ignored her: certainly she saw that she was decently fed and clothed, but otherwise took little notice of her. She never seemed to think that the girl might wish for a little amusement, a bit of gaiety now and then. There were garden parties from time to time in some of the houses nearby, but Ursula hated them—so stiff and formal. The College Races, of course—they were more fun, and she would have really enjoyed them but for the fact that William never bothered about her, never troubled to introduce her to his particular friends. It was Faith whom he looked after and introduced to everyone—he was so proud of his mother. And sure enough, Faith was always the centre of attraction—not the shy, rather dull-looking girl, who was her daughter.

These amusements were the sum total of Ursula's pastimes during the year—with, perhaps, a night at the theatre—and this was seldom, for Faith did not like taking the horses out at night when they had to be out again in the morning, and as the tram then did not go beyond Terenure, the walk to Clodagh at that hour was out of the question. Mrs Weldon had some queer idea that Saturday night was rather a 'common' one, so would not go on that day. Poor Ursula! If she could have looked into the future and seen the girls of today, cycling or driving cars, rushing off to business or other work each morning just like their men folk, earning their own living, mapping out careers for themselves— what would she have thought of them? Such a picture would have been a source of laughter for her and all her generation, just as we today smile when we turn over the leaves of the family album and see the photos of our grandmothers and grandaunts in the quaint costumes of the 'Naughty Nineties'.

Perhaps in London they might have been 'naughty' times, but a girl like Ursula, living her life, protected and secluded, had little chance to earn such a title. Yet a spice of so-called naughtiness might have been good for her.

As she crossed the road and entered the gates of the churchyard, she looked neither naughty nor happy. The life she had to lead was not a healthy one for a girl, and it had made her what we, in modern phrase, call introspective. Not that Ursula had ever heard the term, neither would she have understood its meaning. She only knew that she was unhappy. What she needed was some healthy work, some interest or hobby. She was suffering from the fashions of the time in which she lived. Idleness is good for neither man nor woman, and there is besides, an old but true adage which tells us that a certain person finds some mischief still for idle hands to do.

As she came out of the churchyard to the road again, she noticed a stranger standing on the footpath opposite, glancing through the hedge into the coppice. As he heard the gate open, he turned and saw Ursula. At the moment she made an enchanting picture standing there, tall and slim, in her pretty summer frock, a shady hat covering her dark hair. He stared at her, and she stared at him. There was some indefinite quality in the man which arrested her attention. He was quite young, probably in the early twenties, but looked older on account of the beard which he cultivated so proudly. His flowing necktie and wideawake hat would have proclaimed him the artist, even if he had not carried the usual impedimenta of his art with him.

He at once saw that the girl would make a delightful picture, as she stood there in the sunlight, by the church gate. Such pictures were extremely popular at that time, being in great demand for Christmas numbers, and so on. He wondered if he could make a sketch of this girl. Raising his wide hat with a flourish, he bowed with exaggerated courtesy which he had learned during a year in Paris.

'You will pardon me, I am sure, but is one permitted to enter this charming spot?' He pointed to an opening in the hedge.

'In there? Oh, of course! You can go through that opening. But there is a gate further up the road—that might be better as you have your easel to carry.'

He smiled with easy gallantry.

'You are most kind,' he murmured. 'I wonder would it be too much if I asked you to show me the gate?'

'Not at all—I am going home that way.'

It never occurred to Ursula that her mother might have objected, or, if it did occur to her, she did not worry. She thought that this young man was the handsomest person she had ever beheld. So nice—in fact, the nicest she had met in all her life. An artist, too. The romance of it! It was as if a thread of gold had suddenly become woven into the dull grey of her everyday existence.

So she walked by his side up the hilly road until they reached the little gate, and then, instead of thanking her and passing through the gate and out of her life, he stopped and held her in talk, enchanting her with his easy conversation and delightful manner. Held her as he was to hold her for many years to come, even after romance had fled and the gold threads had turned to grey.

And thus began the ill-starred love story of Ursula Weldon.

Before they parted it was agreed that she should meet him in the coppice on the following day. He had begged and obtained permission to make a sketch of her. His gratitude when she consented had touched her greatly. 'It is not often,' he said, 'that we poor artists are privileged to have a model such as you will make.'

She could only blush and stammer. She had received so few compliments that the flattery was as sweet as it was new. Unlike other girls, she knew few young men, and those she did know had been repelled by her gauche manner and her intense shyness, which they thought was sullenness. But this man was a different type.

During the days which followed—happy days for Ursula, a pleasant way of passing the time for her companion—he told her a little about himself, those things which he knew would appeal to her.

'I was left an orphan, without either father or mother,' he told her, as they sat one morning among the bracken on the hillside, 'and I was given to the care of an aunt, a cold, hard woman, who gave me no love, and with whom I passed a miserable childhood. When I had finished my education she wished me to enter business with her brother—a general shop in a moth-eaten Midland town! I refused of course. Imagine such an existence for one born with the soul of an artist. You can think what I suffered at the mere thought of it.'

'Oh, how dreadful!' said the girl. 'What a cruel woman your aunt must have been.'

'Yes, it was dreadful indeed. But I could not lead such a life. I stayed in the shop for a few weeks, and then one day I fled across the sea to Paris, where I starved in a garret—as so many of us have to do. You have heard of Montmartre and of the Latin Quarter?'

'Just a little. I had a book about it once, but mother took it from me before I had finished reading it. She said it was not a fit subject for a young girl. What is it really like—the life there? Not bad, I am sure, or you would not have lived amongst it.'

Hubert's lips twitched but Ursula did not notice this, and he replied, in serious tones: 'Oh, well, it is hard enough at times—and then gay, too, at times. One learns to take the rough with the smooth when living the Bohemian life. I earned enough to pay for my lessons by selling little sketches to the tourists who think that when in Paris they are bound to visit the "Quartier"—and they are a real godsend at times.' (He did not add that this money was supplemented by sums from his long-suffering aunt in response to begging letters.) 'But as soon as I felt I had a chance of earning my living here, I came back to Ireland.'

'And you are getting on?'

'So-so. I have a commission for some illustrations for the Christmas number of several magazines.'

'But this is summer!'

'Oh, we have to start in good time. What a heavenly day! It is indeed good to be alive!'

With this remark Ursula fully agreed. Not that the day or the place made much difference to her. She would have been happy under any conditions, in any place—if Hubert were only at her side.

But certainly the weather was charming. They would often go off for the whole day, Ursula taking sandwiches with them. She found herself practising her first deception, telling her first deliberate untruth—a terrible thing in her eyes, brought up with all the strictness of that age. But it seemed as if she were no longer Ursula Weldon, but some stranger—some girl who cared for nothing, did not mind what she did, scrupled at no deception, no lie, so long as she might spend those halcyon hours with Hubert L'Estrange.

Her deception could not go on forever; indeed, it was surprising that it had lasted for the three weeks which had passed since the girl's first meeting with L'Estrange. It is not to be expected that in a country place where Ursula was so well known her constant meetings with a stranger should pass unnoticed. She had told the cook that a school friend was staying in Rathfarnham, and that it was with this friend she went for walks and picnics. Mary Molloy was devoted to Ursula and felt pleased that this little bit of pleasure had come her way, so she packed up baskets with all kinds of nice things for the 'two young ladies'. But before long the poor woman was to get the shock of her life. A farmer saw the girl and man sitting on the slopes of Tibradden—saw them there day after day, as he went to drive home his sheep. He spoke of it to the gardener at Clodagh, who, in his turn, told the cook. At first she refused to believe him, nearly giving him a blow with the rolling pin for his pains.

'Ask Miss Ursula herself—can't ye? Or go up the hill and see them sitting together. It's no good blamin' me, Mary—I only thought it right to let you know. Sure what would the mistress say if she knew that ye were packin' up food for a strange man to eat with Miss Ursula?'

Thus spoke the gardener, and Mary Molloy felt cold all over at the words. The mistress. Yes, what would she say if she knew? 'I'll speak to Miss Ursula,' she said, 'and let ye keep a quiet tongue in your head in the meanwhile.'

So on the following morning when Ursula came to the cook and asked for a 'nice picnic basket', Mary Molloy drew the girl into the pantry, closing the door carefully, and there told her what Joe had said.

'Is it true, Miss Ursula? Is it a young gentleman that you are meetin' all the time—and me thinkin' it was Miss Mathers?'

For a moment the girl did not reply, but she quickly realised that it would be useless to try and keep up this deception any longer.

'Yes, Mary—it is a gentleman,' she said, adding: 'But you won't tell my mother? Promise that you will not—please, Mary!'

'Miss Ursula—sure you know I must tell her—'

'Ah—no, no, please Mary! I will give you anything—'

'Will you promise me faithfully not to see him again if I don't tell the mistress?'

How could she do that? To give him up. Never to see him again.

'Oh, Mary—I could not do that! I must see him. I would die if I did not!'

The cook stared at the girl aghast.

'Who is he?' she asked, 'and how did you come to know him?'

'Oh—we just met. Fate, I suppose. He is an artist and will be a great painter some day.'

Mary Molloy gave a sort of grunt. She had not much idea of artists or what they were like, but what little she did know was not too good. But Ursula was talking, her hand on the cook's fat arm.

'He has changed my whole life—I love him so! Oh, Mary, you won't tell mother? If you do, you know that I shall never see him again once she knows. She will send me to Aunt Dorothea—or bring her here.'

'May God forbid!' murmured Mary, fervently.

'There now—you see what you will bring upon yourself. Don't tell mother—dear Mary.'

But Mary Molloy was adamant. Even the vision of Miss Dorothea Rayner, a half-sister of John Weldon's father, a very old Quaker lady, with an inquisitive nose and sharp eyes, who was detested by all the household at Clodagh—even the thought of a prolonged visit from her, could not change Mary from her resolve to tell Mrs Weldon about her daughter's love affair.

'But Miss, darlint—sure you know I must tell her. She would be certain to find it out from someone else and then what would she do? Sure she'd kill me if I kept the like of that from her.'

'Then wait a few days longer—don't tell her at once—give me a little time longer.'

'I'll tell her this evening, Miss, when she comes home; and that's all about it. You needn't blame me for doing what is only right—I must do it Miss Ursula.'

And Ursula could not change her decision. She left the room feeling stunned. If she had thought for a moment, she might have known that this was bound to come, but her obsession had blinded her to all else—she never thought of the probable consequences.

She was to meet L'Estrange that morning in a quiet bit of woodland at the foot of Tibradden. In off the beaten track, one crossed a mountain rill and climbed some hillocks, through furze and bracken, and then came to a clearing under some thorn trees. This was a favourite spot with the lovers, there they felt remote from the prying eyes of the world. Yet, if they had but known it, the place was not so private as they had imagined, and many a time they had been seen wending their steps there. Country people have long eyesight and are always interested in their neighbours' affairs.

Hubert was there before her this morning; her footsteps had dragged, and as she came slowly towards him he saw at once that something had happened to upset her. He partly guessed what it was, as he went to meet her with an air of concern.

'My dearest—what is it? Are you not well?'

Sitting on the hillock beside a thorn bush, she told him, and as he listened, outwardly all solicitude and pity, in his own mind Hubert L'Estrange was calculating what was best to be done—for his own ends. From what Ursula had told him, and from what he had heard from his Rathfarnham friends, he knew that the Weldons must be well off. He knew, too, that she would come of age in a few months, and that she would then inherit the legacy left to her by her father. Ursula had not mentioned the fact that should she marry without her mother's consent before she was twenty-one, she would only receive five hundred pounds instead of one thousand. She had never thought about this. The value of money, the misery of poverty, trying to make ends meet, counting every penny—all this was unknown to her, for she had never experienced such an existence. She had not considered the difference between five hundred pounds and a thousand. And she would certainly never have dreamt, for one moment, that this could count with her lover. How surprised she would have been if she could have read his mind at that moment, and how different her life would have been. But Hubert was astute, and he was careful to say nothing which could give her any inkling of his secret thoughts. He held her hand and told her not to worry—all would come right. And all the while he was asking himself what he should do, how he should act so as to further his own ends, ensure his own comfort. The question was whether he should persuade her to run away with him now—an easy task, he felt sure—or wait until she was twenty-one before marrying her? It was fairly certain that her mother would at once stop all meetings between them; from what he had heard of Mrs Weldon, he guessed that she would be more than a match for any young man whom she might suspect of looking after her daughter's money. And Ursula was afraid of her mother, she would be easily dominated, and if she never saw him, never heard of him, new interests might develop, her mother might even marry her to one whom she considered suitable as a husband. It would be better, much better, to secure the girl at once. Her legacy could not be kept from her when she came of age. They would be married in the Registry Office in London, she could stay with his friends there until all was fixed up. Her mother would not be likely to trace her. But he must walk warily.

'My darling,' he said, when Ursula had finished her recital and was gazing at him, her eyes full of tears, 'what do you think your mother and brother will do when they hear about us?'

'Oh, as for Willie—he does not count! It is mother who matters, and she will certainly be perfectly furious. She will lock me in my room, and then send for Aunt Dorothea to be my keeper.'

'Who in the name of Heaven is Aunt Dorothea?'

'A very old aunt—grandaunt really. She is a very strict Quaker. Some of them are so gentle and nice, but she is terrible—we all dread her visits. She would think nothing of locking me up and giving me bread and water.'

'How terrible for you, my darling! I cannot bear to think of it. I am wondering—' He paused for effect and Ursula asked: 'You were wondering?'

'Whether you had the courage to brave them all—assert your own independence?'

'And how?'

'Will you come away with me? I am going to London—I have just got a commission for some sketches—and if only you would come with me we could be married over there. You could stay with friends until I had arranged everything. Oh, just think of it—think of our life together—no more parting—always together! Dear love—will you come with me?'

The girl could not speak. She sat stunned, silent. But it was with joy. So he really cared for her—this prince who had come from fairyland into her life. She—so plain and stupid. How could he really love her? It seemed too wonderful to be true.

She was silent so long that L'Estrange grew a little uneasy. Was the girl going to develop awkward scruples?

'Well—dear little girl? What do you say?'

'If—if you really love me—'

'I adore you! I swear that you will never regret it if you trust yourself to me now. You will come with me—be my wife?'

She nodded, joy held her dumb.

Hubert, once he had got her consent, went swiftly to the point. She was to meet him that evening at Kingstown, they would cross by the Mail that night. Mrs Weldon would not be home until nearly seven, Ursula was to tell Mary that she was going to see some friends at Whitechurch, she was to try and be natural and not let the woman suspect anything.

'Have you any money?' he asked.

'Very little—a few pounds.'

He hid his disappointment as he said, 'Well, bring it with you. You cannot bring your clothes, of course, but any bit of jewellery.'

'I have only this brooch and a bracelet. Mother does not approve of girls wearing jewellery.'

He cursed Mrs Weldon in his own mind as he said carelessly, 'That does not matter—when you are the wife of a great artist, you can wear what you like.'

He had noticed that she had brought no lunch, so he remarked presently: 'I think you should go home now, dearest, get your lunch, and then say that you are going to spend the afternoon with your friends. Be as natural as you can so that they will not suspect. I shall rely upon you. Keep up your heart—don't look so pale. I will meet you just outside the station at Kingstown. We will be away before your mother has time to be uneasy about you.'

'Oh, that will be all right,' said Ursula, 'she knows that when I go to the Masons I often stay a bit late.'

And when Faith Weldon returned home from business that evening, she had indeed not the slightest suspicion of anything being wrong. When her daughter did not appear at the evening meal, she asked casually where she was, and was told that Miss Ursula had gone to Stone Lodge. Faith nodded indifferently and partook of her meal in a leisurely fashion, her mind on the business, not thinking of her daughter at all.

It was only when she had finished and was thinking of taking a stroll in the garden this warm evening, that Mary knocked and asked if she might speak to her.

One glance at the woman's face told Faith that something had happened.

'Well—what is it?' she asked. 'What is wrong? You had better tell me at once.'

Mary told her in fear and trembling, but was surprised to see how quietly the mistress heard her story. Faith was annoyed, furious with Ursula. But after all, it was just what might be expected with such a girl. However, she would soon stop this nonsense, her meetings with this man would be finished and done with from now on.

'You are much to blame,' she told Mary Molloy, 'you should have looked after Miss Ursula better. You know what a child she is in many ways, rather silly, too. However, it cannot be helped—

what has happened I mean. But it will be stopped at once. I shall write tonight to Miss Dorothea Rayner and ask her to come here and take control of Miss Ursula for the future. And of course I shall speak very seriously to her myself. Where had she gone, did you say?'

'To Stone Lodge, ma'am—to spend the evening with Miss Mason.'

'Oh, well, that is all right. I expect she will soon be home and I will speak to her then. Miss Dorothea cannot arrive before the day after tomorrow, and until then Miss Ursula will keep to her room and you will look after her. You will ask her to come to me in the garden when she returns.'

'Yes, ma'am, I will. I am sure she will soon be back now.'

But Ursula did not return that night—nor the next day. And the days grew into weeks and months and years, but Ursula did not come back to her home at the foot of Tibradden.

CHAPTER V

KATHLEEN

Three years had passed since Ursula's disappearance, and on a warm evening in August, Faith Weldon and her son were sitting together by the open window of the dining-room at Clodagh. The evening meal was over and a rather tense silence had fallen between them. It was broken by Faith.

'If you have anything to tell me, I am ready to listen now,' she said.

William Weldon moved uneasily in his chair. He was just twenty-four, tall, handsome, and intellectual looking. Yet, there was a certain weakness in his character which betrayed itself at times, especially in his relationship towards his mother. He loved her deeply—but the love was tinged with more than a little fear. Faith had ruled him always, just as she had ruled his father, but whereas in the case of her husband the ruling had been done in such a way that John Weldon had never noticed it, her son was made to realise that his mother was the owner and ruler of Clodagh. Had William entered the business, been a man more like his father, things would probably have been different, but as it was, he had left the control of all business affairs to Faith, who had astonished him—and everyone else—by her wonderful business acumen. She paid all his university expenses, dressed him exceedingly well, kept him well supplied with pocket money. She acted, in fact, as a rather indulgent father might have done. On his part, William had done well at Trinity, where he was now in his last year. He had fine hopes for the future, his mother having promised him a decent allowance until the briefs should begin to come in. William had no doubts about his success in his chosen profession.

'Well, Willie—what is it? What do you want to say?'

She could not understand his continued silence, the nervous manner in which he was toying with his spoon. But she was not really anxious; he had never given her the least trouble during his time at university. Since the day of his father's fatal attack, following upon their discussion on national questions, William had never alluded to such matters. Faith took no interest in them herself and seldom spoke of them. She was very devoted to her son, as he was to her, and from the day of Ursula's flight, they had been all in all to each other. At least, until the last few months, when Faith had noticed a change in her son. In what exactly this consisted she could not have said, but there *was* a very definite change, she had realised for some little time now. Then, this evening, he had said that he would like to speak to her after supper.

Yet it was with no feeling of anxiety that she asked again, 'What is it you want to talk to me about?'

He cleared his throat nervously. 'I hope you will not be vexed.'

'Oh, what is it, Willie? How childish you are still! Have you been getting into debt? That is not like you. Still I suppose that all young men—'

'Oh, no, mother—nothing of that sort. The fact is—is—'

'Yes?'

Her voice was colder, and William knew that he had better make a clean breast of it, once and for all.

'Mother,' he said. 'I am in love. There is a girl—'

There was silence. Faith sat as if turned to stone. A girl with whom he was in love. So little had she ever thought of such a thing in connection with her son, that the blow came upon her all the more heavily now. Who was this girl? Why did he not tell her before this? Was it possible that he was going to become involved in some scandal—behave like his sister?

'Just what exactly do you mean?' she asked. 'You had better explain yourself.'

Now that the first plunge was taken, William found his tongue.

'I am in love with her—and she loves me. We want to get married. But you know, mother, that I have given you full control of the business. You have managed it for me—and managed it splendidly—and you understand it thoroughly. I should not dream of asking anyone else to look after it for me. I could not see to it myself.'

'Well?'

Not very encouraging—that 'Well?'

But he went on, determined now to say what was in his mind.

'I intend to go ahead with my profession and leave the business part to you. But now that I mean to get married, I shall want a larger allowance. You see that, don't you, mother? As I have said, I should never think of asking anyone else to look after the business—there is no one could see to it like yourself. But you understand about the money part, don't you, mother?'

'How very kind of you to speak like this! Really, William, I do not know how to thank you. After I have worked and striven, day after day, in order to keep together the business which your father built up for you—to keep it together and to enlarge it, as you know I have done—you are generous enough to say that you do not intend to put anyone else in my place. That is provided, of course, that I make the money for you and your prospective wife to spend as you like. What a kind son! You are, indeed, generous to a fault.'

'Mother—please do not take it like that! I never meant it like that—surely you know that? But don't you understand that when a man marries he must be able to keep his wife? And I have only asked for that. The business kept you and my father in comfort. It can surely do the same for us?'

'May I presume to ask the name of your future wife?'

A barely perceptible pause, then came the reply: 'Kathleen Dillon.'

'If one may judge from her name, the young lady is not of the Protestant faith?'

'No. She is a Catholic.'

'A Roman Catholic. I understand.'

Again silence, broken by Faith's cold tones, saying: 'I suppose that this is the reason why I was not told sooner about my prospective daughter-in-law, and why I was not asked to meet her—to have her here?'

'I was afraid you might be rather vexed at first until you had seen her, that is. But, mother, when you do meet her, you will like her—you cannot help doing so. When may I bring her to see you?'

'Never. I do not wish to meet this person.'

'Mother—you do not mean what you say? You cannot mean it. You will see Kathleen and then tell me what you think about her—please, mother!'

'No—I will not do so. There would be no purpose in my seeing this girl, and we will speak no more about her. With regard to the business, it is your own, and if you do not intend to take an active part in its management, then you had better see George Harvey about the details. I have no intention of working there in your interest any longer.'

'But, mother, I thought you liked doing it? I thought you were devoted to the business?'

'So I was, but the interest I took in it was due to the fact that I was building up a good business for your sons. I need not remind you, William, that your father would never have approved of such a marriage for you.'

It was typical of the woman that she never alluded to her other disappointment, never spoke of his sister's runaway marriage. She remained perfectly cool and self-possessed; she might have been speaking to a stranger or talking about some unimportant detail. What she really felt about the matter would never be revealed to her son.

And from this attitude he could not change her. She told him that he must interview George Harvey and ask his advice. She would not return to the business after the weekend. She would leave everything in perfect order, and if he wished to go over the books with her, he could do so. But George Harvey might be relied upon to supply him with all necessary information. She would retire and live at Clodagh.

Poor William. Gone were all his visions of a happy life at Clodagh. How he had pictured bringing Kathleen to see his home. How charmed she would have been with it. The garden, the delightful, old-fashioned rooms, the peace and serenity of the place. Well—that was all over now. One good thing—he had the business, it was his own, and George Harvey was a good sort and would take all the worry off his shoulders. He knew that the profits were good, he would be well off and able to give Kathleen all those comforts of which he had often thought. Even if they would not be allowed to live at Clodagh, there were plenty of charming houses to be had. It would be fun choosing their own home. What a mercy it was that he was not dependent upon his mother. What would he have done?

Yet her attitude hurt him, and he wished that she had not taken it like this.

'We will talk no more tonight,' said Faith, rising from her chair. 'I think it would be as well if you could find it convenient to accompany me to Capel Street in the morning, and have a talk with Mr Harvey. New arrangements will have to be made, and you will have to discuss the details with him.'

He rose to open the door for her and then returned to his seat feeling more unhappy than he had done for a long time. And as he sat there in a rather wretched solitude, he went over in his mind his first meeting with Kathleen and the subsequent friendship.

At the time he had been spending a few days with friends in Dalkey. One evening he had gone by himself to hear the band play in the Sorrento grounds. The Saturday night bands were a great feature of Victorian Dublin in the 'nineties, and were very fashionable functions. As William Weldon strolled round idly watching the well-dressed crowd, his attention was attracted by a couple who seemed decidedly out of the picture. They were an elderly man with a pointed beard and longish hair, wearing a shabby overcoat and old boots; at his side walked a girl, slim and graceful, but she, too, was shabbily attired, and although her clothes were neat and well brushed, their poor quality could not be hidden. The man was talking rather loudly, and as William passed them, he got a strong smell of whiskey. The girl seemed to be trying to persuade her companion—probably her father— to go home with her, and he was objecting to such an idea.

William felt curiously fascinated by the girl—she appealed to him in some strange way. He could not understand it, but she had stirred his heart as no other girl had ever done—not that he had ever bothered his head much about girls. But this one seemed different in some way, and he found himself watching her, passing and repassing her, as the gay throng moved back and forth near the band-stand. And when the band finished the programme and began to play 'God Save the Queen,' he found himself beside the couple. William had taken off his hat at once when the first strains of the English National Anthem sounded, not that he was particularly 'loyal' —rather the reverse if anything—but it was the correct thing to do. All the men were standing stiffly, their hats in their hands. Yet not quite all. The elderly man in the shabby coat had not taken off his hat, he stood there defiantly with his hat on his head—the only one amongst the fashionable crowd to do so. This was enough, in those queer past days, to arouse the indignation of the 'loyal' crowd, and immediately a hand shot out and knocked off the offending hat, sending it flying up to the rocky heights above the band-stand, where it was lost to sight. But the elderly man saw red, and went blindfold for the young fellow who had thus displayed his attachment to Her Britannic Majesty. A free fight would have followed had not Weldon and some others intervened, and telling the forcible hat lifter that the other was not quite sober, had persuaded him to go quietly away. This he did, but to get the older man to do so was not so easy. At last the combined efforts of his daughter and William were successful and he was persuaded to make tracks for home.

'But my hat—my hat—'

'Oh, don't worry about your hat, father. We will find it in the morning.'

By these words, William Weldon guessed that they must either live in Dalkey, or that they were staying there for a summer holiday.

As they walked down the hilly road to the town, he said to the girl: 'You will allow me to see you home? Your father is not too well, and—'

'I am quite well, sir—quite well. And who the devil are you to come poking your nose where you are not wanted?'

The girl flushed painfully, as she murmured: 'Oh, father—don't! this gentlemen has been so kind.' She glanced at Weldon as if to ask forgiveness for her father.

'Pardon me, if I seemed to intrude,' said he; 'believe me, I did not mean to do so. That young rough was so rude that I just could not help interfering.'

The old man stopped and looked at him. The upset seemed to have partially sobered him, and he spoke now in a more temperate manner.

'You must excuse me, young man, but my feelings got the better of me, and I wish I had been allowed to give that puppy the thrashing which he was asking for.'

'It is over now, father—don't let it worry you. Besides, such people are not worth talking about.'

'You are right, my girl. Come—we will get home. We need not trouble this gentleman any further, so good night, sir, and thank you.'

'But you will allow me to accompany you?'

'No thank you. I am perfectly capable of looking after my daughter myself—good night!'

The girl lifted her eyes to William's face and he saw that they were full of gratitude, as were also the tones in which she murmured: 'Good night—and thank you so much.'

That was William's first meeting with Kathleen Dillon. They met for the second time a few days later, and this time the girl was

alone. Although rather shy and reserved, she was plainly glad to
see him and they fell into a friendly chat, sitting on the rocks of
Sorrento. She told him that her father was not well and he had
been ordered to stay in bed for a little while. She was evidently
anxious about him, and never was able to stay away from him for
long. William thought he guessed the reason and felt profoundly
sorry for her.

By degrees he grew to know a good deal about these two who
interested him so much.

The man was one Patrick Dillon, a journalist of sorts, a freelance,
eking out a livelihood by writing articles and short stories, and
helped by his daughter who gave music lessons at one of those
small 'private' schools, which abounded at the period. She also
had a few pupils whom she taught at their own homes. The Dillons
lived in Rathmines and had only come to Dalkey for a fortnight,
Mr Dillon having been ill from 'overwork'—probably too much
drink, thought William—and the doctor had ordered change of
air. They were staying with a Mrs Kelly, who had once been a
servant in the house of Kathleen's mother; she had a cottage in
Dalkey and took the father and daughter for next to nothing,
being devoted to the girl for the sake of her dead mother.

William had gathered, how he never knew—he just sensed it—
that some mystery existed about Patrick Dillon's younger days.
Something had happened to embitter him. He was as one who
had his hand against everyone, and he seemed to think that
everyone's hand was against him.

William and Kathleen met often. They would sit on the rocks
at Sorrento or go for walks up Killiney Hill, but all the time, the
girl was anxious about her father, hoping that he would be all
right when she was not with him—not that she was ever very long
away from him. William guessed that her anxiety arose from the
fear that Patrick might take more than was good for him when
she was not there to restrain him. That she was devoted to her
father was plain to be seen; she lived only for him—or had done
so until she met William Weldon. Before the fortnight was up, she
and William had grown fond of one another, and when they
returned to town, the friendship was continued. Patrick Dillon
had grown accustomed to William and rather liked him. Many a
tale would the older man tell as he sat, pipe in mouth and glass at
his elbow. Once his tongue was loosened he would chat away on

many subjects—with the one exception of politics or any reference to the national movement in Ireland. Truth to tell, politics were not very exciting just then, and the national spirit, if not dead, was sleeping. William Weldon never suspected that Patrick Dillon had had any connection with that movement, and it was not until he had mentioned the matter to Kathleen that he heard any details. Then she told him quite simply that her father had been concerned in the Fenian Rising, of the late 'sixties, had suffered imprisonment, and had never been the same man again. Her mother had died several years ago, and she had looked after him ever since.

'He may take a little too much at times, as you know,' she said, 'but it is to try and forget what he suffered in that English jail. He hardly ever speaks of it, and if he did so, mother would try and turn his mind away from all that. The Rising was such a disappointment, you know—it was over almost before it began.'

'Yes, I know. The people who lived in our house, Clodagh Cottage, near Whitechurch, were mixed up in it. The son of the house got away to America and his mother sold the place and followed him. That is how my father bought it as he was looking for a house at the moment. It is a lovely place, Kathleen—you will just love it.'

And when William visited them in their lodging in Upper Rathmines, he wished more than ever that he could carry Kathleen off to Clodagh at once, and set her down there amongst the flowers and beauty of his loved home. The Dillons occupied two rooms and had the use of the kitchen. Kathleen's bed was in the sitting-room, being one of those uncomfortable chair-beds which folded up by day in an unconvincing attempt to pass as an arm-chair. The girl kept the place as clean and neat as possible, washing and cleaning when not slaving at her music teaching.

Yes, William wished she was away from it all, and the result of his wish had been his interview with his mother and the unexpected and unpleasant sequel.

However, he did not allow his mother's attitude—much as he deplored it—to interfere with his plans for the future. On the following morning he accompanied her to Capel Street and explained matters to George Harvey. Harvey was now an old man and seemed much upset at the news.

'You see, sir,' he said, 'Mrs Weldon has been simply wonderful and knows all about the business from every standpoint. The trade has increased enormously under her management. I do not know what we shall do without her—I really don't!'

'Oh, but surely you can manage all right?' replied William. 'You know it all yourself so well, and then you can have help from the other clerks.'

'That will not be the same, sir—not the same at all. And I am getting an old man, I am not as I was in your father's time. If you were coming into the business yourself—'

'But I am not doing so—I hate business. I should be no use anyway, so put that idea out of your head. I intend to follow the profession which I have chosen. Why should I waste all my study—all my years at Trinity?'

'It is a pity, sir, a great pity! All I can say is that I will do what I can—you may rely upon that. But the place will not be the same without Mrs Weldon—not the same at all.'

Harvey was not the only one who thought so. All the staff were sorry. Faith had been a just and kind employer; she was so capable, too—such a business head. The idea of 'Old Harvey'—really old now—being at the head of affairs was disturbing. Why, he had no memory these days; he would be useless by himself.

It was intended to make a presentation to Mrs Weldon before she left altogether, and steps were taken accordingly. They were sure that she would take a formal farewell of the staff before leaving altogether. But this was just what Faith felt that she could not do. She left her office for the last time on Friday evening without saying that she was not returning on the next morning. She saw no one before she left, going down to the waiting carriage by herself as had been her custom for all the years during which she had worked there. Capel Street saw her no more. Faith Weldon's work there was finished. The years during which she had been the mastermind of the business had been splendid ones for that business and happy ones for her—the happiest of her whole life as she now realised but too well. It was a broken-hearted woman who drove for the last time back to Clodagh along the familiar route. Yet she would not continue to take charge of the business; she would not work in order that the sons of a woman whom she did not know—and did not wish to know—should profit by her stewardship.

As the carriage drove past the churchyard at Whitechurch, her eyes turned towards the spot where her husband was buried.

'I did my best, John,' she whispered. 'I took your place and I worked hard and the business has prospered and grown. It is not my fault that all my work has been useless.'

She never saw the house of business in Capel Street again.

CHAPTER VI

A CHRISTMAS GIFT

There are few parts of London more drab and depressing than that of the district surrounding the Euston Road. Third-rate lodging-houses abound there, and their sordid rooms could tell of many a tragedy. Such places are bad enough for those who are strong and hopeful, but for a sick penniless woman such a spot must be a very hell. And it is in one of these houses that we find Ursula L'Estrange. Seven years have passed since her ill-starred marriage, and she is now twenty-eight, but one would easily guess her age as being ten years more. She is worn and haggard, her lovely colour gone, her eyes shadowed by care and sorrow. The past seven years have been ones of disillusionment and misery, of grinding poverty and failing health.

She and her husband had been in Paris when she had come of age, and both had crossed to Ireland and interviewed Mr Manton, the solicitor. Ursula produced proofs of her marriage and asked that she should receive her legacy. She would not tell Mr Manton where she was living—she was of age and her own mistress and wished to have her money at once. Thus she spoke by her husband's instructions. He accompanied her to the lawyer's office and he did not make a good impression upon that astute man. However, Mr Manton could only hand her a cheque for five hundred pounds and this she cashed before leaving Dublin. Not that she saw much of it—a few pounds only. The rest went to L'Estrange. But that was not the worst for poor Ursula. Mr Manton happened, unfortunately, to mention about the clause in her father's will by which she had lost the other five hundred by marrying without her mother's consent before she was twenty-one. L'Estrange had turned upon her in a fury, not caring that the lawyer was a witness to his outburst.

'Why did you not tell me this?' he shouted.

'You were within a few months of twenty-one and you have lost five hundred pounds. What were you thinking about to be such a fool? Have you no common-sense at all?'

'I—I never thought about it. I had forgotten. Besides, I did not think that the money mattered so much—then.'

The last word was a tribute to the fact that already, after a few

months as his wife, she realised the importance of money and of
how much it did matter.

Mr Manton had stared at the man in disgust and amazement.
That poor child. How she had ruined her life! He drew Ursula
aside just before she left, saying coldly: 'Excuse me Mr L'Estrange,
I wish to speak to your wife.' He asked the girl to confide in him,
tell him where she was living, allow him to inform her mother
and to see if the breach between them could not be healed. But
she only shook her head.

'It would be no use, Mr Manton—no use at all. I am his wife
now and must stay with him. And mother would never get on with
Hubert.'

She tried to smile, to seem happy, but she did not deceive
Samuel Manton.

'Will you not give me an address to which I may write?'

Again she shook her head. 'It would be no good. We are always
on the move. Please do not ask me.' Then as an angry cough
sounded at the other end of the office, she said hastily: 'I must go
now—goodbye, and thank you so much.'

That scene had taken place over six years ago and Hubert and
his wife had wandered from one continental town to another.
Living was very cheap and he managed to eke out enough to
keep them, partly by his sketches, and partly by giving drawing
lessons. For Ursula it was a wretched existence and her health
and spirits soon broke down. She was completely disillusioned by
her husband, and saw him as he really was—a selfish, untruthful
man. She knew that he had married her for her money and that
he had never forgiven her for not telling him about the clause in
John Weldon's will. And now they were in London—at least she
and little Faith were there. L'Estrange had left her three days ago,
and only that morning she had received a letter from him, short
and to the point. He did not intend to return to her, he was
returning to Paris, she had better go back to Ireland. There was
another woman in Paris, of course, she had known it for some
time. And so he had gone away, leaving his wife and child to shift
for themselves. Just like Hubert, as she realised.

But she realised, too, that her position was well nigh desperate.
She was in bad health and almost penniless. What was she to do?
How could she support herself and Faith? She could hardly drag
herself across the room, so weak did she feel.

The room in which she sat was of the usual dingy lodging-house type—what is known as a bed sitting-room. A small fire burned in the grate, and out of doors snow was falling in the London streets—falling and turning into a mass of hideous slush even as it fell. The horse buses and hansom cabs of the period were plodding through this slush, and ladies in long skirts and wide hats were picking their way along, as they went shopping, gazing into the windows in search of Christmas presents, for the next day would be the eve of Christmas.

Ursula was not thinking about Christmas. She was simply wondering what she was to do. The landlady had asked for her rent that morning; she wanted the money, she said, and there were now three weeks due to her. Ursula could no longer say that this would be paid when Mr L'Estrange returned. She knew that he would return no more. And she was glad—glad. She did not deny the fact to herself. She never wished to see him again. But were she and the child to starve? What were they to do? If only she did not feel so desperately ill she might be able to think of something, evolve some plan.

'Mammy, will Father Christmas send me anything for Christmas? Mrs Ruddles' little girl is hanging up her stocking and says he is going to fill it for her.'

Mrs Ruddles was the landlady.

'I am afraid that he does not know us, dear,' was Ursula's bitter reply.

'But why doesn't he, mammy? Besides, last Christmas Santa Claus filled my stocking—and it's all the same, isn't it?'

Last Christmas, as Ursula remembered, they had been living in a small village near the Black Forest, with some fellow-artists who had been kind to the child in their happy-go-lucky way. But it was different now. Few cities are so hard to the poor, she thought, as London. Charity there was—of a kind. But its bread tasted bitter. Ursula had never contemplated looking for help, yet suppose she had to do so or starve? What then?

'Did Father Christmas fill your stockings when you were a little girl, mammy?'

Before the mental vision of the unhappy woman seated by the wretched fire, came pictures of Christmas at Clodagh in the long ago. Centuries away those Christmas Days seemed now. Christmas at Clodagh when she was a child—a little thing as young as her

daughter Faith. But how different, and what a different childhood
hers had been.

Christmas at Clodagh. The awakening in the early morning
when it was still dark; groping for her stocking, always bulging
with gifts, lying across the foot of the bed—Father Christmas having
thoughtfully removed it from the mantelpiece where she had left
it overnight. What a lovely feeling as she pulled it up and began
to take out the things, one by one, until—right down at the toe
she would find a shilling wrapped up in paper. Breakfast, with her
plate loaded with gifts; the walk to church holding her father's
hand, while Willie went in front with his mother; joining in 'Hark
the Herald Angels Sing'; the Christmas dinner, the lovely evening
afterwards, sitting beside her father looking at her new picture
books. Willie generally knelt on the rug beside his mother—at
least that was the picture that came before her now. The pleasant,
old-fashioned room, the leaping fire, the Christmas cake for tea.
Where was Willie now, she wondered? Had he married? She
supposed so, and in that case he and his wife would be at Clodagh
now. Perhaps there were children there now. Happy children,
not like her Faith—poor little mite. She had heard no word of
her home for she had never written a line to anyone. Somehow,
she could not bear to do so. Had her marriage turned out
differently, had she been happy, had Hubert been a better
husband, then she might have tried to make friends with her
mother. But as things were she simply could not bring herself to
write home. At least up to the present moment. But now, faced
with a hungry and fireless Christmas, she found her thoughts
going across the Irish Sea with a bitter longing for all that she had
left behind her on that mad summer's day when she had run
away with a strolling artist. And suddenly came the resolve. She
would go home—back to her mother; for the sake of the younger
Faith she would humble herself in the very dust before the older
one.

But how to manage it? Where was the money to come from for
the fares? Let her think. Oh, she *must* think—*must* pull herself
together. There was so little time. Tomorrow would be Christmas
Eve and she wanted to arrive at Clodagh on that day. Surely her
mother would never turn her away then? And she must love Faith—
her grandchild who was named after her, and who was so like her
in many little ways. Ursula turned her head now and looked at

her small daughter.

Faith L'Estrange was at this time six years of age, but she might have passed as being much older, so demure and quiet was she in her ways. She was, however, small for her age; her fair hair—so like her grandmother's, as Ursula often thought—was loosely tied with a bow, and she had altogether a decided resemblance to the pictures of Alice in the 'Wonderland' and 'Through the Looking Glass' stories. An old-fashioned Victorian child. Her life had been passed mostly in the company of adults; she had been used to moving from place to place with no settled home and no home life of any kind. She was half fond, half afraid of her father, who, when he had money to spend would throw her a shilling or two for herself, but at other times would come home drunk— 'sick' she was taught to call his condition then—and make her mammy cry. The worst of it was that the child was by temperament a second edition of the older Faith, except that her character was not so strong. She already showed her love for order and neatness, being a very tidy little person, and a settled routine would have suited her to the ground. But she had never known such an existence—did not know that people living such lives were numerous—and Ursula could foresee that as the child would grow older so, too, would grow her dislike of the nomadic life which she had been leading since her birth in a Paris pension just over six years ago. She had so far received no education beyond her letters and a few words of one syllable, but she was an intelligent child and her mother had often wished that she were at school. But now, if they could reach Dublin and things turned out as she hoped they would do—then the child would have a proper education and be able to take her place in the world.

And now how was she to get the money for their fares so that they could start for Ireland by the morning mail?

She had exactly two shillings in her purse and not a penny more, and she owed her landlady fifteen shillings. She had nothing worth selling or pawning; even her wedding ring had gone long ago and been replaced by a worthless one. Not that she would have parted with it. Hubert had taken it one night so that he might have money to spend on drink. How then was she to pay for the journey?

'Stay here and be a good girl until I come back,' she said to little Faith; 'I have to go out for a short while.'

It was like the child that she never asked to be taken, too; she just said, 'Very well, mammy,' and sat down on a low chair at the window, from where she could see the snow falling on the streets below. Ursula put on her hat and coat and went out—not knowing where she was going and with but one fixed idea—to get enough money for the journey tomorrow, somehow, someway.

It was bitterly cold and the coat was threadbare. She walked as fast as her strength would allow, trying to get warm, and all the time wondering how she was to get possession of five pounds. That was the sum upon which she had decided. With care it should do for the journey and to pay Mrs Ruddles her rent. Ursula remembered that she had heard that street singers made quite a lot of money. Suppose she were to try? At this season, too, people's hearts might be easily touched. But she had never tried to sing in the open with traffic all around her and her efforts were doomed to failure. She just essayed a few words of a carol which were inaudible even to her own ears, and gave up the attempt in despair. The dusk was falling, and panic seized her. She would never get the needful sum. What was she to do? A stout, prosperous-looking man was coming swiftly towards her and she went forward, her lips shaking as she tried to ask for help. He brushed past her carelessly, she was only a beggar and he was in a hurry. The same result followed her next few efforts, but then she had a bit of luck. A lady with two children stopped and gave her sixpence, and after another hour she had nearly five shillings in hand. Five shillings—and she wanted five pounds. It seemed so hopeless that she almost gave up in despair. But there is a desperate courage which is born of despair—the courage which holds on till death.

Frozen with cold, weak from hunger, Ursula determined to buy some food and return to her room where poor little Faith must be wanting something to eat also. After a meal she would put the child to bed early and come out again to beg. That she must and *would* obtain the required five pounds was now an obsession with her.

She bought some food at a cheap eating house and carried it back with her. The fire had gone out and Faith was shivering with cold. Ursula made her get into bed for there was no coal to relight the fire, and once the child had eaten she fell asleep almost at once. Ursula forced herself to eat a little and then once more sallied forth on her desperate errand.

The streets of London, when one is alone in them, are always hard and cold; the throngs of hurrying people intent on their own business push past, unheeding and uncaring. Ursula, tired and faint, began to lose heart, she knew that her physical condition would not allow her to keep on much longer.

She was almost on the point of returning to her room when her attention was attracted by a group of revellers, just emerging from a brightly lit public-house. It looked warm and cosy in there. Ursula—the once proud, aloof Ursula—would have gladly gone inside for a rest in the warmth. The men lurched towards her but she did not ask them for help, she had always been afraid of drunken men and her married life had served to add to this fear. She drew to one side to let them pass her, which they did, singing the tipsy chorus of some music-hall song. But as the last one went by, he reeled slightly, and as he pulled himself together, Ursula saw that he had dropped a small wallet. He did not notice, indeed, he kicked it aside as he went on his way. It lay there, in the slush, and Ursula stood and stared at it. Only for a moment, then she stooped swiftly and picked it up.

A little later, by the light of a candle in her room, she opened the wallet. A five pound note stared up at her. To the sick and desperate woman it seemed not to be money which she had stolen, but an answer to prayer. Not that prayer had been of much comfort to her lately, neither had she put up any verbal petition to Heaven to send her this money, but she knew that the unspoken prayer had been in her heart all the time during which she had tramped those terrible streets outside. They could leave for Ireland in the morning.

She hardly slept that night, and when coming towards the dawn she dozed for a little, she dreamt that she was back at Clodagh again—as a child, as a young girl. Her father was with her, and as is the way in dreams, she suddenly remembered that she was married, and was telling him all about it. 'I thought that I had gone away, far away, and would never see you again. Oh, father— I am so glad that it was only a dream after all, and that I am safe at home!'

Then, as her mind groped through the mist of her dream, she cried: 'I thought you had died! You are not dead, father?'

And then came the well-remembered voice, that voice which had never spoken to her in anger: 'No, I am not dead. You can see I am with you, little girl. Do not worry—all is right now.'

The dream faded and she was back to reality, lying on a lumpy mattress in a dingy London lodging. And soon it was time to get up and heat water on the gas ring to make tea and get ready for the journey. How ill she felt! Worse than yesterday. It must be the cold—the bitter cold.

'Are you very cold, darling?' she asked Faith as she helped her to dress.

'Yes—a little, mammy.' The child's teeth were chattering as she spoke.

Presently they were out in the street walking to Euston, then sitting in the train on their way to Holyhead and the boat. Ursula got some lunch for Faith and tried to swallow some herself but was not hungry. Only cold and terribly weak. It was warm on the steamer, and Faith fell asleep, but her mother could not warm. She would have liked to go on deck for the first sight of Ireland, but felt too weary to mount the cabin stairs before it was necessary.

Kingstown at last, and the train to Westland Row—and there she was in the streets of dear old Dublin once more. She was too ill—too tired—to realise it. Her one desire was to get home to Clodagh, and she hurried the sleepy and weary Faith into a Terenure tram. She hardly noticed each familiar landmark as it went past, only rousing herself by an effort when the tram stopped at the Terenure terminus and the walk to Clodagh had to begin.

Little Faith was never to forget that walk. There was a reason why it should be for ever stamped upon her memory, but apart from that reason, the cold and darkness made it like a walk in a nightmare.

Just as they reached Whitechurch, after a long and weary walk from Terenure, snow began to fall heavily, and if Ursula had not known every step of the way, she would never have been able to keep to the right path. She plodded on, her breath getting shorter and more difficult, her steps faltering at times, while the child with a stoicism unnatural in one so young, trudged at her side. Only now and then she would ask: 'Will we soon be there, mammy?'

'Very soon now, dear. Are you very tired? I wish I could carry you, darling—but I am not able.'

'I know you are tired, too, mammy.'

'But we will soon be at Clodagh now, Faith. And there will be a grand fire and a lovely hot cup of tea.'

So she tried to keep up her own spirits and those of the little one. It is not really a long walk from Terenure to Clodagh. A hiker, setting off on a summer's day, would think nothing of the distance. But on a winter's night, with a heavy blinding snowstorm beating against one, the road all uphill, and the walkers a sick woman and a weary child, the journey might be called an epic one. Only the thought of little Faith kept Ursula from falling down and going to sleep—the sleep of death—in the snow.

At last the turn of the road leading to the house. How dark and still was the slope of old Tibradden just then. Could it be the same hill as that upon which she and Hubert had sat and talked during those summer days of a hundred years ago? Then the sun shone, the bracken and heather were under their feet; now there was only darkness and cold. She could not see the gate and had to feel her way along by the wall until she reached it.

She pushed the gate open, and holding her child by the hand went up the garden path to the door. Then, a great weakness came upon her, so that even as she was reaching for the knocker, she swayed and collapsed upon the threshold of her old home.

'Mammy! Mammy!' The child's cry fell upon the silence of the night. And then little hands beat upon the door of Clodagh and a terrified voice cried out: 'Open the door—my mammy is sick! Open the door!'

CHAPTER VII

THE PASSING YEARS

Two people heard the child's cry that Christmas Eve.

Faith Weldon, sitting alone by the fire in her cosy sitting-room, heard it, and Mary Molloy, now an old woman, over seventy, who was also sitting alone in her kitchen, heard it. Delia, the other maid now at Clodagh, had gone to Rathfarnham that evening and had not yet returned. Both women hearing the cry, raised their heads in astonishment, and Mary made the Sign of the Cross with shaky fingers. The voice of a child, on this night of all others, and crying to them to 'Open the door!' A child out in the snow!

She went along the passage as quickly as her old legs would carry her, and into the sitting-room to her mistress.

'Did ye hear that, ma'am? A child crying! At the door!'

'Yes, I heard it. Some tinker's child, I suppose. You had better see, Mary.'

Mrs Weldon spoke in her usual serene tones. She would not let Mary see that the cry, in the silence of the late evening, had stirred her in any way. Yet it had done so. Faith Weldon was a lonely woman now, but if she felt her loneliness, she did not allow this to be seen; she went her own way, living her quiet, uneventful life, apparently content. If there were moments—those secret moments which come to all of us at times—when the truth faced her in all its nakedness, and she had to admit to herself that life had disappointed her, she allowed no one else to guess this fact.

Her daughter's runaway marriage had hurt and vexed her, but she had not loved the girl very deeply. Ursula had always been a source of annoyance to her, and so she was not surprised that she should make such a wretched marriage. Since the day when Mr Manton had informed her that he had paid Ursula the five hundred pounds, Faith had heard nothing more of her daughter. It was William's marriage that had hurt her most, she had felt his conduct bitterly, it had been a frightful blow to her pride and to her love. His marriage had been bad enough, but two years ago—just after the birth of his little son—he had himself become a Catholic. She had not seen him since, had told him not to cross the threshold of her house again. She had never met his wife, had never seen her little grandson. A hard woman in the eyes of the world; a just and deeply wronged one, in her own.

Faith Weldon, in this year 1898, was forty-six, and hardly looked her age in spite of the fact that the clothes of the period did not help to make a woman younger. She lived such a quiet life that it might have helped to keep her young, yet she knew that the years in Capel Street, when she had been at the head of a good business, every hour of the day filled with work and with varied interests—she knew that those years had been far happier than her present existence. Certainly, she could have continued in the business had she liked, William had made that clear, but the resolution taken on the day when he had told her of his intended marriage had not been broken. She had never entered the premises in Capel Street since the day she had left, to be driven home to Clodagh from her office for the last time. Neither had she ever made any enquiries as to the progress of the business. Her interest in it was gone.

She lived her quiet life at Clodagh now; her only interests her garden, poultry, and reading. She was a great reader. Sewing of any kind or 'fancy work' she detested; and although like all girls of her generation, she had been taught these things when young, she never bothered with them now. She preferred reading—it took her mind off other things. She could forget her loneliness when deep in a book—not that she would ever confess to being lonely. But tonight was the eve of Christmas, and although Faith Weldon was one of the least sentimental of women, even she could not but feel the atmosphere surrounding this—the Holy Night, the Silent Night. Ghosts from the past—childish voices, tiny hands—seemed to be in the quiet room with her.

And now, cutting across that silence, had come the cry of a child, a shrill voice calling—'open the door!' Who could it be?

The next moment there came a great cry from Mary.

'Miss Ursula! Is it you? Miss Ursula!'

A strange trembling shook Faith Weldon, but she rose from her chair and with shaking limbs went out to the hall. There she saw Mary bending over a prostrate figure which seemed to have fallen on the doorstep. A small child, with snowflakes on her shabby little coat, trembling with cold and fear, stood by.

'What is it, Mary?'

The quiet tones interrupted Mary's lamentations, and as Faith spoke, the little girl turned to look at the mistress of Clodagh. Mrs

Weldon found herself looking into eyes as blue as her own, as bright as her own had been once; caught a glimpse of honey-coloured hair under an old hat. The child came towards her.

'I am sorry if I made a noise—but mammy is sick.' Then as the older woman stared at her, she went on: 'Are you my grandmother? I hope you are, because we are so hungry and cold.' The little lips quivered and Faith Weldon stooped and took her in her arms.

'Yes, I am your grandmother,' she said, 'come into the sitting-room and get warm.'

She placed the child in a big arm-chair drawn close to the blaze. 'Wait there until I see after your mother—I will soon be back.'

Helping Mary to bring Ursula into the house and along the passage to the spare room—once her own—Faith could hardly realise that this thin, haggard woman was the girl who had left Clodagh only a little over seven years ago. This worn, poverty-stricken woman, in her thin clothes and broken shoes, who looked as old as Faith herself—could this be Ursula? Mary was sobbing bitterly; the poor soul was quite broken at the sight of the girl she had so loved coming home like this. The voice of her mistress pulled her together.

'Go round to the stable and see if Dan is there. Send him for the doctor at once.'

Dan Brophy was still at Clodagh, an old man now, but able for the work—little enough these days. He was found and dispatched to Rathfarnham, and Ursula was undressed and put to bed, hot jars to her feet, hot milk to drink, and a big fire set blazing up the chimney. It was long since she had seen such a fire. She lay there, without speaking. It seemed as is she were too exhausted to talk, but she smiled now and then, content just to be warm and comfortable. Leaving her to Mary, Mrs Weldon went back to the room where she had left her grandchild.

The little girl was sitting on the hearthrug, and in her arms she held a small black cocker.

'My dear, I am sure you must be cold. I have brought some warm wraps for you and we will take off those wet things. I was busy with your mother.'

'How is my mammy, please?'

'She is in bed, where you will be as soon as you have had some supper, and are warm.'

'I am warm now, thank you. The fire is so lovely—I never saw such a lovely fire! And the doggy has warmed me, too. What is its name please?'

'That is Judy. And now, what is your name?'

'I am Faith.'

So Ursula had called her Faith. As she stooped to kiss the child, Faith Weldon found herself trying to remember how long it was since she had last kissed anyone. It must have been Willie—many years ago now, or so it seemed to her.

From that moment little Faith crept into her grandmother's heart, and there remained through all the years to come.

Ursula had come home to die. She lived a couple of weeks, and then, in spite of all that care and skill could do for her, she passed quietly away. It was as if she were glad to lay down her weary burden of life—glad to go. The child missed her very much at first, crying softly to herself, but making no outcry, as was her way. But before long the memory of her mother faded, and her grandmother became all in all to little Faith. And of a surety, she was everything to her grandmother—the joy of her life, her one comfort.

Mary and Dan often spoke of the difference the child's coming had made to the mistress of Clodagh.

'Sure it's young again she's gettin'—so it is!' said Dan. 'Since Master Willie went agin her, I never saw her lookin' so happy.'

'Well, it's to be hoped she won't have the same disappointment with Miss Faith,' replied Mary, adding: 'not that such a thing is likely. A more obedient little girl I never saw in all me born days!'

'That's true for you, Mary,' replied the old man. Then he added, with a pessimistic shake of the head: 'All the same, ye niver know with faymales—niver!'

'Such nonsense you talk, Dan Brophy! Well you know that Master Willie did more to hurt the poor mistress than Miss Ursula ever did.'

'That was bekase she loved him the best,' replied Dan, wisely.

The years went past, and Faith the child became Faith the young girl. The nursery governess who had taught her at first was succeeded by a more advanced lady, and Faith's education went forward. Her grandmother knew that the girls of that day received more liberal teaching than had been the case in her own time, and she spared no money on Faith. She had special lessons in French from a French woman, and went into town for her music and dancing. She was, however, by no means a clever girl as far as intellectual attainments went, much preferring gardening and knitting, content with her life at Clodagh, devoted to her grandmother.

Her education finished, Faith lived the usual life of girls of her class and money before the war. She went the social round of visits; tennis in summer, dances in winter. She had her bicycle and also her pony trap. Billie, the pony, was a great pet, but the greatest pet she possessed was a black cocker named Judy—a granddaughter of that same Judy who had warmed her that cold night when she arrived at Clodagh.

There were changes at Clodagh as the years passed. Dan was dead, and so, too, was Mary Molloy. In her place was her niece, Kate Doyle, with Delia Flanagan to help. Two gardeners were employed. The carriage had been given up some years ago, and when Mrs Weldon wished to drive out, she went in the pony trap.

A quiet, uneventful life for a girl, but Faith, as we have said, was content.

And then she fell in love.

Perhaps that is too strong an expression to use in connection with Faith, so cool and detached, so quiet always, so self-controlled. But certainly she was very fond of Charles Draper, junior partner in the firm of Draper, Lee and Draper, Solicitors. The elder Draper was well off, and his son a steady young fellow who should go far in his profession. His family were pleased with his choice of a wife, and Mrs Weldon, although grieved to lose Faith, was glad that she was making such a sensible match. The wedding took place in the summer of 1912, when Faith was just twenty. Fortune seemed to smile on the young couple. They went to live in a house in Rathmines, a delightful house, with garden and tennis court ('but never can it be like dear Clodagh,' thought Faith to herself). The furniture was given by Mr Draper, and Mrs Weldon supplied the linen. There they set up house and were perfectly happy for two years.

And then came the war of 1914.

Mrs Weldon at once threw herself heart and soul into every project for helping 'the boys at the front.' She knitted and made bandages, sent off parcels, held meetings at her house. Faith joined the V.A.D. and attended classes, she too knitted and sent off parcels to the front.

Early in 1915, her husband joined up, and then Faith went to Clodagh to stay with her grandmother until her baby should be born. Mrs Weldon wanted her to remain with her until the war was over, but nothing had been decided on that June day when a baby girl arrived at Clodagh Cottage.

The baby cost the mother her life. At first Mrs Weldon could not believe the doctor when he told her that Faith was dying. It seemed incredible—too terrible to be true. Yet it was true, as she was soon to realise. The girl who had been so dear to her—dearer far than either of her own children—was taken from her. Taken away in a moment of time. Her son and daughter had left her for strangers, treating her in a heartless manner, hard and selfish—both of them. That she herself had been in any way to blame she would never allow.

And then Faith had come. The little girl who had crept into her lonely heart on that snowy Christmas Eve seventeen years ago. Faith would never have disappointed her. And Faith was taken from her.

The bitterness of death came upon Faith Weldon in that hour.

CHAPTER VIII

CLODAGH: 1916

They shall grow not old
As we that are left grow old:
Age shall not weary them, nor the years condemn.
At the going down of the sun and in the morning
We will remember them.

There is an old house standing at the corner of Lilac Lane, in Rathfarnham. It is built of red brick, mellowed by age, and the garden reaches down to the Dodder river, where it flows past on its way to Dublin City and the sea. A dear old house. One had only to look at its windows to know how friendly it was, for they seemed to smile in welcome to all who came up the short path to the door.

It was to this house that William Weldon had brought his wife when they were married that summer in the nineties of the last century. The house had been well furnished then, there had been fine linen and silver; and William had provided his wife with a pony-carriage and had a fashionable dog-cart for his own use.

Today, the furniture was a bit worn and the carpets shabby, the linen patched and darned, and the pony-carriage and dog-cart had been replaced by bicycles or the humble train.

Things had not gone too well with William Weldon. All had been well while George Harvey was alive, but when he had died William found himself without a manager for the business. It so happened that his father-in-law had recommended a friend of his own—one Gerald O'Malley—for the position. This man was supposed to be an excellent man of business, but his management had been disastrous for William Weldon. Affairs had gone from bad to worse, and almost before he had time to realise it, he saw his business going from him. He was no use himself, and he knew it; he had relied upon this man who had proved himself to be a broken reed. Now, when it was too late, William knew that O'Malley had always been too plausible. He had contracted bad debts, had fought with the rest of the staff, had kept his books any way. The result was that, in a few years' time, William Weldon had to go through the Bankruptcy Court, and was glad to sell what was left of the business to a big soap combine. When he had settled with his creditors, there was little left from the wreck, and he was dependent upon his profession. He managed to live, but never made a name for himself; there were times, too, when briefs were few and far between, and he and Kathleen had a tough enough fight to keep their heads above water.

Yet they were happy—wonderfully happy. Three children had been born to them—two girls and a boy. The eldest girl had died when but a few years old; the boy was just twenty now, and his sister two years younger. The boy had been named after his two grandfathers—John Patrick. Kathleen would have wished that the order of the two names had been reversed, and that he had been called Patrick, but her husband had stood out for John, so John took the place of honour, although he was always 'Jack' to his family and friends. He was a clerk in an accountant's office in the city; he had always had a good head for figures and wished for such work himself, and, in any case, his father could not have afforded to give him a profession. His sister, Maureen, was in a florist's—a shop owned by a school friend of her own—and seemed quite content. She was also able to sell some of the flowers from their garden. Both Jack and herself were devoted to gardening.

Kathleen was an ideal wife and mother. The years seemed to have changed her but little, and her husband, looking at her sometimes, would think that she had but grown more gracious with the passing of time; in his eyes she was as lovely as on the day he married her. The loss of their business and the income from it had not troubled her much; she had always been used to poverty, and would not have cared for riches. Her old father—now going on for eighty—lived with them, and in spite of being troublesome at times, and more or less of a burden, he was a favourite with them all. His grandchildren were devoted to him, and never tired of listening to his stories of years gone by. It was only William who remembered at times that he might blame the old man for the loss of his business.

But he was too just to put all the blame upon Patrick Dillon; he knew that he should have looked after things better himself. And then he would wish—as he had so often wished before—that his mother had remained at the helm of his ship of trade. What a splendid captain she had made!

William and his son were great pals—more like brothers than father and son. After all, William Weldon was still in the middle forties, and young for his age, as was his wife also. But although he and Jack were such friends, the older man had not the boy's entire confidence. He had known, in a vague sort of way, that Jack belonged to the Volunteers, but hardly took the matter seriously. His wife and father-in-law could have opened his eyes. But, as it was, William Weldon got a bit of a shock one morning in April 1916, when his son announced that he was under orders to report at the General Post Office for duty. Jack looked well in his Volunteer uniform—a boy of whom any father might have been proud. Kathleen had paled as she held him in her arms for a moment.

'God keep you, my son. You will do your duty for Ireland—I know that—and I am glad.'

At that moment Maureen rushed in.

'I am off!' she cried. 'We will cycle together, Jack, if you like. Oh, come on—we must hurry!'

'You are going, too, Maureen?' Her father stared at her in dismay as he spoke.

'Why, of course, daddy! I am in the Cumann na mBan—I have just had a message. We are all mobilised.'

'But *must* you go, Maureen? A girl like you——'

'Certainly I must go—and I am so proud. We are going to fight again—the country is up——'

She was interrupted by a great shout from the threshold. There stood their grandfather, his head thrown back, his eyes shining.

'The country is up!' he cried, raising his hands above his head as if thanking Heaven. 'The country is up! Thanks be to God that I have lived to hear those words again!'

And long after the young couple had flown off on their bicycles, the old Fenian could be heard repeating to himself:

'The country is up! The country is up!'

Neither William nor Kathleen could ever forget the days which followed, they were burnt upon their brain to return at times in the form of terrible dreams.

On the Saturday evening, Maureen returned, wan and haggard, but of Jack there was no sign, and no news reached them. Maureen told them that she had parted from him when they reached the College of Surgeons at St. Stephen's Green, where she had to report for duty, while he proceeded on his way to the GPO. They discussed amongst themselves what his fate had been.

'Some of the men escaped,' said Maureen, 'they got away by the side streets. It is just possible that Jack may have been one of these.'

Kathleen said nothing. She had no hope. Even as he had paused for an instant at the garden gate and waved back to her—even then she had known, a premonition had come upon her, that she would not see her boy again for a long time—if ever. But she said nothing to her husband; after all, it might only be her imagination—just a case of nerves. It was strange though that she had not had the same premonition with regard to Maureen. She had not felt very anxious about her—had expected her to return. But the boy—she had no hope of seeing him again for many a long day.

Her father tried to cheer her up, for to him she had confided her fears. He could not believe that Jack would not come back safely. But then, neither would he believe for quite a long time that the Rising was over, that the gallant band who had kept such overwhelming numbers in check, were really at last forced to surrender. So Kathleen did not heed him much when he told her that Jack was sure to come home some day soon.

But the days went by, one after another, and there came no tidings of him.

Instead came the reports of the executions, one after another, as Britain took her vengeance; the imprisonments; the round-up of all suspects, as the British military hunted for all who took part in the fighting.

'And it is to be hoped that they will find every rebel! Such a disgrace to the country and the decent people in it—to take advantage of our being at war to make trouble here! I would hang every one of them. Any other death is too good for them—they should be treated like the curs that they are.'

Faith Weldon—now a woman over sixty—looked grim enough to do the hanging herself, as she gave voice to these sentiments one afternoon when some friends had called. Her callers quite agreed with her.

'Do you not feel nervous—living here alone, dear Mrs Weldon?' one lady asked, as she plied her needles swiftly, doing the eternal knitting, then so fashionable with her class. 'Comforts' for 'our boys at the front.'

'Nervous? Certainly not. Why should I be nervous?'

'There are so many of these rebels going through the county, trying to escape. This would be an ideal house for them—they could hide here.'

Mrs Weldon set her lips.

'If one of them tried to hide here it would not be for long,' she said; 'if I had to walk to the police barracks myself I would see that he did not escape the law.'

'That is very brave of you, dear Mrs Weldon,' gushed an elderly spinster; 'but poor little me would be terrified!'Then as she saw her hostess glance rather contemptuously at her, she hastened to change the subject. 'And how is the darling, *dear* little baby?'

'She is quite well, thank you.'

'And may we see her before we go?'

'Certainly. She is in the garden with her nurse.'

Tea finished, the ladies went into the garden with Mrs Weldon. The baby was asleep in her pram, the nurse—a middle-aged, old-fashioned person—sat sewing beside her. Mrs Weldon would have nothing to do with those 'new-fangled' children's nurses, of whom she did not approve. Little could be seen of the infant but a rosy face and a dimpled hand. Baby Ursula was now almost a year old, a well-cared-for and thriving child. Faith Weldon saw that the child was properly looked after, but she had no love for it. This child had cost the life of the one being whom—since her son had left her—the old woman had really loved. Her grand-daughter's death had been a bitter blow, one she could not forget, and although she saw that the child had all that was necessary for its comfort and well-being, she gave no love or affection to the little thing.

The baby duly admired and praised, the ladies took their leave, and quietness descended upon Clodagh.

A few hours later, Mrs Weldon was seated at her evening meal. Very lonely was Faith Weldon now. As has been said, she took little interest in the child who might — had she allowed it — have helped to fill the aching void in the woman's heart. But she simply did her duty by the infant—no more and no less. So far as love or affection was concerned, the child would have received as much if left to the care of a conscientious matron attached to some home for foundlings.

Of her son, Mrs Weldon knew little, except, of course, the bare facts of where he lived, and that three children had been born, of whom one was dead. This much the newspapers had told her. She knew, too, about the failure of 'Weldon's', and this had been a sorrow only second to the death of Faith. Her husband's business. The business for which he had worked and planned—all brought to nothing—gone with the wind. And only for the want of a proper person at the head of affairs. Small wonder that Faith Weldon, remembering her successful years in Capel Street, should bitterly upbraid her absent son for his carelessness. Never would she forgive him for that—nor for his hated marriage. Never! Over twenty years had passed since he left her, and she was as hardened against him now as she had been then.

She drank some milk and had some biscuits to eat. She was not hungry and the day had been very warm for May. She would take a stroll in the garden and retire early to bed. She felt tired.

Outside, the evening was beautiful; the dusk was falling, the darkness made fragrant by the scent of the flowers. The sweetness of the lilac trees came to her as she went slowly along the path at the side of the house. Her garden. She loved it above all else. It was the one thing that brought some peace and serenity to her tired soul.

Tonight she felt really tired—really old. And with her advancing years she felt the loneliness which comes with age.

She began to think about her son, as she seldom thought now. She found herself thinking how good it would have been if only he had married a woman of whom she could have approved; the business would have still flourished, his children would have been with her— here at Clodagh. She felt that she could have loved those children. Perhaps she would have loved them almost as much as she had loved little Faith. As 'little' Faith she often thought of her now. The little child who had come to her on Christmas Eve. It was as that child that the old woman loved to remember her, even though she had grown up to be a wife and mother, and her child was now sleeping in the quiet house behind her. There had been no one like Faith—no one. Yet if William——

She suddenly paused in her walk and stood still as voices came to her ears. She was walking by a hedge which separated part of the kitchen garden and was surprised to hear these voices. They were speaking in low tones, but after a moment she had no difficulty in recognising one of them as belonging to Kate Doyle. The other voice was that of a young man, and Mrs Weldon noted that the accents were those of an educated person. Who could it be? Who was talking to Kate at an hour which was late for the household at Clodagh; talking, too, in a secretive manner. Surely Kate had not a 'follower'? This was strictly forbidden at Clodagh. Besides which, she had noticed that the man's accent proclaimed him to be a better class than Kate. Mrs Weldon was not an eavesdropper, she was moving away with the resolve to speak to Kate tomorrow, when some words from the cook made her pause.

'Oh, Master Jack—why did you come here? Sure it's not safe! The mistress is so bitter and——'

'I had to come, Kate. They were hot after me. I felt sure that you would hide me for my father's sake. This house will never be suspected—that is why I thought of it. I am sure you would help me.'

'Sure you know I'll do all I can—there's nothing in the world I wouldn't do for you——'

'Then find me a place to hide in for a few days. I hope to get over to America then. There's just a chance I'll be able to get away. You will take a message to my mother, won't you—to let her know that I am all right?'

'Oh, of course, Master Jack—you know I will. But now let me think where to hide you. There's the loft over the stables where old Dan used to sleep—it's not much, but——'

'As if it mattered! Anywhere will do.'

'Well, it might do if only the mistress doesn't find out——'

'But she is not likely to go there—is she? And as I said, this house should be above suspicion just *because* of her. Everyone knows Mrs Weldon's sentiments.'

His voice was bitter, and the listener wondered once again who he could be? But one thing was certain. One of the rebels was trying to escape from justice, and was actually going to hide in her stable. Well—let him try.

They moved away, passing close to her where she stood behind the hedge. She heard Kate say: 'You do look bad, Master Jack! You must have gone through a terrible time. I'll get you a bit of supper and bring it out to you as soon as the mistress is safe in bed. Come now, and I'll show you the loft.'

They passed by, leaving her in the garden—alone.

Now, what was she to do? There was a rebel at Clodagh. At Clodagh of all places.

The angry old lady, standing in the gathering darkness of her beloved garden, had quite forgotten that, long before that evening of 1870, when she had come there as a bride, there had been 'rebels' at Clodagh. Had not young Owens fled to America after the Fenian Rising? Was there not a story that Robert Emmet had lain hidden there one night on his way to Wicklow? But Faith Weldon neither knew nor cared about all this. Clodagh represented to her all that was most 'respectable'; it was a bulwark of that Victorian tradition which she saw crumbling to pieces before her horrified eyes; it stood for decent society, for loyalty to King and Empire. It was simply unthinkable that a rebel was to find shelter at Clodagh while she was mistress there.

But how was she to send a message to the authorities? The servants she knew could not be relied upon. She had no telephone. She supposed that the police barracks at Rathfarnham would be the proper place at which to report. How could she get there herself at this hour—nearly ten o'clock—quite late for Mrs Weldon? It would be a long walk and she could not take the pony trap out without being seen. She would have to walk—there was nothing else for it.

But even as she was making up her mind to start at once, she heard the tramp of feet coming up the road to the gates. The tramp of drilled men, marching together. Going to the gate, she found a small band of British military, and the sergeant from the RIC barracks at Rathfarnham was with them. He saluted on seeing Mrs Weldon.

'I beg pardon, ma'am, for troublin' you,' he said. 'I told the officer that there was no need to search here—no need at all—but he—'

'That will do, sergeant,' interrupted the young officer, abruptly, 'I have my reasons for supposing that one of the wanted men is here. My information comes from a reliable source. We shall have to search your house ma'am.'

Mrs Weldon drew herself up, very erect and dignified. She did not like the manner of this young man, nor his way of addressing her. There was a want of that deference to which she was accustomed from all around her. But her duty must be done.

'You will not need to search the house,' she said, 'if you will follow me I will show you where I think you will find the man you want.'

The officer was surprised.

'It was a rash thing for you to hide any of these rebels,' he said. 'You can be severely punished.'

She turned on him like a flash.

'How dare you, sir! Do you mean that you suspect *me* of harbouring any of these men? Only that you happen to be a stranger, you would know better.'

'I beg your pardon, I am sure,' replied the other, 'but you must admit that the circumstances were suspicious.'

'I admit nothing of the sort. I would not have a rebel inside my gate—as Sergeant Gately can tell you. But I suspect that my servants have given shelter to one of these men. I think that he will be in the loft over the stables.'

From the kitchen windows, Kate and Delia watched the soldiers crossing the yard.

'God forbid that they think of the stables!' breathed Kate.

'That is just where they will go,' replied Delia. Exclaiming the next moment: 'Look—there they go—and may God save us—the mistress herself is guiding them! Oh, if she knew—if she knew!'

Kate rushed out and reached the stables just as the soldiers were preparing to enter.

'There's no one in there!' she cried. 'No one at all, I tell you!'

Her mistress interrupted in tones of ice.

'That will do, Kate. I happen to know that you have dared to give one of these men shelter in my house.'

Kate stared at her in dismay. 'Oh, but he has gone, ma'am, he did not stay a moment!' she lied quickly.

'He is not gone—he is here. Hidden in the loft above the stable, as you know.'

'He is gone, ma'am! Tell them he is gone! Oh, for the love of Heaven ask them to go away. For the love of God——'

Mrs Weldon stared at the white face of agonised appeal and was conscious of feeling puzzled and uneasy. It was queer that Kate should act like this. Could the fellow be her lover? That was not likely. Mrs Weldon remembered how she had addressed him as 'Master Jack.' There was nothing of the lover business there. He must be someone of importance amongst the rebels. All the better that he had been prevented from escaping. Pushing aside the detaining hands with which Kate tried to hold her, she said to the officer in charge: 'I am sure you will find the man you want in that loft—above the stable.'

They entered the stable as directed. The ladder leading to the loft above had been pushed aside and lay in the straw. To lift it up and mount was the work of an instant. There came the sounds of a sharp scuffle, and then the soldiers appeared coming down the ladder, pushing before them the man who was now their prisoner.

The stable was lit by the electric torches of the military and Mrs Weldon caught her breath as she faced the boy, standing there between two soldiers. He looked straight into her eyes, and she returned the gaze, staring at him. Looking, looking—trying to remember where she had seen him before; asking herself why his countenance was so familiar. This boy, in the dusty, torn uniform, tired and haggard, yet with head erect and eyes steadfast—of whom did he remind her? His expression, a slight movement of the head—and his eyes. They seemed so familiar. It was almost as if they spoke to her.

The British officer was stepping up to the boy.

'Well—so we have you at last!' he said. 'And now—what is your name?'

It was then that Faith Weldon understood why she thought that she had seen this boy before. His reply came clearly, with a proud lift of the head.

'John Weldon is my name.'

There was a little cry from Kate Doyle, but Faith Weldon made no move, uttered no sound. She stood there, like a figure of stone while he was taken away.

As he passed her Jack raised his hand to the salute. 'Goodbye, grandmother,' he said.

They marched away, the British soldiers and the RIC sergeant, with the grandson of Faith Weldon walking as a prisoner in their midst.

CHAPTER IX

THE OTHER URSULA

Ursula Draper sat on the steps of Clodagh Cottage on a certain warm afternoon in June, 1933. She was supposed to be engaged in the task of darning her stockings, but the work was momentarily suspended while she stared in front of her with eyes that saw nothing of the beauty which surrounded her, or the glory of the garden in June.

Truth to tell, Ursula was heartily wishing that she could get away from it all and live in the city with congenial friends and within easy reach of the cinemas. She regarded her present existence as slavery—'slavery on a desert island'—was how she put it to herself and her particular friends. If only her great-grandmother would allow her to take a commercial training so as to fit herself for a secretarial post or something like that—how delightful it would be. She would then be independent, able, perhaps, to share a small flat with friends in the city, get away from this monotonous existence—be free to live her own life in her own way.

Ursula was now eighteen and resembled her grandmother—that other unfortunate Ursula after whom she had been called—in appearance; like her she was dark and graceful and lovely to look upon. But there the resemblance ceased. Her grandmother had belonged to a different period with different traditions. The granddaughter was a modern girl with all the modern girl's love of independence and freedom of action, and her life at Clodagh with her great-grandmother was hard to bear. She was thinking at the moment how delightful it would be if only Mrs Weldon could be got to see things in a modern light.

'How awful to be dependent upon an old woman who lives in the past and who cannot realise the life of the modern girl—cannot be made to understand that we want to work—to be free to do as we like! Grandmother is a century behind the times!'

Even as she was so thinking, Ursula heard her name called sharply, and turning round saw the old lady at the window.

Mrs Weldon was now eighty-one years of age, yet in many ways she seemed younger; she was still active and walked with an upright, erect carriage. Her health was good and she seldom had a day's illness. In matters of religion or politics she remained an old-fashioned Victorian, such as we often hear described as a 'diehard.' The new Ireland which she had lived to see, was anathema to her, as indeed was the whole present-day world. In the ears of Mrs Weldon the slogan of 'youth must be served,' had never sounded, and had it done so, she would have regarded it as little short of blasphemy. She ignored all new ideas and lived her own life after the fashion of pre-war times. Unfortunately, she wished her great-granddaughter to live this life also.

'Have you not yet finished that darning, Ursula?' she now asked.

'Nearly, grandmother—I'll be finished in a few minutes.'

Ursula always called Mrs Weldon 'grandmother,' it was so much simpler.

'You should have finished by now. I want you to take a letter to Mr Clayton and bring me back the reply.'

The girl jumped to her feet, glad of an excuse to be off on her bicycle, but Mrs Weldon held up her hand.

'Finish your darning first, and then you can come to me for the letter.'

'How like grandmother—so tiresome!' thought Ursula, but she sat down again and finished her darning—not too carefully, it is to be feared.

A few moments later she was cycling down the hilly road to Rathfarnham, where Mr Clayton lived, in one of the numerous new houses which had sprung up there recently. He had been introduced to Mrs Weldon by a mutual friend, and she had been greatly struck with what she regarded as his sound business knowledge; his accounts of various investments in which he was interested had especially appealed to the old woman. Of late, she had seen her income dwindling at an appalling rate; since the war it had been diminishing, and recently it had become smaller and smaller. Dividends which at one time had been good, were poor enough now. Then the cost of living had gone up and never come down; wages, too, were higher; she had had to increase the wages of the maids and the gardener. She had been compelled to give the increase because, at her age, she could not bear the thought of strange servants at Clodagh. Kate Doyle and Delia Flanagan had been many years with her now, they understood her ways, and they were not like those young girls of whom she had been told, who wanted so many free evenings in the week and late leave to go to the pictures. Sometimes she would think of the wages paid to the domestic staff when she had first held the reins at Clodagh; of the cost of living; of the good old Victorian traditions which were now all gone. Altogether, the world had gone mad, in the opinion of old Mrs Weldon, and as time went on things seemed to be getting worse. That they were worse for her, from a financial standpoint, she could not deny, and she had wished for some time past that she could augment her income, even a little. Since her marriage, she had never been compelled to count every penny, but lately that was what it had come to. She still kept all the household accounts, and looked after the house and garden down to the smallest detail. As for Ursula, she regarded her as almost a child, and would never have thought of consulting her in any way. Yet, had she done so, she might have been spared much worry and also the trouble which was to come, for, although Mrs Weldon never dreamt of such a thing, Ursula had inherited much of the old lady's business capacity.

This Mr George Clayton had told her that he was a stockbroker and she had decided to consult him about her investments. He might be able to advise her, might be able to suggest better investments for her money than had been done by Mr Manton. It would have been different if Mr Manton, senior, had been still alive. But he was dead, and Mrs Weldon did not like the son who had succeeded to the practice. She generally referred to him as 'that young puppy'. The unfortunate young man—who was not so young after all, being in his thirties—was terrified of the redoubtable old woman, but his conscience and common-sense would not allow him to let her make a fool of herself by investing her money in some wild-goose scheme. He had been amazed to see that of late Mrs Weldon seemed to be losing that sound business instinct for which she had been noted all her life. She was getting senile, of course, he thought. Yet what could he do except try and save what little capital was left, so that the girl would not be left penniless when the old lady died. If he had known that she contemplated consulting Mr Clayton, he would have driven out to Clodagh on the instant. But he knew nothing until it was too late.

Mrs Weldon was determined to see what her new friend would advise, and so sent him a letter by Ursula, asking him to call at Clodagh as soon as convenient.

Ursula did not like Mr Clayton. She thought that his nose was too long and his manner too oily. He lived alone with a housekeeper, and as he greeted the girl she thought that he held her cool hand in his warm moist ones much longer than was necessary.

'Well, my dear—and what can I do for you?' As he spoke, he led the way into what he called his 'study'. This was a small, newly furnished room, the windows, on this warm evening, all tightly closed.

'I have brought you a letter from grandmother, and you are please to give me an answer.'

She spoke exactly like a prim schoolgirl, for so she had been taught, and in spite of her modern outlook, the manners of childhood still clung to her. But in her own mind she was thinking what a horrid man he was—slimy, like a slug!—and wishing that he would hurry and reply to the letter, so that she might escape from him, from this stuffy room, out into the pure air again.

At last, he did write the reply, just a few words, saying that he would do himself the honour of calling upon Mrs Weldon at eleven the next morning.

And then, just as Ursula was walking swiftly to the door, he asked her, casually: 'And what do *you* intend to do with yourself, Miss Draper? Have you decided on your future career?'

Ursula paused and stood by the door in silence for a moment. This Mr Clayton was a horrid man, but her grandmother thought a lot of him from a business point of view—she knew that. Supposing he could help her by speaking to Mrs Weldon—asking her to allow her granddaughter to take this commercial course, explaining to her that nearly every girl was working for her living these days? Little as Ursula knew about Mrs Weldon's affairs, she had guessed of late that she was worried over money matters. In that case, surely she would be glad to allow her granddaughter to earn some money.

Impulsively she spoke.

'Oh, Mr Clayton,' she said, 'I am very anxious to take a course at one of those commercial colleges—one that would fit me for a secretarial post or something like that. But grandmother will not hear of it. You see, she is very old-fashioned and does not understand that girls nowadays are earning their own living just the same as young men. I wonder if you spoke to her—explained to her how things are in the business world—how many girls are in positions today—I wonder would she listen to you and let me do as I wish?'

He smiled at her. She did not like his smile, but put up with it in the hope that he might speak for her.

'Why, of course, my dear! I shall be delighted to help you in every way possible. As you so aptly remark, girls nowadays earn their own living in practically every walk of life. I could tell you of ladies who are earning more than their husbands or brothers. I am sure, too, that you have the ability and that you would do well at business. I shall certainly mention the matter to Mrs Weldon when I see her tomorrow. But it is, of course, a little secret between us?'

'Oh, of course! And thank you so much!'

She could not now withdraw her hand too quickly when he held it in a moist grasp, but she was glad when she found herself once more on her bicycle, speeding homewards.

In a few moments she saw a small two-seater car coming towards her and a hand waving to her to stop. At the wheel sat Greta Mason, granddaughter of one of those 'Mason boys' with whom Ursula used to dance and play tennis in those far-off days of the 'nineties'.

She drew up beside Ursula.

'Hello, Ursula—you are the very girl I wanted to see! What about the old dame? Is she still adamant about your future? Are you to be allowed to earn your own living and enjoy a bit of life? Or must you sit at home and sew a fine seam all the rest of your days—or hers, which comes to the same thing, because, as far as I can see, the ancient crone will live for ever.'

'I don't know what to say about it, Greta. I have done all I could to make her change her mind, but she won't. However, now I have a hope—a faint one—but still a hope.'

'Well—go on, tell us more about this ray of hope. It sounds interesting.'

'I have been talking to a Mr Clayton. He is a stockbroker, and is going to advise grandmother about some investments—at least I think so. He asked me what I was going to do, what sort of a career I would like? So I told him that grandmother would not hear of anything of the sort, and I asked him to speak to her and try and get her to understand how different things are now to what they were when she was young. Grandmother is so fearfully old-fashioned!'

'Yes, I know—a fossil! All the same, Ursula, don't you know that when she was left a widow, she took over control of the business in Capel Street? I often heard dad speak about it. He says she was a wonderful woman.'

'I know all that—Kate has told me many a time. Only for her I wouldn't know much of my family history as grandmother never talks much to me. You see she has never forgiven me because my birth caused the death of my mother and she was devoted to her. But it is the present and the future—not the past—which interests me. I only hope that Mr Clayton will persuade grandmother to see reason.'

'And I hope so, too. That is what I wanted to talk to you about. I am taking a flat near Fitzwilliam Street and sharing it with that Brown girl. Flower, she calls herself—such a name for such a girl—there's nothing of a flower about Miss Brown. However, she works in a smart hat shop, and as I am starting my course in beauty culture and hairdressing, we are sharing the flat. I was just thinking that there would be room for you if you could come. It would help us, too, for the rents of those flats are enormous.'

Ursula's eyes sparkled.

'Oh, Greta—I would just *love* it!'

'Yes—wouldn't you? A latchkey of your own at last; no questions asked when you come in or go out—keep any hours you like. Then we are close to the cinemas, and there would be plenty of dances, too. Now, do you think your grandmother will ever be brought to consent?'

'It all depends upon Mr Clayton. She thinks a lot of him.'

'What is he like?'

'A horrid man—slimy and oily! I detest him, but I had to be polite to him just now in the hope that he would speak for me tomorrow.'

'Of course. Always get what you can out of a man whether you like him or not—that's my motto.'

'I think it's a horrid motto.'

'Oh—bunkum! When you know as much about men as I do you will know that they always take all they can from us—and don't give us much in return. However, I must be off, I have to meet Miss Flower Brown in town—No, it's not poetry!—to make final arrangements about the flat. I suppose you wouldn't throw your bike into some shop in the village and come along with me? We could do the pictures and a dance afterwards—what do you say?'

'Oh, Greta—if I only could! But you know how impossible it is.'

'Well, we will hope for better luck soon. Cheerio, Honey—I'll be seeing you!'

And with a bang and a snort the two-seater went roaring on its way.

Jumping on her humble bicycle, Ursula was soon at home. The old lady was quite pleased when she read Mr Clayton's reply and seemed in good spirits for the rest of the evening. Ursula was almost tempted to bring up the matter so near to her heart, but having asked Mr Clayton to speak for her she thought it best to leave it so. And this proved to be the better way.

The following morning while he was with her grandmother Ursula wandered into the garden, too anxious to sit still anywhere. Pat Doyle—a relative of Kate's—was busy weeding. He was an old man and almost past his work, but of late he alone had had to do all the work of the gardens at Clodagh. Mrs Weldon could not keep another man—or even a boy to help. Ursula paused beside him. 'You have a lot to do—haven't you, Pat?' she asked idly.

The old man straightened himself as he replied.

'A dale too much, Miss Ursula. I mind the time when there were two gardeners and a boy here, but now I have all to do meself, and no wan man could do that same. The mistress says she can't afford any help, so since Jimmy left last month I'm tryin' to do what I can. But sure the place is goin' to rack and ruin.'

'Yes—it's a pity,' replied Ursula. 'But times are getting so hard. I wish I could help you, Pat, like Miss Short up at Lilburne—she is a great gardener.'

'Mebbe—mebbe. But I don't hould wid women doin' gardening—they were never fit for such work.'

'I don't agree with you. If only I had been taught I would have been as good as any man. Just like those land girls who do such a lot.'

'Yerrah, is it them bould hussies? God forbid, Miss Ursula, that you ever were like them. But I must be gettin' on wid me weedin' now.'

Ursula wandered around, remembering what a lovely place the gardens had been when she was a child—indeed up to quite recently, just before the old lady had begun to talk about her money troubles. It was a pity that the gardens were not properly looked after, as surely they would have paid for their upkeep. But somehow, grandmother seemed to have lost heart over the garden lately. And she had been so devoted to it, loving every flower—every tree—that grew there.

Presently, Ursula turned and went back to the house. She felt that she could stand this uncertainty no longer. Surely they would have finished their talk by now?

The sitting-room door was ajar as she passed it, and Mr Clayton must have heard her footstep, for he opened the door wide as she reached it, calling out:

'Is that you, Miss Draper?' and before she could reply, had shaken hands effusively and pulled forward a chair.

'You are just in time,' he said. 'Mrs Weldon has been talking to me about your desire to take a commercial course, and I have taken the liberty of advising her to allow you to do this. I hope that you do not object—do not consider that I have intruded in any way?'

No one could have ever thought that all this had been planned beforehand. Yet, although Ursula was grateful to him for his help, she did not like his manner, his deception of her grandmother. He must be laughing in his sleeve at the old lady—his tongue in his cheek all the time. No doubt he thought that Ursula was enjoying the joke also. But the girl was too loyal to do so. She hated deceiving Mrs Weldon in this fashion, and if only that lady had been more reasonable, not quite so far behind the times, she would never have done it. But how could any girl be expected to put up with the sort of life which she was compelled to lead? No cinema or dances, the hours of every day planned and mapped out for her; sewing, reading, going for walks or a ride on her bicycle; indoors by nine o'clock—summer time!—in bed at ten. It was too much. She must get free at any cost, and now was her opportunity.

'Oh, grandmother—do you really mean it?' she cried.

Mrs Weldon replied in the cold tones to which the girl was accustomed:

'Yes, I have decided to allow you take this course. I hope that you will concentrate and try to do well. My means are not what they were—as I have just been telling Mr Clayton—and I could not afford to waste any more money on you except I thought that it would be of some real use.'

'But I think that before long your money worries will be a thing of the past, my dear Mrs Weldon,' interposed Mr Clayton; 'and in any case I feel sure that Miss Draper will do well at her studies, and when the course is finished I may be able to find her a suitable post with some good business firm.'

'Oh, thank you, Mr Clayton! And you, too, grandmother, it is so kind of you!'

'Well, that will do now. We will speak about it later.'

Ursula knew herself to be dismissed, and as she ran out again to the garden to think it all over, it seemed too good to be true. Was it possible that her grandmother had given way at last and was going to allow her to take this course at Mallon's Commercial School? What a marvellous man this Mr Clayton must be. She had been begging her grandmother for months and months for this same thing and had always met with a curt refusal.

And so it was arranged. The school opened early in September, and greatly to Ursula's astonishment, Mrs Weldon consented that she should share the flat with Greta Mason and Miss Brown. It was Mrs Mason who had got round the old lady to agree to this. She said how nice it would be for the girls to be together, and after all Tibradden was rather out of the way for a girl to cycle backwards and forwards twice a day. And then Ursula would have to take her lunch in town, while if she shared a flat she could share with the others, and it would really be the cheapest in the long run. So Mrs Weldon, rather against her will, allowed herself to be persuaded, and on the first day of September, Ursula left Clodagh and went to live at 99 Elton Street, close to Fitzwilliam Square.

CHAPTER X

THREE GIRLS IN A FLAT

'Gosh! Such weather!'

Miss Brown hung her mackintosh and hat on the bathroom door and put her umbrella in the bath to drain. Having washed her face and changed her shoes she went into the sitting-room. She was the first home on this wet October evening, and she plugged in the electric fire with a vicious jerk. She hated the rain, it always put her in a bad temper, and as she threw herself into a chair she was wishing that she could win the Sweep and be off to sunny climes before the real winter set in.

Flower Brown was a short, thick-set girl in the early twenties. She was rather plain, with smallish eyes—'boot buttons', Greta called them—and a sallow complexion. She used no make-up except lipstick, and this she put on so thickly that it was like a deep gash across the paleness of her face. Her hair was her best point, being thick and naturally wavy. She was a clever woman of business and a splendid saleswoman, persuading elderly ladies to buy hats that were only meant for the very young, and making the young buy two hats where one would have been enough—at the price. Anyone less like a flower, it would have been hard to imagine, but a fond mother had so dubbed her only child when she was a baby and the name had stuck. Her mother lived in Waterford and Flower was a good daughter, spending most of her short holidays with her, and helping to augment Mrs Brown's slender means.

Flower was just thinking of getting her own tea when Greta Mason and Ursula entered, having met on the doorstep. Greta was a great contrast to Miss Brown, being extremely pretty and extremely smart; instead of Flower's drab mackintosh and plain umbrella, Greta wore a scarlet waterproof cloak with hat and umbrella to match. Ursula, needless to remark, had no such attire, being as plainly garbed as Miss Brown.

They just put their heads around the sitting-room door on their way to change, and Greta called out: 'Hello—you in, Flower? Plug in the kettle like an angel and make some toast.'

The flat was small but compact; a large sitting-room, two small bedrooms, a tiny kitchenette. Ursula had been six weeks at Elton

Street and was growing accustomed to a life which was so different from that lived at Clodagh. She was attending Mallon's Commercial School and trying to study hard, but this was not easy. Nearly every night there was some distraction; they were going to the pictures or a dance, or friends would drop in and stay talking until late. Ursula, accustomed all her life to the early hours and quiet routine of Clodagh, had at first felt out of place in this new existence. But she was becoming accustomed to it, and if at times she had doubts about her studies and examinations, she put the thoughts behind her and continued to enjoy her liberty and life as it was lived at 99 Elton Street. She was changed, even in that short time, in some indefinite way; she seemed older, was becoming more modern in her opinions, wore her clothes better. Greta had introduced her to a number of young people—all ultra-modern in their ideas and manner of life; the girls modelled on whoever happened to be their favourite film star for the moment; the young men trying to be as sophisticated as possible.

'Well, Flower,' said Greta, as they sat down to tea, 'have you asked Harry Dalton if he can come on Thursday?'

'Yes. He says that he will.'

'Good! And what about you, Ursula? Who will be your guest at our own particular bean feast?'

'I should like to ask Maureen O'Dwyer—she is such a nice girl.'

'Oh, gee—that Gaelic person! Do you think she would mix with the rest of the crowd? We are not her style, you know.'

'She is all right, Greta. Great fun, too, when you know her.'

'O.K.—so long as she is not too straitlaced. We will be a bit latish—or earlyish—breaking up. Where does she live?'

'I think it's somewhere in Rathfarnham.'

'Oh, well, she will probably be gone before the noisy crowd get into their stride. But have you no boy friend you want to ask?'

It was Miss Brown who made the last remark, and Greta laughed as she replied: 'Ursula has no use for boyfriends. If only she were a Roman Catholic she could retire into a convent—I really think she would be quite happy there.'

Flower smiled loftily.

'I don't care much for boys myself.'

'That's a pity!' replied Greta, with a wink at Ursula. It did not go unnoticed by Flower, who said at once: 'Oh, I know I am not attractive in the general sense of the word. But I am smart and well groomed, and what is best of all—I possess *chic.*'

Miss Brown was very fond of saying she possessed this quality; the remark had been made about her by a wealthy client and it had never been forgotten by Flower. A chic shop—Madame Moderne's was surely that—chic hats and a chic saleswoman to sell them. Flower considered all this entitled her to hold her head very high indeed.

'Don't let us fight, anyway,' said Greta. 'I do hope our party will be a success.'

'But of course it will!' cried Ursula, who was quite thrilled at the thought of it. The girls had arranged to hold a bean feast to celebrate setting up housekeeping together, and each was to invite two or three—not more—friends to come to supper on the following Thursday. This was Tuesday and they were deep in preparations for the event. The flat was small, but this did not deter Greta. There would be no cooking as they were having sandwiches and cakes only. As for drinks: 'I suppose we will be boiling kettles all the time?' asked Ursula with a laugh.

'Boiling kettles? Not on your life!' replied Greta.

'But they will want tea or coffee?'

'No. This will be a cocktail party, my sweet innocent. And Grant Foxall is a champion mixer and shaker!'

Ursula did not know what Greta was talking about, but not liking to display her ignorance—which was so often the cause of merriment to the other two—she kept silent. But she was certainly surprised when she saw the amount of drink which arrived on the day of the party.

The guests had been asked for eight o'clock, but only one arrived anywhere near that hour. This was Maureen O'Dwyer. The others drifted in about nine or after.

'I hope I am not too early?' said the first guest, 'I thought you said eight o'clock.'

'Yes—that is all right,' replied Greta, 'the others are not very punctual people. Ursula will show you where to take off your things—you will have to throw them anywhere, this place is so small.'

As Maureen O'Dwyer followed Ursula from the room, Greta made a grimace.

'She will be shocked if the crowd are noisy,' she said, 'such a prim young lady—not our sort at all.'

'Oh, she's not too bad,' replied Flower; 'pretty, too—in the Celtic way. Would do for an advertisement for one of our latest Galway hats.'

In the next room Maureen was taking off her coat and running a comb through her dark hair which she wore in a big knot. Her eyes were large and dark grey, and her cheeks had the colour which mother nature—and the Dublin hills—had bestowed upon them. She was absolutely natural, no make-up at all. A rare sight in these artificial days. Ursula, too, had hardly any make-up, just a little powder. She had not yet dared to venture on rouge or lipstick. The vision of old Mrs Weldon was too real, too near to her. One does not get over the training of a lifetime in a few weeks.

'I hope your party is not very smart?' said Maureen. 'I always think that when a party starts late it is a grand one—very posh! And you know I am not that. Will I do? Am I all right?'

'You are lovely, Maureen! I like your frock so much.'

'I am glad. I was afraid it might not be smart enough. Mother made it for me.'

The frock was of some soft material, rose coloured, the elbow sleeves being the only concession to so-called 'evening dress'.

But Maureen felt decidedly out of the picture when the other guests began to arrive. The girls wore such smart frocks, they had so much lipstick and rouge, they smoked so many cigarettes. Maureen was, as Greta had opined, rather 'out of it'.

When presently she refused the cocktail offered, Ursula made tea for herself and her guest, and as they drank it sitting by themselves in a corner, they began to talk, more intimately than they had done before.

'How gay they all are!' said Ursula. 'I feel rather in the way here at times. I was brought up very strictly and in an old-fashioned way by my grandmother. I was never at a party like this until I came here.'

'Do you think that they are really gay?' asked the other. 'Their good spirits seem to me rather forced.'

'Do you think so? I had not noticed it.'

But she saw now that Maureen was right. There was an atmosphere of artificial gaiety, the laughter was too loud, too metallic to be real.

'Do you like living in town?' asked Maureen.

'Oh, yes—I love it!'

'How strange. I should just hate it.'

'You live in Rathfarnham, don't you?' asked Ursula.

The girls had met at the commercial school and had become very friendly; although not alike in any way, they were drawn to one another from the first day they met.

'Yes—at River House. It is at the corner of Lilac Lane. Do you know Rathfarnham at all?'

'Well, I should think so! I have lived all my life at Whitechurch—or just beyond it at Tibradden. Clodagh Cottage is my home. That is where my grandmother—Why, what is the matter?' For Maureen O'Dwyer was staring at her as though she had been a ghost.

'Then you must be Mrs Weldon's granddaughter—or rather her great-granddaughter?'

'Yes, I am. But I always call her grandmother. Do you know her?'

Maureen smiled.

'My grandmother was married to her son,' she replied. 'My mother was Maureen Weldon before she married my father. Did you not know about us? We are cousins, you know.'

Ursula stared at the other girl in amazement. So this was her cousin, one of the family—the disgraceful family according to Mrs Weldon—who lived in the old house at the corner of Lilac Lane. She remembered how often she had passed it and thought what a nice homely place it looked. In summer the sun would be shining on the river as it flowed by the foot of the garden and there was a crazy pathway leading to a queerly built summer-house. Her grandmother never spoke of those who lived there, but from Kate Doyle she had heard a good deal. But she had never been told of that evening in 1916, when Mrs Weldon had watched her grandson being taken away—a prisoner between two British soldiers.

'Do you live there with your mother?' she asked now. 'And is your grandmother still alive?'

'Oh, yes—dear granny! She is such a dear. But of course you know what a granny is like——' She stopped suddenly in some confusion, recollecting all that she had heard about the terrible old lady at Clodagh Cottage.

'Yes—please go on,' prompted Ursula, who wanted to know more about these cousins.

'My Uncle Jack lives with us, too. He was arrested and imprisoned in 1916, but released afterwards when the amnesty came. He is a chartered accountant. And then mother still works at Casey's—the flower shop, you know. We sell quite a lot of our flowers to Mrs Casey. And I am training for a business career, as you already know. Now tell me about yourself.'

'There is not much to tell. I have always lived with grandmother. My mother died when I was born, and I think that grandmother never forgave me because I cost my mother her life. She loved my mother very much—more than anyone except perhaps your grandfather. I believe she was very fond of him—at least until he——'

Ursula paused, but Maureen finished the sentence for her.

'Until he married my grandmother, you mean?'

'Yes—that is what I mean. As for myself—she just tolerates me. She thinks it is her duty to look after me for my mother's sake. But she does not care for me.'

'Oh, but that is nonsense. There are but the two of you—she must love you. I wonder she ever allowed you to leave her and come to live here. I go home every evening, but then Rathfarnham is more convenient than Tibradden and there are so many buses going there—which there are not to Tibradden. Still your grandmother must feel lonely now without you at Clodagh.'

'I do not think so. She is always so self-sufficient—or appears to be so. Very serene and quiet. Lately I think she has been worried about money matters, but I do not suppose it is much. She is a strange woman. No one can really understand grandmother. I have heard that she was a wonderful business woman herself, and when my great-grandfather died, years and years ago, she took over the control of his place in Capel Street—and at that time, of course, women were not in business like they are now. Yet when I asked her to let me take this commercial course at Mallon's she would not listen to the idea. It was not until a business man, of whom she thinks a lot, advised her to do so that at last she consented.'

'How queer. Well, anyway, you and my humble self must be better friends than ever—now that we are cousins. You must come and see us at the River House.'

'I wonder if I could?'

'Why not?'

Ursula was silent. How could she explain that her grandmother still felt bitter animosity against all those at the River House? And then they were Catholics.

'Well, we will see about it later,' she said. 'I would just love it, but there is grandmother to consider.'

At that moment Greta came towards them with a young man.

'Now I think that you two are most unsociable,' she said, 'sitting here by your two selves all alone. Anyhow, here is a gentleman who wishes to be introduced to you, Ursula. He thinks that he should know you.'

Maureen slipped away to where she saw a girl whom she knew sitting alone, and Greta having made the necessary introductions, left Ursula and the young man together.

'Do I know you?' asked Ursula, rather puzzled. The name 'Owens' conveyed nothing to her.

'Well, I guess not—yet,' was the reply, spoken with a slight, but not unpleasant American accent. Greta, the film fan, would not have noticed this, but Ursula was not accustomed to the accents of the films, and her ears were quick to catch the American inflection.

'You are an American?' she asked.

He laughed. 'So my speech betrays me?' he said. 'I did not think it was so bad!'

'Oh, I did not mean *bad*——' The girl flushed, fearing that she had hurt his feelings.

'No harm done,' he said, with a smile. 'I am not an American really, but having been born and brought up in New York it would be hard for me to escape altogether from the accent. You could hardly expect it—now could you?'

'No, of course not. I am so sorry——'

'Not at all. May I sit down?'

Taking her consent for granted, he seated himself beside her as he spoke. 'I wanted to meet you,' he said, 'because, quite accidentally, I heard Miss Mason telling the friend who brought me here, that you lived at a place called Clodagh—away in the Dublin hills somewhere—isn't it?'

'Yes, I was born there. I have lived there all my life. Do you know it?'

'Never seen it—yet. But my folk hailed from there. My great-grandfather was out in the Fenian Rising—you can bet I am proud of the old chap!—and he escaped to New York afterwards. His son, my grandfather, made his pile there, and later my old dad added his bit to it. I am here on a holiday before taking my place in the business. Some holiday, too!'

'How strange,' murmured Ursula. Racking her brains, she could faintly remember some story about the Owen family. Kate had heard it from old Mary Molloy and old Dan Brophy, who was said to have been concerned in the Rising himself—always such a queer secretive man that the other servants never liked to ask him anything.

So this was the great-grandson of that Terence Owens who must have been a young man when Faith Weldon had come as a girl bride to Clodagh. How strange to think of it all. Now Faith Weldon was an old, old woman, living alone with her memories. And Terence Owens dead. Dead like so many others who had been 'out' with him, and who had seen the failure of their fight for Ireland.

She turned to him with a smile.

'How queer it must be for you, Mr Owens, to be seeing Ireland now for the first time.'

'Queer enough. But I think I shall like it. I only arrived in Dublin yesterday. By the way, do you think that your grandmother would allow me to see Clodagh if I ran out there tomorrow? I have a car, of course, though it is not like the one I have at home. I could ring her up, I suppose?'

Ursula's lips twitched at the idea of anyone alluding in that casual way to Mrs Weldon. And as to ringing her up!

'There is no telephone at Clodagh,' she replied; 'and I think you would want to write a formal letter to my grandmother and make an appointment to see her. But even then I do not know, I could not be certain——'

'In fact the old dame is a bit on the crotchety side? A bit of the ancient beldame—is that it?'

Ursula was really shocked. 'Oh, please do not speak like that,' she said; 'Mrs Weldon is very particular and a little old-fashioned. That is all. Besides, your people were rebels——'

'Rebels?' He interrupted her at once. 'I guess you are making a big mistake, if I may be allowed to say so. A rebel is one who fights against his own government—isn't that so?'

'Why, yes——'

'Well, I reckon that my great-grandfather was no rebel. He did not rebel against an Irish government or his own people, but against the British. And that is a different story.'

Ursula stiffened slightly. This was such a queer young man. She did not know whether to like him or not.

'I am afraid we must agree to differ on those questions,' she said, speaking as primly as even Mrs Weldon could have wished.

'As you wish, fair lady. And in the meantime, I will write to Mrs Weldon and ask her gracious permission to visit the home of my ancestors. Is that quite correct?'

'You are laughing at me,' replied the girl, and made as if to leave him.

'No—don't go, please! Forgive my Yankee talk and stay here a little longer. You see I don't know anyone here except my friend, and he has disappeared, and to tell you the truth, I don't care much for this crowd. They are so unlike what I expected to find in Ireland, I feel kind of disappointed.'

It was her turn to laugh now.

'Why? What did you expect?' she asked. 'The girls dressed like the Colleen Bawn and the men in knee breeches——'

His stare of amazement made her pause.

'But of course not. I am not so ignorant as not to know that stage Irish characters are gone. But I certainly thought that I would hear the Gaelic spoken and see some Gaelic costumes.'

'Oh—that kind of thing! You would have to go to the Gaelic League crowd for that. You have come to the wrong place.'

'That is what I have been thinking. You see it is not easy for a stranger to understand Ireland. I had heard that there was an anglicised crowd here, but I had never met them before. In New York we Irish *are* Irish.'

'I must introduce you to Miss O'Dwyer, she is one of the Irish-Ireland people. She will talk away in Gaelic to you—but I suppose you would not understand a word she was saying?'

'But indeed I would. I can speak the Gaelic fairly well. We have Irish classes in New York and are great enthusiasts in the cause. It seems to me, indeed, that we are more Irish over there than you are here.'

'You are with the wrong people—that is all,' she replied. Then she asked, curiously: 'How did you happen to come here at all?'

'I had an introduction to young Dalton, and as he was invited here this evening, he asked me to come also. He promised me some pretty girls and a jolly evening. But it seems to me that you are the only girl here I would care to know—that is with the exception of your friend—the one who was with you when Miss Mason introduced us.'

'That is the Miss O'Dwyer of whom I told you. She is my cousin. Come and look for her. You will find her as Irish as yourself.'

'There is no hurry, surely? Let us stay here a little while longer and then we will go and look for your cousin in the pink frock.'

As they sat and talked, the time slipped past, and when at last they rose and went to look for Maureen, it was only to be told that she had gone home.

'Her uncle called for her at half-past ten,' said Greta. 'You would think she was a child at a Christmas party! I asked him to stay and join us, but he said it was late enough and his sister was not used to late hours. Wouldn't even have a drink!'

'Say—I'm sorry I missed seeing your cousin,' said Owens. 'I should have liked to meet her.'

'So you can,' replied Ursula. 'Any time you like to make an appointment, I will ask her here to tea.'

'A thousand thanks! I will let you know when I can come.'

CHAPTER XI

THE SHADOW OVER CLODAGH

Terence Owens—Terry to his friends—did not take Ursula's advice regarding his visit to Clodagh. He did not write, asking if he might call. Instead, he set off a few days later in the car he had on hire, to explore the neighbourhood from which had come his father's people so many years ago.

The rain had gone, the day one of those delightful ones which we sometimes get in October, fine, bright, with a touch of frost and a blue sky overhead, while on hedgerow and tree the leaves showed in their autumnal shades of russet and gold. So Terry saw the lovely road to Whitechurch under ideal conditions. His car was no time passing through Rathfarnham and on to Whitechurch. On his right he saw the old Catholic burying ground, to his left the Moravian Cemetery, dark and gloomy, then the Protestant Church, with its tall spires. Further on, he asked the way from a woman standing at her cottage door, and soon afterwards he was at the gate of Clodagh.

He thought that he would have recognised the house from the description which he had so often heard, and when he looked upon it now and remembered that it was from those very doors his great-grandfather had been obliged to flee after the Fenian Rising, he caught his breath suddenly, his Irish blood coming to the surface, bidding him salute the Fenian dead.

The place was very quiet as he stopped the car and got out. Pushing open the gate he was approaching the house, when a small black cocker came rushing towards him, barking furiously. However, Terry happened to be a dog-lover and so a few words exchanged between them put matters right. Judy's bark was now one of welcome and she ran before him to the door as if they had been old friends.

Terence stood on the steps for a moment to look around him before lifting the old-fashioned knocker. On the left he saw the gardens stretching away to the back, in front a fine herbaceous border ended in a rock garden and summer-house. In the distance could be seen the smoke of the city, and when he turned round, the Dublin hills were standing in all their beauty, clear against the horizon. A lovely home, there was no doubt about that. And it had once belonged to his people.

In answer to his knock, the door was opened by an old woman, very clean and tidy, in every detail the old-fashioned servant about whom one may read nowadays, but never meet. To Terry she was a new character, and anyone more unlike the American servants could hardly be imagined.

'You rang, sir?'

'Yes—can I see Mrs Weldon?'

'I could not say, sir, but if you will give me your name and state your business, I will ask her. The mistress does not see many people at present, she has not been very well.'

'Say—I'm sorry to hear that, but here is my card, and if you will tell her that I happened to be in this neighbourhood and thought I should like to call upon her, I shall be greatly obliged to you.'

Kate Doyle was gazing at the name upon the card, and when she had read it, she looked up at the young man with a puzzled expression.

'Do you know me?' he asked with a smile.

'I know the name, sir. An old aunt of mine often spoke of a Mrs Owens and her son who owned this place once. He—he had to go away——'

'Yes—to America. That was my great-grandfather. He was a Fenian, you know——'

'Oh, speak easy, please sir! If the mistress heard that sort of talk she would never see you, nor let you cross the doorstep. She is very bitter entirely about them things. Will I ask her now if she will see you?'

'Please do—if you will be so kind.'

Kate looked at him for a moment without speaking.

'I am an old woman, sir,' she said then, 'over seventy. Will you shake hands with me—for the sake of those old times when your people were here at Clodagh, and my people were working for them?'

Terry extended his strong hand and took her old one in a firm grip, as he said: 'And I am proud to shake hands with you—shake and shake again!'

'But look at me keeping you standing all this time on the doorstep! Come in, please, and wait in the sitting-room while I tell the mistress you are here. She is upstairs.'

'Try and get her to see me—like a good soul.'

Left to himself, Terry gazed around him at the old-fashioned furniture, the old prints on the walls—everything good and well cared for, but definitely 'dated', as he would have phrased it. And the date was that of the late Victoria of England. He was thinking what a pretty room this would be if only refurnished in a more modern manner, when the door opened and the mistress of Clodagh entered. She came towards him, her keen eyes fixed upon his face.

'Mr Owens? You wished to see me?'

'Yes, Mrs Weldon. I belong to the family from whom I understand your late husband bought this place.'

The old woman motioned him to a chair and sat down herself.

'That was a long—a very long—time ago,' she said; 'it must have been your grandfather who was here last—or rather his mother from whom we bought the house?'

Terry smiled. 'My great-grandfather,' he said.

'Ah, yes—that would be it. You are young and I—I sometimes forget the passing of the years.'

She was silent, and after a moment Terry ventured to ask if he might see over the gardens?

'I shall be very pleased to allow you to do so. But will you not rest for a while first? You must be tired after your walk—or did you get a bus?'

'Oh, I came in my automobile. I ran out from the city very quickly, so I am not tired.'

'You mean a motor car?'

'That's correct, Mrs Weldon. We have different names for things over the herring pond, you know.'

'And how do you think you will like Ireland?'

'Quite a lot, I guess. By the way, I had the pleasure of meeting your granddaughter a few nights ago.'

'You mean Miss Draper? She is my great-granddaughter.'

'Some girl—if I may say so. We had quite a talk together. She was introduced to me by a Miss Mason—I think they share a flat.'

Mrs Weldon stiffened a little. She hoped that Greta Mason was not inviting all and sundry to the flat, she would have to make enquiries. Perhaps she should never have allowed Ursula to live in Dublin.

'If you wish to see the garden, I will come with you now,' she said.

'But I should not like to tire you—I can go alone——'

She drew herself up. 'I may be an old woman, young man,' she replied, 'but I can still walk around my garden.'

As they left the room, Judy, who had been sitting before the fire, got up and accompanied them.

'I see you have made friends with Judy,' remarked Mrs Weldon.

'Oh, yes—I am fond of dogs—we keep quite a number of them at our place in Long Island.'

'It is a good sign when a man likes dogs,' said his hostess, graciously; 'we have had cockers here for generations—the Clodagh breed are quite famous. But I think that this Judy will be the last here, as I have given up keeping them now.'

'Say—what a pity! This is a little beauty.'

'Yes, she is a good dog, and a splendid watch.'

They were strolling down the garden path between beds of asters and dahlias which seemed to be flaunting their beauty in a brave attempt to pretend that summer was still in the land. But Terry's sharp eyes were quick to note the neglect all around; he saw that the garden wanted more work put into it, and thought what a pity it would be if the place had to remain uncared and untended. Mrs Weldon seemed to sense what he was thinking.

'I am not as well off now as I was some time ago,' she said, 'and I cannot afford to pay for the labour which this place needs. Wages have increased to such an absurd amount, and the price of everything also, so that I really find my income insufficient to keep this house and garden in proper condition.'

'Would you not think of selling it?' asked Terry.

She turned upon him with flashing eyes. 'Sell it? Sell Clodagh! You must be mad, young man, to even suggest such a thing. If I had to starve I would rather do so here, within sight of the hills which I love so much—here in my own dear garden—than live in luxury elsewhere.'

She stopped suddenly, her thin voice breaking. Terry gazed at her in dismay.

'Say—I'm real sorry!' he exclaimed. 'Won't you forgive me. I had no idea—I did not know——'

'You need say no more,' she replied, speaking more quietly. 'I quite understand that Americans cannot have the same feelings that we have—I mean towards their homes——'

'Pardon me, but I think you are mistaken. My great-grandfather often spoke to his son about Clodagh, and he, in his turn, told my father. So I have heard a lot about this house, and when I came to Ireland for a holiday, my old man——'

'Your old man?'

'Pardon the American word! I mean my father. He told me to be sure and see the old place, and if it were for sale by any chance, I was to make the first offer.'

'It is *not* for sale, and never will be as long as I own it.'

'There is no more to be said, then. Just forget it!'

They walked along in silence for a few moments, Judy at their heels. Presently they came to where Pat Doyle was working and the dog ran to greet him, she was very fond of the old man. Pat straightened himself as his mistress and the young man—about whom Kate had already spoken—drew near. He touched his forehead as he said: 'A fine day, ma'am, thanks be to God!'

'A lovely day, Pat. This is Mr Owens from America. He is the great-grandson of that young man who went to America when my husband bought Clodagh.'

'D'ye tell me that, ma'am? You are welcome to Ireland, sir—to the home of your people—if I may say so.'

'Thank you, I guess it's mighty kind of you to say so. Shake!' and in his American manner Terry held out his hand. Pat was supremely gratified. He could faintly remember the story of that other Terence Owens who had been 'out' with the Fenians. He wondered if this young fellow had the same notions? Hardly likely—after all these years. Still you could never tell. Pat stood looking after him as he walked away beside the mistress.

Returning to the house, Mrs Weldon said: 'You will take a glass of wine before you go?'

Terence, feeling like a character from a Victorian novel, thought it best to accept, and was presently sipping a glass of sherry and nibbling a piece of cake. He found himself liking the old lady. That they were poles apart in their outlook on every possible subject under the sun, he knew, but it did not seem to matter. One had to allow for age and changing view-points. He liked her. She was a quaint old dame, but the goods all the same.

And Mrs Weldon, on her part, also found herself inclined to like this queer young man. She had not met anyone resembling him before, and she liked his frankness, his outspoken speech.

As they talked, Terry put a few carefully-worded questions

regarding her circumstances. To his surprise, she told him that she hoped soon to be much better off than she was at present, that she had a friend who was now looking after her interests and was about to invest her money to greater advantage. Terry listened in some uneasiness. Was the old lady allowing herself to be fooled by some shark?

'You know this man well?' he presently ventured to ask. 'For a good while, I mean?'

'Not for very long, but I was introduced to him by friends in whom I have the utmost confidence—and I have the same confidence in him. He is a wonderful business man. Perhaps you are not aware that I was at one time in control of a business myself—here in Dublin. Of course I am now too old to take any active part in business matters, but I think I can still recognise a good man of business when I meet him.'

'Well, I hope it will turn out real well for you and that you will soon be quite rich. And now, don't be angry with me—please, but if ever you *do* want to sell Clodagh, I ask you as a great favour to let me have the first chance.'

She looked at him, partly vexed, partly astonished.

'Mr Owens,' she said then, 'I do not know what your means may be but the person who wished to purchase Clodagh would require a couple of thousand pounds. There is a good deal of land attached to the house.'

'I think I could manage that amount if necessary,' replied Terry with a smile. He could have laughed to think how little that sum would appear to his wealthy father. Rising to his feet, he told Mrs Weldon that he must go now as he had an appointment to keep in the city.

'And I want to thank you for your kindness. I shall not forget to tell my father all about it.'

'You were very welcome,' she replied, ceremoniously. 'I was happy to be able to show you the old place. Perhaps when you come again it may be looking more like the Clodagh which I remember best.'

Mrs Weldon accompanied him to the front door, standing on the steps to watch him as he went away. Judy followed him to the gate, and as Terence reached it, he saw another car slowing up. In it was seated a man to whom Terry at once took a strange dislike. He was in the middle forties, stoutish, sallow complexion, with a prominent nose. Involuntarily, the young man found himself thinking of a fat spider, whom he had once watched spinning his web in a corner of the ceiling in a New York lodging-house, where he had gone to visit a poor Irishman. As the man got out of his car, Judy ran forward, barking furiously.

'Get out—you little beast!' cried the visitor, aiming a kick at her. The little dog was too quick and dodged the smart shoe in time, and the man strode up the path to the house. Terence flung him a look which was quite lost upon him. 'Beast yourself!' he thought, as he stooped to pet Judy. 'That fellow is no good, whoever he is.'

It never crossed his mind that this could be the trusted adviser of whom Mrs Weldon had spoken. Had Terry but known that fact, it is quite probable that he would have retraced his steps and had a few words with the old lady and her visitor. As it was, however, he said goodbye to the cocker, and jumping into his car was soon speeding along the road to the city.

In the sitting-room at Clodagh, Mrs Weldon and the caller were seated. He was speaking.

'Yes, my dear Mrs Weldon, I am happy to tell you that I have been able to negotiate the investments of which I spoke. You will be pleased, I think, with the dividends which you will receive— rather more substantial, I can assure you, than those being paid to you at present. It was not easy to obtain the shares, but I have a good business connection, and after a little difficulty I was able to manage. If you will kindly sign these necessary papers for me, I shall make the final arrangements tomorrow with my stockbroker.'

The old lady looked very pleased as she took the papers which he held out. Then, as a faint recollection of some remarks passed by her last visitor returned to her, she asked 'They are quite safe?' Mr Clayton laughed in what he meant to be a genial manner.

'Safe, my dear lady? They are as safe as the Bank of England itself!'

And, as in Mrs Weldon's mind nothing could be safer than the British concern, she was perfectly reassured and obediently signed as requested. Her invitation to partake of a glass of wine was politely refused by Clayton, who told her that he had not literally a moment to spare, having to return to the city as soon as possible.

'These shares are being simply snapped up,' he said, 'and we do not want to lose our chance.'

'Then you are investing in them, too, Mr Clayton?'

'I should say I was! Why, my dear lady, there is not a business man in the city who would not buy them if it could be managed at all. And now good morning—I shall see you again in a few days.'

As he passed close to Judy where she sat before the fire, the dog snarled at him, baring her teeth, her hair standing up.

'Why, Judy—what is the matter with you?' said Mrs Weldon. 'She is such a friendly dog with most people, I cannot understand why she is so cross with you.'

Clayton tried to smile as he stepped gingerly past the dog, he even spoke to her in would-be friendly tones.

'Good dog then—good dog!' and he made silly clucking noises with his tongue. Judy was having none of it. She bared her teeth more than ever and rolled the whites of her eyes at him in cocker fashion. It was plain to be seen that she was both angry and afraid.

'Really, Judy—I am quite ashamed of you! Please do not heed her, Mr Clayton.'

'It is quite all right—quite all right! And now once more, good day!'

But as he reached the door he flung back a look at Judy which she considered to be so insulting that she made a rush for the door—which, however, was shut in her very face. Shaking herself vigorously, as if to get rid of the atmosphere of the horrid visitor, she returned to her seat on the hearthrug.

After George Clayton had gone, Faith Weldon stood at the window looking out at her beloved garden and to the road beyond, along which, in her young days, she had so often driven or walked with her husband at her side. She often thought now of those far-off days, the older she grew, the nearer did the days of her youth seem to be. She could remember them more vividly that the days of a few years back; she liked to re-live them over again, to see herself in crinoline and bonnet walking to church on Sunday; working in her garden, managing her house, driving in her pony carriage, on the other days of those happy years.

It was strange that it was to those days her thoughts turned the most frequently. Happy and content as she had been during the time she had spent as head of the Capel Street business, her mind seldom reverted to that time now. It was as a girl bride, a young mother, that she liked to think of herself now. Now—when her days on earth must surely be numbered.

How thankful she was that she would now be able to do what was needed so badly to both house and garden. Once more Clodagh would be its own self. And when Ursula inherited, she would surely look after the place and keep it in order. Faith Weldon was glad to know that the girl would have Clodagh. Not that she had ever loved the girl as she had loved the mother. She could never do that. But, for the sake of that mother—the little Faith who had come to her out of the snow on Christmas Eve— for her sake she was glad that Ursula would have a comfortable home of her own. She would leave her Clodagh, of course. There were others who some people might think had a better right to the place, but no Roman Catholic should ever inherit Clodagh.

She only hoped that Ursula would make a suitable marriage. She wondered what her husband would be like? She sighed as she realised that in the matter of marriage, Ursula would go her own way. There would be no choosing of a husband for her—no matter how suitable he might be. She was too modern to allow any interference of that kind.

'This modern world—how terrible it is! Young people doing just as they like—not even consulting their elders. How different things were when I was young.'

Yet her own marriage had been of her own making, she had planned for it in a determined, quiet way. Not openly, of course. In fact she had seemed quite surprised when John Weldon had proposed to her! She had almost swooned. But that was how those matters were arranged in those days of long ago. Days of peace and tranquillity—so far away, so almost unbelievable to us who live today.

'I must only pray that Ursula will choose someone who will make a good master for Clodagh,' she thought. 'Come, Judy—we will go for a stroll before dinner.'

CHAPTER XII

LOVE—OR FRIENDSHIP?

During the weeks that followed, Ursula saw a great deal of Terence. He was always dropping into the flat of an evening; sometimes they would just sit and talk, other nights they would go to the Abbey or the Gate. On a few occasions, Greta or Miss Brown had gone with them, but these young women preferred the pictures as a rule. Rather to Ursula's surprise, Terry seldom offered to take her to a cinema—only if she expressed the wish to see a certain picture. 'The movies? No, I'm not keen on them,' he said.

'But why?'

'Oh—I don't know, we get too many of them in the States. Besides, the theatres here are a change for me.'

November came in cold and foggy. 'What a pity it is not summer,' remarked Ursula to Terry one evening, as they were sitting together by the fire, waiting for the other two to come in for tea.

'Well, I reckon that I am enjoying myself as it is.'

'But there are so many lovely places around Dublin and we could have had such jolly outings at the week-ends. Perhaps you will be able to stay for the summer?'

'Not an earthly, I'm afraid. In fact I should be thinking of going home now. You see my old man is not too strong—has had a real hard life—too much business—rush and strain all the time. You folk over here have no notion of it.'

Ursula was silent. She felt very cold suddenly. It was as if happiness had fled for the moment leaving her lonely and forlorn. He was going away, crossing the Atlantic. He thought nothing of the journey, she knew that—no more than she would think of crossing to Holyhead. He would be miles and miles away. But of course he was nothing to her. Never would be, she supposed. Yet he had seemed to like her, had never bothered about Greta or Flower beyond being civil to them and all that; she had been the one of whom he had made a friend. And now she was going to lose him. Well, she would not let him see that she cared—that she would miss him. His voice broke the silence that had fallen.

'Have you seen your grandmother lately?' he asked.

'I am going to Clodagh next Sunday.'

'I wish I could come with you, but perhaps I would not be

welcome.'

'Would you like me to ask grandmother?'

'I should be delighted.'

'Then I will. Clodagh is rather gloomy in the winter—in this kind of weather I mean. It is lovely when it's dry and frosty. Of course I am used to it at all seasons.'

'I hope Mrs Weldon will say it's OK for me to come with you. If she does, I'll drive you in my car. By the way, that is a swell little dog you have there.'

'You mean Judy? She is a dear. I missed her so much when I left home, and Kate said she fretted after me, too.'

'Your grandmother told me that the Clodagh breed of cockers were quite famous?'

'They are—or rather *were*. I am afraid that the present Judy will be the last—at least the last at Clodagh. Grandmother is not going to keep them any more.'

'There were other Judys then?'

'Oh, yes—that is the name we always give the mother dogs. This is Judy the Tenth! There was a Judy in my Grandmother's time, and when she and my mother arrived at Clodagh one cold Christmas Eve, the Judy of that day was there to welcome my mother who was a poor little girl of about seven years old.'

'Tell me about that.'

So she told him the story of that Christmas Eve, as she had heard it from Kate, who, in her turn, had had it from the lips of Mary Molloy. Terry was keenly interested, and they were both so happy, sitting chatting by the fire, that they were quite surprised when the other two returned from business, anxious for their tea.

'Well—I do think you might have had the kettle boiling and some toast made!' cried Greta. 'How long have you been there—gassing away?'

'Oh, not long,' replied Ursula, rising hurriedly to plug in the kettle.

'Say—let me make the toast,' said Terry. 'I'm a real swell hand at that kind of thing!'

'Sure mark!' replied 'The Flower', ironically. However, she cut the bread and Terry toasted it all right.

Mrs Weldon was graciously pleased to allow him to visit her on Sunday. Indeed she invited him to partake of the early dinner at two o'clock, suggesting that he and Ursula should meet her at the church for morning service. Mrs Weldon did not like to miss the service, and, as she was not now able for the walk, Pat Doyle drove her to the church and back every Sunday when it was possible for her to go. In very bad weather or if she was not well, she did not attempt to drive, but if she could attend at all, Faith Weldon would not miss church on Sundays.

It had not dawned upon her that Terence Owens was a Catholic, and Ursula had not thought of it either. She was quite surprised when he said: 'I am glad that Mrs Weldon will have me. I generally go to early Mass, so I can meet you afterwards at the flat and drive you to Whitechurch. I can wait in the car while you are at church.

'You are a Catholic?'

'But of course. Surely you knew that our family was Catholic?'

'I had forgotten, and I expect that grandmother has forgotten also. If you don't mind, Terry, I think it would be better if you said nothing about religion to her. Or about politics either. She lives so much in the past—Victorian and all that.'

'I will watch my steps all right.' Then he asked, rather tentatively: 'And what about you, Ursula?'

'Oh—I do not bother one way or another. When I am at home I have to go to church every Sunday, but I have got a bit slack since I came here—you see the others don't bother about anything like that.'

'And your politics?'

She laughed.

'I have not got any. If you want to discuss that sort of thing, then Maureen is the person for you.'

'Oh, yes—your cousin. I had nearly forgotten about her. You were to introduce me.'

'Yes—I had forgotten, too. Never mind, I will arrange soon to have her here for an evening.'

Sunday was fine and dry. Ursula and Terry were in great spirits as they drove out to Whitechurch, laughing and talking together. At the gates of the church Ursula got out, and Terry went for a drive by himself, coming back in time to meet her after the service. Mrs Weldon was just getting into the pony trap and seemed pleased to see him, but she refused his offer to allow him to drive her in his car. So he and Ursula were at Clodagh some time before Browney, the pony, had made his leisurely way along the hilly road home.

Dinner passed off well, and afterwards they sat by the fire in the pleasant room and chatted until tea time. Terry found himself liking Mrs Weldon more and more, and, on her part, she liked him also. He had to be careful about religion and politics, but, on the whole, managed to steer clear of these dangerous subjects.

Twilight came, and before the lamps were lit—there was no other light at Clodagh—the old lady unbent and began to talk about her earlier days there. Ursula was astonished, she had never known her grandmother to be so communicative.

'Of course you must understand that the Clodagh of those days was a different place from what it is today. My late husband could afford to keep it up in good style, and I was able to see that the house and gardens were well looked after. Especially the gardens. People used to come and ask to see the Clodagh gardens, and I was so proud of them. I love my garden still. But it is not the same—not the same——'

The old head sank for a moment, the eyes closed as if in a reverie, and the two young people were afraid to interrupt. Presently she looked up, a brighter expression crossing her face.

'But we must not regret what is past and cannot be recalled,' she said. 'Besides, I have good hopes that I shall soon have all the money needed to do the repairs to the house, and to keep the gardens as they were some time ago.'

Terry felt suddenly uneasy. Those investments of which she had spoken vaguely on the occasion of his last visit. Was this what she meant? If so, could he obtain from her any reliable information?

'That is good news,' he said. 'May one ask if you expect to win a prize in the Sweep—or have you come in for a fortune?'

Mrs Weldon smiled.

'Neither,' she replied. 'But I have made arrangements to sell out some of my capital, and to re-invest it in a more profitable way. I shall soon expect to receive quite a large income.'

So it was as he had feared. 'I wonder if I know the name of your stockbroker?' he asked. 'I am in touch with a good many in Dublin—my father gave me some introductions.'

For an instant the old lady hesitated and then replied: 'Mr George Clayton. He lives in Rathfarnham, having bought a new house there. He has offices in the city, and I am sure you must have heard of him, as he is extremely well known on the Dublin Stock Exchange.'

George Clayton. The name seemed familiar in some vague way.

Then as his mind was groping for a clue, he remembered. Only the previous day he had heard that name mentioned in connection with some decidedly shady transactions. He had been sitting in the office of a business man with whom his father had some dealings, and a remark had been made, and this name spoken. Forgotten at the moment, it had passed from his mind, only to return now in full force.

'George Clayton?' he repeated.

'That is the name. Do you know of him?'

'I have not met him,' was the cautious reply.

'But you have heard the name? You know he is a fine man of business?'

Terry hesitated before speaking. Was it wise to tell her or not? He did not want to annoy or upset her, yet he felt in duty bound to warn her.

'Mrs Weldon,' he said, 'I am afraid that you will not care to hear what I have to tell you.'

Again he hesitated, and Mrs Weldon said, tartly: 'Please continue, Mr Owens. I do not like people who hem and haw!'

'Now grandmother is more like herself,' thought Ursula. She had not the slightest conception of what the next few minutes would bring.

'Well—as a matter of fact, I *have* heard of this man,' replied Terry, slowly, 'and I am sorry to say that what I have heard is not to his credit.'

'As how?'

'He has been involved in some rather shady work on the Stock Exchange. He managed to keep out of trouble himself—making another his scapegoat. I would not have known about the matter myself, only that I happened to be in an office where the affair was mentioned. The man upon whom I was calling was warning a friend of his not to trust this man Clayton with any business. "No further than you can see him—and not as far!" Those were his exact words.'

Mrs Weldon smiled in a superior manner.

'I think that you must have been entirely misinformed,' she said; 'Mr Clayton is a wealthy man. He has gone out of his way to get me those shares about which I told you. I understand that they were very difficult to get—being snapped up so quickly. He said that I was lucky to get them and that the investment would be a most remunerative one.'

So it was the usual story. Terry felt terribly sorry for the old woman. Another bubble floated by a few sharks; a trap set to catch people who wanted more money, now that the cost of living had gone up. He hardly knew what to say to her. If he offended her now it would do no good. Yet could he let her rush headlong to disaster without trying to prevent her?'

'Mrs Weldon,' he said, 'please do not mind what I am about to say—or take it in the wrong spirit—but I do wish you would allow me to make enquiries about this George Clayton. I could easily do so quietly and find out if he is OK or not. After all, a lady like yourself living more or less out of the world, and who has not taken any active part in business matters for so long——'

He stopped suddenly as he saw Ursula making frantic signs to him behind Mrs Weldon. Terry did not know that he could not have gone a worse way to influence the old woman. On account of the years when she had ruled in Capel Street, she still considered herself a capable woman of business. And now to hear this young man speak to her as if she were practically senile was more than Faith Weldon could stand.

She looked him up and down. 'My dear Mr Owens,' she said, 'you must kindly allow me to be the best judge of my own affairs. I have the most perfect confidence in Mr Clayton. If I have not known him for long—I have at least known him for a longer period than I have known you.' She smiled frostily as she added: 'Do not think that I wish to be rude—you are my guest—but you are also a young man of little experience, and I was head of a large business before you were ever thought of. And now shall we talk of other things?'

And Terry, feeling rather like a whipped schoolboy, mumbled a reply. He could do no good by trying to convince Mrs Weldon of her foolishness—or even persuade her to be a little careful. He appeared to have done harm instead of good. So for the rest of the evening, conversation was about other matters, all of no importance.

Later, when he and Ursula were driving home in his car, she spoke about her grandmother.

'If you had *wanted* to offend her, you could not have gone a better way to do so,' she said; 'you know she forgets at times how old she is, and just because she was a wonderful woman of business— or thinks she was—umpteen years ago, she still imagines that she has a business mind, and is able to manage her own affairs.'

'I am real sorry I spoke as I did,' he replied, 'but I'm anxious about the old dame—and that's a fact. I do not think that this Clayton is all he should be, and I shall make it my business to find out all I can about him.'

'It will be useless—no matter what you find out,' replied the girl; 'once grandmother makes up her mind to do a thing—it is as good as done. She firmly believes that this man is all right, and as far as I know, she has already made over part of her capital to him for re-investment. I think he is an odious beast—like a slug! And I only hope that she has not trusted him with much money.'

'I will let you know if I hear anything about him,' promised Terry, 'and then we can consider what is best to be done.'

They drifted into talk about sundry other matters—pleasant, desultory talk—and the drive was enjoyed by both. To one of the two, indeed, it seemed all too short. When they reached the flat in Elton Street, it was only nine o'clock, and Ursula asked Terry to come in for a little while. He parked his car and followed her in. They had the place to themselves as the other girls were out for the evening, and Ursula did not expect them home until fairly late. She plugged in the fire and she and Terry sat down comfortably on each side of the radiator, for a chat and a smoke. The smoking was mostly on his part. True, the girl took a cigarette, but after a few whiffs put it down. She had only lately tried to smoke—just to be in the swim—and had not yet become used to it. Terry liked his pipe and leant back puffing away, while Ursula talked. She could always talk to Terry; she did not know the reason, but she felt so completely at her ease with him, he seemed such a real friend that she never tired of telling him all about her work at the commercial school, and how she hoped to get on later when she had finished the course. She told him, too, how fond she was of Clodagh.

'I used to think it dull—and it is *dull*, of course—but it is my home, and I know now that there is no place I could like as well.'

'I do not wonder at that,' he said; 'it is a dear old spot. I never saw a house that seemed to appeal to me like Clodagh does.'

'That is because you know that your ancestors lived there once.'

'Well—that may be the reason—partly anyhow. The call of the blood and all that. But the house itself is delightful, and the garden would be fine if well looked after. Gee! But I would have Clodagh a swell spot if I owned it.'

Ursula laughed. 'You will never do that,' she said; 'grandmother would die rather than part with Clodagh. She once said to me that the old home was bone of her bone and flesh of her flesh.'

'A queer way of putting it—but I know what she was getting at all right. Would you be surprised to hear that I asked her to let me have the first offer of the place if she ever did have to sell it?'

'You—*what?*'

'Just what I said. You see if she gets into a mess with this Clayton guy there's no saying where it may end.'

'She would never sell Clodagh. Besides, it would cost a lot to buy it.'

'I guess I might manage that part all right—or rather my old man would. He is keen to have a place in Ireland to spend a holiday in, and there would be no place he would rather have than Clodagh.'

Ursula was silent. When her great-grandmother died she supposed that Clodagh would be hers. That the old lady would ever allow it to be owned by any of her son's family was out of the question. The girl knew how bitter were the feelings felt by Faith Weldon towards all at River House. Yet, if she herself were to inherit Clodagh, would she be able to keep it up? She did not know what money her grandmother had, what investments, not even what her yearly income was. She had often wished that Mrs Weldon would be more open with her, but instead of that, she was treated almost as a child, while the girl was perfectly aware that she was quite capable of discussing financial questions with her grandmother, had she been given the chance to do so. But Mrs Weldon did not think so—and there it ended.

She glanced at Terry as he sat opposite to her, his gaze on the electric fire. And suddenly—unbidden, unsought—had come the wish that they were sitting by their own fireside. She would not care where that might be. She had hardly believed Terry when he had spoken of buying Clodagh; besides, she did not want her grandmother to die yet, she was fond of the old lady in spite of the fact that Mrs Weldon had never shown much affection for her. No, she would not care where their home might be—so long as *he* was there. She could even give up Clodagh to be with him. She wondered would he have to live in New York?

'But would your father come from New York just to spend a holiday at Clodagh?' she asked.

'Why not? It is no distance now—if one travels by air it takes only a few days. Perhaps the old man might sell out and settle in the old country when he sees it. Not that I think there is much chance of that, he is too typical of New York to be really happy anywhere else. Now if it was yours truly, *I* would not mind coming here to live.'

Ursula did not know whether he were jesting or not—that was so like Terry. But how gay he was! And how comforting in some queer way.

There was silence for a few moments, each one busy with their own thoughts, which were worlds apart had they but known it. Then Terry looked up and met Ursula's eyes. He was by no means a conceited young man, but there was no mistaking the expression which for a second he had surprised on the girl's face. It was gone in an instant. But that he had seen it—and been able to read its meaning—was plain to Terry. He hastily withdrew his glance and turned again to the electric fire.

The silence remained unbroken for a few moments until it became so tense that he hastily broke it by remarking: 'These electric fires are not like the real thing—are they?'

Ursula was herself again now, and replied at once in careless tones: 'No, but I thought that in New York——'

'Oh—yes. There we have central heating, besides every electric gadget under the sun. But in Ireland—I *did* hope to see a turf fire.'

'Well, you will see one at the River House. I forgot to tell you that I have an invitation for you next Saturday. Will you come?'

'Indeed I will.'

'You will not mention to grandmother that I took you there—or went myself? I have only been a few times, but I am very fond of Maureen and her mother. It is absurd for grandmother to object to them because of their religion—don't you agree?'

'You bet I do. I shall be real pleased to make the acquaintance of the folk at the River House. And now I must be off—you will be tired and want to get a rest.'

But as Terry Owens drove to his hotel that night, he felt far from easy in his mind. He did not care for this girl as a man should care for the woman he marries. Did she care like that for him? And if so, was it his fault? Terry was long before he slept that night.

CHAPTER XIII

AT THE RIVER HOUSE

'And who is this young man whom you have asked to tea?'

The family at the River House were seated by the fire on Saturday evening, in the charming low-ceilinged room, with the diamond-paned windows which looked out at the garden and away to the river beyond. In summer that river flowed placidly by, its water murmuring softly as it meandered to the sea; but in winter there would sometimes be floods and it would overflow its banks, rushing past as if raging against everything within reach, and often doing a fair amount of damage. This November evening was calm and the river quiet enough.

It was Mrs Weldon who had spoken. We saw her many years ago, at a Dalkey band in the 'nineties, when she was lovely Kathleen Dillon. She is an elderly woman now, over sixty, quiet and even-tempered, always one to throw oil on troubled waters, and beloved by all her family. The passing years have taken their toll of her good looks; her hair is grey, her face lined, but in the eyes of her husband she is still as beautiful as ever, and doubly dear.

William Weldon, just a year older than his wife, if still practising as a barrister, and not doing so badly. Time has dealt kindly with him; his home is peaceful and serene, and with advancing years, he had become more absorbed in his books, asking for nothing better than to sit and read after his return from his city office—by the fire in winter, in the garden in summer. He had been a little upset, and a trifle troubled, when his granddaughter had brought Ursula to the house. He was glad to welcome her for the sake of his dead sister, but she recalled memories of the past, visions of his mother and her bitter parting with him. How hard she was, that old woman, who still ruled at Clodagh when over eighty years of age. He did not like the thought that Ursula was visiting at the River House without Mrs Weldon's knowledge. Yet what could he do? The girl was plainly afraid of his mother, she was a nice girl, his own flesh and blood, and she and Maureen were devoted to each other. He could only let things slide and hope that Mrs Weldon would not hear of the visits to River House.

William Weldon's daughter, Maureen, whom we saw speeding off on her bicycle on that April morning of 1916, lives with him.

She is a widow, her husband, Michael O'Dwyer, having died when the only child—Maureen the younger, as she is sometimes called—was a few years old.

Also at the River House was John Weldon, but he was not amongst those who were waiting for Ursula and her friend. The old man, Patrick Dillon, had gone to his rest in the winter of 1916. The excitement of that year, the bitter disappointment, had been too much for him, and he had not lived to see the fruits of that Rising.

'He is an Irish-American of whom Ursula thinks an awful lot,' replied Maureen now. 'I have not spoken to him, just saw him for a moment at one of those silly cocktail parties which Greta Mason gives at the flat. I was bored stiff, and don't mean to go again. Of course I did not know what it was going to be like when Ursula asked me.'

'I am glad to hear you say so,' remarked her grandfather. 'I do not know what the young people of today are coming to!'

His wife smiled.

'Oh, Willie,' she said, 'how often do I remember my father saying the same thing about the young people of our day.'

'Ah, well—I suppose it is the same with each succeeding generation,' assented her husband.

At that moment the bell rang. 'Here they are!' cried Maureen, running to open the front door.

'How are you, Ursula? How nice of you to come.'

'Sure I am always glad to come and see you! This is Mr Owens, Maureen. He wants to meet what he calls real Irish people, and real Irish girls—not like the imitation film stars which he says he meets at our flat.'

Laughingly, Maureen shook hands with Terry, and as he followed her into the sitting-room, he thought what a pleasant, unaffected girl she seemed to be. Not pretty. Her best friend would not have described Maureen O'Dwyer as good-looking—that is, good-looking in the usual acceptance of the word. Her eyes were her best feature—big grey eyes which could look the whole world in the face with utter fearlessness; but her nose was far from classical or Grecian, and her straight, mouse-coloured hair was worn brushed back from her forehead in an uncompromising fashion. But once Maureen began to talk and laugh, one forgot her lack of mere prettiness, and sensed the

clever, interesting character of the girl. Many a young fellow had
found her plain, clever face, and honest grey eyes, more attractive
than the uniform, doll-like, painted prettiness which is so common
today.

That first evening at the River House was never forgotten by
Terry. He was delighted to meet a family like these, where he
heard the Gaelic spoken and joined in song and story around the
fire. He thought the old people charming and fell in love with
Mrs O'Dwyer.

'Have I met all the family?' he asked smilingly, as they sat down
to tea.

'All except my brother Jack,' replied Mrs O'Dwyer, 'and he will
be in any moment now.'

Even as she spoke, the door opened and Jack Weldon entered.
Terry, looking up, met the gaze of a pair of deep-set eyes, which
seemed to be looking into his very soul.

'This is Mr Owens, Jack,' said Mrs O'Dwyer; 'he is from New
York. His people lived at Clodagh once.'

Terry was surprised to see that John Weldon's face seemed to
darken at the mention of Clodagh. He did not know that John
was looking back, seeing the old stable there, and himself marching
out, a prisoner, between two British soldiers, saluting, ironically,
as he went, the hateful old woman who still ruled Clodagh.
However, he greeted the guest politely as he sat down to tea.

'You are late, Jack,' said his mother.

'A little—I was detained in the city.' He said no more, and
none of the family ever thought of questioning John Weldon's
movements. He was a law to himself, reserved, taciturn. Morose
and bad-tempered, too, at times. Only to his mother was he always
kind; he adored her and was the best of sons.

During tea, Terry was conscious of John Weldon's scrutiny, and
wondered what it meant. In his turn, he found himself studying
John, when he could do so unobserved. He saw a man in the late
thirties, tall, well set-up, decidedly good-looking, but with an
expression of settled disappointment, discontent, unhappiness.
Yet Terry liked him, and was attracted towards him in some strange
way.

After tea, as they grouped around the blazing turf fire, William
Weldon spoke of Clodagh and what he knew of the Owens'
connection with the place.

'It was old Mary Molloy who told me,' he said; 'at that time I was at college, and there was a group of us there imbued with the national spirit. I suppose you know that Trinity has always produced such spirits from one generation to another. I am afraid I was not very much in earnest, although I thought that I was at the time. Anyway, after my father died I did not bother further. Certainly, my sympathies were always Irish, but I took no active part in any movement. You see my father and myself had some angry words on the very night that he was taken ill—it was a stroke, I think, and he died before morning. My sister, Ursula—your grandmother, Ursula, as you know—blamed me bitterly, we never got on together. I blamed myself, too, for I was a bitter disappointment to my father. But my mother tried to comfort me and did not put the blame on me. We were very devoted to one another in those days, and that is why she felt my marriage so much. However, I am wandering from the point. I was going to tell you that Mary Molloy, who was our cook for years and stayed at Clodagh until she died, had also been in service with Mrs Owens. Her son was your great-grandfather. Mary remembered him well, and often spoke of him to me—never, of course, to my mother. She knew he had been out in the Fenian Rising, hiding in the hills, nearly frozen from the cold. His mother, Mrs Owens, was a fine woman, and used to bring him, and the boys with him, some food, walking through the snow to a cave in the mountains, where they were hidden for weeks. Then, later on, the son was got safely across to America and she followed when she had sold Clodagh to my father—then a newly-married man. He bought a good deal of her furniture, too—there must be several things of interest to you still at Clodagh.'

'Say—I wish I'd known that and I would have asked the old lady to show them to me, when I was up there a few days ago.'

'You were at Clodagh, then?' asked Mrs Weldon.

'Yes. Ursula here wanted me to write and make a date, but I thought I would take her unawares and see if she would see me. And she did—was quite friendly, took me round the garden, and gave me a glass of wine and some cake. Gee! I thought I was living in one of those Dickens' novels! I liked her a lot, and for that reason, I should like to put a few questions to you, Mr Weldon, if you have no objection?'

'Go ahead!' replied the other, smilingly.

'Well—first of all. Do you know much about your mother's business affairs?'

'Nothing whatever. We have not spoken—or even met—for many years. I can only tell you that my mother should be fairly comfortable—in fact, quite well off.'

'You do not know how she has her capital invested?'

'I have not the remotest idea. I know that there had to be readjustments when she left her post in Capel Street, but how she arranged about her capital, I do not know. I was rather surprised when Ursula told me that there seemed to be a shortage of money at Clodagh, and that the house and garden both needed attention. I was rather of the impression that my mother was growing miserly in her old age. That is often the case, you know.'

'It is not the case with grandmother—I'm sure of that.' interposed Ursula. 'She is quite worried about money—or she was until this Mr Clayton turned up. Now she thinks he is going to make her fortune!'

'That is just what I wanted to speak about,' said Terry. 'I am afraid that this man is not all right—not by a long way. He seems to be a shady customer, and I'm sorry she has got herself mixed up with him.'

'Have you asked her about him?'

'He has indeed!' said Ursula, with a laugh. 'He put his foot into it, too, when we were there on Sunday. Grandmother will never allow any interference with her business arrangements, she thinks she knows the right thing to do. I tried to make signs to Terry to stop before he offended her, but it was no use. The harm was done, and now she will never allow him to talk about the matter again. You see, Uncle William, she has the utmost confidence in this George Clayton.'

'And do you know him, Ursula?'

'I have met him.'

'And you don't like him?'

'Oh, no! He is a horrid creature—like a slug!'

They laughed at the description. All but Terry. He did not laugh, but said, in serious tones, 'Something should be done to prevent Mrs Weldon from allowing this man to get control of any of her money.'

'No one could do that,' replied William Weldon; 'my mother would never allow it. Besides, I can tell you that she was always an excellent business woman, and I simply cannot imagine her being fooled by any man.'

'But you must remember how old she is now. At her age she could hardly retain those business faculties which were hers when she were younger. I will tell you what I know about this Clayton.'

He told them then about the conversation which he had heard with reference to the man in question, and was sorry to see that it appeared to make little impression on his hearers. Mr Weldon shook his head.

'I cannot believe that my mother would allow herself to be taken in by anyone. I know how old she is, but even so, I feel sure that her mind is as clear as ever. What do you think, Ursula? You have known her all these latter years.'

'I think that grandmother is as clear-headed as any of us here, and she is so clever. I do not think she would make a mistake if she understood the facts, but, all the same, I am terribly afraid that Mr Clayton will dupe her in some way. He seems to have got such an influence over her in such a short time—I simply cannot understand it.'

'Well, will you do what you can to find out some details about this man?' asked Mr Weldon. 'We could see then if anything could be done. But if once my mother gets a thing into her head—' He did not finish the sentence, but they all knew what he meant.

Before he left, Jack Weldon drew Terry aside for a moment. 'May I come and see you some evening? I should like to talk with you.'

'But of course. Any evening you say. Will you come tomorrow?'

This was agreed, and the next evening at seven o'clock Terry was awaiting his guest in his private sitting-room in the hotel. The young man believed in comfort, money was no object to him, and he had been told by his 'old man' to enjoy his holiday. This he was determined to do, he knew he would have little time for pleasure when he was harnessed to work in his father's office.

Jack glanced around in some surprise as he entered the room. It was evident that this young man had money to burn, but as he had never boasted or even alluded to his financial position, Jack had not expected such luxury as a private room in one of Dublin's most expensive hotels. Terry came forward to meet him with hand outstretched. 'Take this chair—it's fairly comfortable,' he said, 'and now what will you drink? A cocktail—or plain whiskey and soda?'

'Neither, thank you. I don't drink—at least those kind of drinks,' and he smiled.

'Coffee then—tea? Say what you would like.'

'A cup of coffee then, if I may. No—I don't smoke either—thanks all the same,' as Terry handed him a cigarette.

'Ah, well, I suppose most of us drink and smoke too much,' said Terry. In his own mind he was thinking: 'You might be a little more cheerful if you indulged a little.' To his intense surprise he heard Jack say immediately: 'No—I should not be any the better for it—I am sure of that.'

Terry could only stare in amazement, seeing which Jack explained:

'Oh, I just guessed what you were thinking. I have a rather uncanny habit of doing this, as my relatives and friends could tell you. A bit awkward at times. And now I am sure you are wondering what brought me here?'

'Not at all. I am only too pleased to see you. Here is the coffee—do make yourself comfortable.'

'You know,' said Jack, 'you are not a bit like an American. As a rule I cannot stand them, so boastful, thinking they own the world. You are so different. How is it?'

'But I am *Irish*—not American really. Of course, I can claim American nationality and all that, but I am Irish—heart and soul.'

'Are all your people like that?'

'Yes, the men all married Irishwomen, and the children have all been brought up in the real Irish tradition.'

'That is good hearing,' said Jack, and for a moment the gloom on his handsome face seemed to lighten. But only for a moment, almost at once the bitterness returned to his voice as he said:

'There is little that is Irish left in the Ireland of today.'

'You mean?'

'I mean that English propaganda in the form of books, newspapers, the cinema, dances and so forth, have combined to do more spiritual and cultural harm to our people, than did years of the penal laws. In fact, the penal laws only strengthened our faith and nationality, while these things are killing it, slowly and surely.'

'But you have the Gaelic League, and there must be plenty of people with Irish ideals.'

'A certain proportion, I grant you—and thank God for them. But the vast majority of our young people take little interest in Irish questions. Ask any ordinary girl or young man whom you may meet in a casual way, to give you some details of Irish history, Irish heroes—even about the men of 1916—and I would be ashamed to hear their replies. But ask them the name of some film star and their history—including divorces etc.—and you will get correct replies. Look at the modern dances and singing. *Singing*—save the mark! And that in Ireland—in *Ireland*. Oh—it makes me sick to think of it!'

Terry stared at him.

'But you have your own Government now,' he said; 'they could make their own laws about such things as this English propaganda. Why are there not Irish film companies, controlled by the State, and State-aided when necessary? They could produce Irish films of history and books. And then the scenery—where could you beat it?'

'All you say is true, but it does not alter the fact that ninety-nine percent of the films shown in this country are American or English. Their influence must be definitely anti-Catholic and anti-Irish; at the best they may be harmless, in so far as not being actually bad from a moral point of view, but their effect upon the culture of our people is lowering beyond words. Now and then we may get a film which could influence for good, but their number is so small that they are negligible. But do not let us talk any more about these things—talk can do no good and action is not forthcoming. Tell me about your home in New York and about your people.'

Before the two men had parted that night, a warm friendship had sprung up between them which was never to be broken while life lasted.

CHAPTER XIV

THE PASSING OF A DREAM

November went by and December came, soon it would be Christmastide. One evening a few days before Christmas Eve, Ursula was alone in the flat. The others had gone to a cinema and Ursula was busy with pencil and paper, making a list of her Christmas gifts. When one is strictly limited in the matter of cash, this is not an easy task, and Ursula was so absorbed in trying to make ends meet that she jumped up in surprise when she heard the bell. Terry Owens stood on the threshold.

'Oh, come in—I am so glad to see you! We were just saying at tea-time that you must be lost—or gone back to New York.'

And indeed, Ursula had not seen much of Terry during the past few weeks—not since she had introduced him to the River House. Yet she had not felt in any way anxious, nor in the slightest degree jealous. Never for an instant did it cross her mind that he might be interested, in any but a friendly way, in Maureen. Poor, plain Maureen. What man could think about her when a prettier girl was near?

Had Terry been to blame in his attitude towards Ursula? Afterwards he often asked himself that question, but could never get a satisfactory reply from his conscience. He had not meant to let her imagine for one moment that he cared for her, indeed, since the time when he had surprised that glance from her eyes, he had been careful to be just friendly and nothing more.

But, unfortunately, she took his friendliness for something deeper; how it was that she had grown to believe he loved her, it would be hard to say. Perhaps the wish was father to the thought, or it might have been because Ursula had known so few men while under Mrs Weldon's supervision that she was ready to imagine any man in love with her. Then, Terry had all the American's frank comradeship where the other sex were in question, and his manner might have given her a false impression. Whatever was the reason, Ursula really thought that Terence loved her and would soon tell her so.

Terry, on his part, was rather annoyed when he found that Ursula was alone. He had taken care to avoid this whenever possible. However, it could not be helped now, but he determined that his visit should be a short one.

'I can only stay a moment,' he said. 'I called to say that I have a box for the pantomime on the 28th, and I hope that you three will be able to join us.'

'Who else will be going?' she asked, rather surprised that he had taken a box.

'Maureen and her mother. Mrs Weldon has a bad cold, and Jack, as you know, does not care for the pantomime.'

'I am glad you have asked Maureen,' said Ursula. 'Poor girl, she does not get much amusement in her life—except for those Gaelic League affairs.'

He stared at her in amazement.

'Not much amusement?' he repeated. 'Why, Maureen is the soul of fun and laughter. And as for what you call those Gaelic League affairs, I have been to a few, and I can tell you I enjoyed myself no end.'

'Oh, well—if you care for those sort of things it's all right, I suppose. I would be bored to death.'

She was thinking that it seemed a pity he should be so obsessed with these Irish amusements. Anyway it was a waste of time talking about them now. Quickly she turned the conversation.

'I suppose you will come and see me at Clodagh during the holidays?' she said; 'it will be pretty deadly there now, especially after these few months in town.'

'But it is a lovely spot. Surely you will be glad to be there again?'

'Yes, I love Clodagh. But it will be lonely with only grandmother.'

'Oh, I shall take a run out—you may be sure of that.'

'Where are you spending Christmas Day?' She was wondering if she could possibly persuade her grandmother to invite him for dinner that day? His next words surprised her.

'At the River House,' he said. 'It was real good of them to ask me—wasn't it?'

She did not reply at once, the disappointment was keen. Why had she not thought of speaking to her grandmother sooner? He was speaking again.

'Ursula,' he said, 'there is something I want to talk about— something I want to ask you.'

Her heart seemed to stop for an instant, then raced rapidly on. Was he going to speak about their future? Had the moment really come at last?

She could not speak, only smiled as she waited for him to continue. He hesitated and seemed embarrassed, then said, diffidently: 'It is about a Christmas gift.'

So he wanted to give her a present, and did not know what to choose. That was it, of course. What should she suggest? Nothing very valuable, even although by now she knew that money was no object to this young man. The next moment she was disillusioned.

'I wanted to give Maureen a present,' he said, 'and I thought that you would know what she would like best. She is not well-off, and I want to give her something useful and yet nice to look at. But I was afraid that she might not like an expensive gift—or her mother might not like it.'

'What were you thinking of giving her?'

'A fur coat—a good one. It would be a suitable gift for the season—wouldn't it? Do you think she would like it?'

A fur coat! An expensive present like that. For the first time a feeling of uneasiness crept over her. Was it possible—*could* it be possible—that Terry cared for Maureen? Had she been mistaken in thinking he cared for her—Ursula? But no, she could not believe it. Had it been Greta Mason, with her sophisticated charm and prettiness, she would not have been so surprised. But Maureen—so plain and unattractive. She liked Maureen, always had liked her, but it had never entered her head to regard her as a probable rival. He was waiting for her reply.

'I am afraid,' she said, 'that Mrs O'Dwyer would think a fur coat rather an unusual present. I do not know about the custom in New York, but here such a present is generally only given by a man to a girl if they are engaged to be married.'

He grinned at her cheerfully. 'That is just what I hope we will be,' he said. 'I mean to ask her on Christmas Day—and somehow I don't think Maureen will be surprised. But whether she will look at a fellow like me or not—that's another question.'

There was no reply from Ursula. It was not possible for her to utter a word at the moment. She felt as if a band of ice had settled upon her heart, slowly squeezing it dry of every drop of blood. But her pride came to her aid, crying to her not to show the white feather, not to let this man see that she cared, that he had wellnigh broken her heart. With stiff lips she forced a smile.

'I hope you will be very happy,' she said. To her own ears her voice sounded like that of a stranger coming from a distance, but Terry did not seem to notice anything amiss. He was pleased that she was smilingly wishing him happiness. He had been a trifle upset at the thought of telling her, had rather shirked doing so, and then got it over in a rush. And she was not troubled at all. Taking it perfectly coolly—he must have imagined a lot of nonsense.

'Thank you, Ursula,' he said; 'if she will have me I shall be the happiest man in the States!'

'Shall you be going back to New York?'

'I mean to run over and see my old man. He has been so good to me, and I should not like to spring a thing like this upon him by cable—I want to talk to him. Then, if things are "OK" I'll come back, get married, and take my wife across.'

'Will she like New York, I wonder?'

She was still talking in that stiff, automatic way, talking for the sake of talking, talking because she dare not stop—that would be fatal. But would he never go? How much longer would he stay?

'Well—I guess she can run across—or fly for that matter— whenever she likes. We don't think anything of the journey these days. But I must be going. I am tiring you—you look quite fagged.'

For the first time he noticed how pale she was, and she hastened to reply, to make excuses.

'I am all right really—just the usual Christmas rush. You know what that means! Trying to think of suitable presents and all that.' She smiled again with lips that seemed frozen so stiffly that it was a pain to move them.

'Well, I must be off.' But at the door he paused to ask:

'Then you think that I may buy that coat?'

'Yes, of course, now that you are nearly engaged.'

Dear God—would he *never* go?

'And you think, too, that Maureen will like it?'

'I am sure she will.'

'That's good! Well—cheerio, Ursula—and thanks so much for your advice and good wishes. Don't forget the panto—we will make a night of it!'

He grinned cheerfully and was gone. Gone at last, and she was alone to fight this terrible thing that had come upon her.

The others might be in before long, she felt she could not meet them yet, so going into her little bedroom, she locked her door and sat down to think.

Just for a few moments, she was not able to think clearly, she was dazed and stupid. Then, by degrees her brain began to function and she was able to see the plain facts, to understand all the last half hour had meant. He did not care for her, never had done so—that was plain enough now. What a fool she had been to allow herself to love him. Yet could she have helped doing so? Wasn't there some old song which said that love came unsought?

And now could she make herself forget him? He would be going away soon—thank Heaven for that! Then, when he returned for Maureen perhaps she might manage to avoid seeing him. Oh, she must try to do so in some way! Suppose she were to be asked to the wedding—as she probably would be? She must stop thinking about it all—she would be driven mad if she went on like this. If she could wake up and find that she had only been dreaming! But it was reality and no dream. She knew that only too well.

The minutes went past; the other girls came home and she heard them laughing and talking. They knocked at her door and she said she was tired and had gone to bed. The hours went by and the traffic without grew less until almost complete silence fell. Peace came over the city. But there was no peace in the heart of the girl, lying awake, dry-eyed and wretched through that long night.

In a couple of days Ursula went to Clodagh to spend the holidays with her grandmother. She had managed to pass herself before the two girls by saying that she was not feeling very well. They had not known about Terry's visit to the flat, so did not connect him with Ursula's poor spirits. Had they known of the visit they might have suspected something, as they had guessed Ursula's secret long ago.

However, if her unhappiness had escaped the notice of her friends, it was not so with Mrs Weldon. That astute old lady saw at once that something was wrong.

'Are you not well, Ursula?' she asked, the first morning at breakfast.

The girl started from the miserable reverie into which she had fallen. 'Quite well, thank you, grandmother,' she replied.

'Then why are you so quiet—so unlike yourself?'

'I am all right, grandmother.'

The old lady said no more, but she was not satisfied.

'You will be glad to know,' she said presently, 'that I have already received some very satisfactory results from the investments which Mr Clayton arranged for me. I hope soon to have augmented my income considerably.'

Ursula murmured a response, she took little interest in what her grandmother was saying. With the selfishness of one in love, her only interest was focused entirely upon herself.

Christmas day dawned and Ursula presented her gifts; presents for the servants and a pair of bedroom slippers for her grandmother. Mrs Weldon gave her granddaughter a winter coat. It was badly needed, for Ursula's old one was worn and shabby. The girl thanked her dutifully, and at another time would have been really glad of the gift. The old lady was disappointed at the manner in which her gift had been received; the coat was a good tweed, and she would not have bought it had she not been so sure of that augmented income of which she had spoken. She could not know that Ursula was seeing Maureen wearing a fur coat. The kind of fur coat which most women dream about—and only dream.

Ursula sent an excuse for not going to the pantomime, she just felt that she could not bear seeing Maureen and Terry together. Later on, perhaps, but not now.

Maureen had written telling her about the wonderful thing which had happened to her. She seemed very happy but not at all excited or overelated in any way. She had evidently known that Terry loved her and meant to ask her to marry him.

Yet, had Ursula but guessed it, Maureen was feeling uneasy about her. She had known that Ursula liked Terry—liked him quite a lot—and it must have been a bitter blow to her to hear that he was to marry another girl. Still what could Maureen do? Pray for her—that was all.

And she did pray for Ursula, fervently and often. When coming home each evening from town, she was in the habit of entering the Carmelite Church in Whitefriars Street for a few moments' prayer. And there, before the wonderful statue of Our Lady of Dublin, she now knelt daily to ask for comfort and consolation for Ursula.

'Dear Mother,' she would pray, 'you can comfort her. You know it was not my fault that he cared for me and not for her. I love her, too, and I think she is very unhappy and she has not the faith. Please take care of her and comfort her—dear Mother!'

When Ursula returned to the flat the others had already arrived. Greta Mason had had a jolly time at Stone Lodge and reproached Ursula for not coming to her Christmas Party.

'I was sure you would come, Ursula—and I had a number of nice boys. I think it was really shabby of you—considering what friends the Weldons and Masons have been for umpteen years! What happened you at all?'

'I was not very well—I am sorry, Greta.'

'Oh, you could have made an effort, surely—you are not that bad—' began Greta. Then she stopped suddenly and stared at Ursula as if seeing her for the first time. 'Well, now that I look at you, I see that you are not exactly in the pink—far from it, indeed. What have you been doing to yourself?'

Flower Brown lifted her eyes from her eternal knitting. 'Yes—I noticed her at once,' she said; 'what is wrong, Ursula?'

'Oh—nothing—nothing! For Heaven's sake leave me alone—can't you? Poking and prying like that! What does it matter how I feel? What has it got to do with you?'

She flung out of the room, leaving two astonished people behind.

'Well—I'm jiggered!' remarked Miss Brown, and Greta nodded in agreement.

'But I can guess what is wrong with her,' added Flower, and again Greta nodded as she said: 'Yes—it's Terry Owens and his engagement to Maureen O'Dwyer.'

'I'm sorry for her,' said Flower; 'he is such a nice fellow—and with money to burn. But then there is the religion, and besides, he is Irish mad, so of course the O'Dwyer girl would appeal to him.'

'I suppose so—and to think that Ursula was the one to bring them together. Well, it can't be helped now.'

'No—it can't be helped, and Ursula will get over it in time—we all do.' And Miss Brown sighed, sentimentally.

There was a party at the River House for Terry and Maureen before he went to New York. Ursula was asked and accepted the invitation. Afterwards, she used to sometimes try and remember the details of that night, but was never able to do so. It was just a blur of pain and suffering, an eternity of misery which seemed as if it would never come to an end. Yet she must have hidden her feelings for no one appeared to notice anything amiss, and she knew that she talked and laughed and danced—or some other individual who was inhabiting her body at the moment did it for her. But there was one who saw—and understood.

Jack Weldon drove her home in his small two-seater. He had sensed her suffering with that uncanny intuition which he possessed and felt terribly sorry for the girl who was trying to show such a brave front to her little world. He talked on casual subjects during the drive, and it was not until they were nearing Elton Street that he remarked, quietly: 'It is a sad world at times, Ursula. None of us can hope to come through it unscathed.'

She turned her head to look at him, but Jack was staring straight ahead, driving carefully, and rather slowly, through the city streets.

'Yes, it is sad,' she replied, almost in a whisper. 'Too sad to be borne sometimes.'

'No not that, although I have thought so at times. But I know better now. We could not bear the sadness and the greyness by ourselves, but we can always look for help where it is to be found.'

'I am not religious.'

'No?' he smiled 'yet we cannot afford to do without religion. It is the only bit of comfort that we have. Tell me—looking at her with his penetrating gaze—have you ever been inside a Catholic church?'

'Oh, no—never! Grandmother would have a fit if she thought I would enter such a place.'

She was trying to laugh it off, to take it lightly, but he replied seriously: 'Then the next time you are passing one of our churches—just go in a spend a few moments on your knees. Now, here we are at your flat—no, I can't come in, thanks very much all the same. Good night, Ursula—and remember.'

CHAPTER XV

'OUR LADY OF DUBLIN—PRAY FOR US'

The month of January went by and February came. Ursula was working hard now at the commercial school; she had withdrawn into herself, seldom joining in any of the amusements of the other two, taking little interest in their concerns. After trying, time and again, to cheer her up and take her out of herself, they had given up the attempt, going their way while she went hers.

Terence Owens was in New York, and Ursula had heard from Maureen that his father was very pleased at the news of his engagement, and that Terry hoped to be back in Dublin before long. He would have returned at once only for the state of his father's health, which was not good, and he did not like to leave him until he was better.

Maureen was really troubled about Ursula, although she did not let her cousin guess that she was worried. They only met now at the school; there they met daily, but Ursula always had some excuse ready when Maureen asked her to the River House. Mr and Mrs Weldon and Mrs O'Dwyer often asked Maureen about her, they could not understand why the girl, whom they had made so welcome amongst them, now never came to see them. Except Maureen, only Jack Weldon knew the reason. He spoke to Maureen one day, asking:

'Do you see much of Ursula these times?'

'I see her every day, Uncle Jack, but she does not talk much to me.'

'That is a pity. I need not ask you to be as kind and gentle with her as possible. You see, Maureen, I know how she is suffering.'

'Yes. I understand; and really, Uncle Jack, I *have* tried to make friends with her—real friends—and to get her to come to the River House. But lately, ever since—'

'I know. Ever since your engagement to Terry. Well, it is quite understandable. Poor girl—she was badly hurt. We can only pray for her. You do that, I am sure, Maureen?'

'Yes—every day.'

But as the days passed, Ursula seemed to have fallen into a sullen apathy: nothing seemed to matter to her, there was nothing of importance going on around her; empires might have crumbled into dust, great events have befallen the world, but they would have appeared of little or no import to this girl who was living entirely to herself, daily growing more introspective, more egotistical.

As in duty bound, she paid a visit to Clodagh every week, but so wrapped up was she in herself, that she failed to notice a change in her grandmother, which would have been plain to any observer. It was Kate Doyle who drew her attention to the matter.

'Miss Ursula,' she said, one early spring day when the crocus was making a brave show in the garden, and the trees beginning to think of their new frocks, 'have you noticed the mistress lately?'

'Noticed her? How? In what way do you mean Kate?'

'Well, Miss Ursula, she's not herself these times—not herself at all. She seems terrible worried over something.'

'Does she?' indifferently. 'I had not noticed.'

'But I wish you would, Miss Ursula. You know she is an old lady now, and there should be someone to help and advise her—'

'Such nonsense, Kate!' interrupted Ursula. 'You should know well that grandmother would not allow any interference in her affairs. She would soon put me in my place if I tried anything like that.'

'Miss Ursula,' said Kate, then, lowering her voice instinctively, 'I don't like that Mr Clayton who comes here. I don't trust him.'

Ursula seemed to wake up at those words.

'But does Mr Clayton come often?' she asked. 'I thought he had finished grandmother's business about those investments?'

'Not at all, Miss. He does be out here very often—several times a week—bringing papers for the mistress to sign. I don't like it at all, and that's the truth.'

Neither did Ursula like it. In her own trouble she had almost forgotten about George Clayton. What was he doing, still bothering her grandmother? He was a man to whom she had taken a strong dislike—in spite of the fact that only for him she would probably never have been allowed to leave Clodagh and study at the commercial school.

'I will speak to grandmother, Kate,' she said.

'I'm glad of that, Miss Ursula. But sure you won't mention my name, or let on I was talkin' to you?'

'Of course not. I know better than to do that.'

It was a Saturday evening and Ursula was staying over the night, returning to Elton Street by bus on Sunday afternoon. So this evening, as she and Mrs Weldon sat by the fire, she began very cautiously to feel her way.

'You are not looking well, grandmother,' she said—as indeed was the truth, now that she noticed it. 'Are you feeling all right?'

The old lady sat up sharply, fixing her still keen gaze upon the face of the girl sitting opposite. Ursula, knowing that glance of old, tried to keep her expression innocent, to look as if no ulterior motive lurked behind the words.

'I am fairly well, thank you, Ursula,' was the reply. 'But I am beginning to feel my age.'

Still with caution, Ursula went on: 'But now that you have no financial worries, you should be feeling young again.' She laughed lightly as she spoke, but carefully watched the old face on the other side of the fire. With something like dismay, she saw it change and seem to grow haggard and worn before her very eyes. She feared to say more, only waited for her grandmother to speak. It was a few moments before she did so.

'Ursula,' she said then, 'I think it but right to tell you that, owing to unforeseen circumstances, the shares which Mr Clayton secured for me have become practically worthless. It has been rather a blow to me—and to Mr Clayton who had a much larger number of shares himself. However, he has great hopes of being able to secure some excellent shares in a new company which is just being formed and of which he is one of the promoters.'

Ursula's heart sank. This sounded bad, worse than she had anticipated.

'But grandmother,' she said, 'surely you will not sell out any more of your other shares to reinvest in this new concern? It would be better, don't you think, to leave what you have untouched? You know that even if the dividends are small, the money is safe.'

Mrs Weldon straightened herself, her eyes flashing in the old way. 'Kindly allow me to manage my own affairs, Ursula,' she said, in tones of ice. 'A young girl, such as you are, is not capable of understanding these matters. I consider that, old as I am, I am still a good woman of business. And as regards Mr Clayton, I have the utmost confidence in him.'

Ursula was silent for a moment, but she felt that she simply could not let the matter pass without making one more effort. So, greatly daring, she said: 'But grandmother, won't you first consult Mr Manton? You know he has been our solicitor for so long, and then you have known him for years, while this other man is a stranger and ——'

'Be quiet, Ursula! I will not be dictated to by you. As for Herbert Manton, he is a young puppy. I have no confidence whatever in him. Mr Clayton is well known in financial circles—his reputation is world-wide. Now please say no more on the matter—all this is beyond your comprehension. You may rest assured that I will do what is best as regards all financial questions.'

Ursula could say no more, she knew it would be useless, but she felt decidedly uneasy. She wondered should she call and see Mr Manton. She would have liked to do so, but fear of her grandmother was too strong. She knew that Mr Manton would be sure to take steps at once, he would immediately interview Mrs Weldon—and the fat would be in the fire. Even now when she was more or less on the road to independence, Ursula Draper could not face her grandmother in one of her angry moods.

No, she must just let things slide for the moment until she saw what would happen. She could not believe that Mrs Weldon would be so foolish as to lose much of her money.

She went to church by herself on Sunday morning as the old lady was not feeling too well. So Ursula cycled the familiar road to the Protestant Church, and as she was rather early, went across to the grave where were buried her great-grandfather, John Weldon, and her grandmother, Ursula L'Estrange. So accustomed was Ursula to call Mrs Weldon 'grandmother,' that it seemed queer now to remember that her real grandmother lay there, in the quiet country churchyard. Her grandmother of whom she knew but little. Mrs Weldon never spoke of her—only of her daughter, the girl whom she had loved so dearly. Ursula knew, of course, the bare outlines of that home-coming on a Christmas Eve so long ago—back in those strange days when there were no taxis, no bus running to Whitechurch and Tibradden, and when her grandmother and the little Faith—who was to become Ursula's mother—had been compelled to walk through a blinding snowstorm from Terenure to Clodagh. She had sometimes wondered about that other Ursula, and now, as she stood beside the grave—covered with the purple and white and yellow of the crocus flower from the garden at Clodagh—she found herself thinking of that girl and of what life must have been like to her, living at Clodagh in the early nineties of the last century. There had been so little for girls to do then, and her grandmother must have been even worse off than others; her father dead, her mother at business all day, and a brother with whom she did not agree. How funny to think of Mr Weldon of the River House as a young man—a mere boy. What was her grandmother like then? How did she dress? In a particularly hideous manner if the few photographs which Ursula had seen were to be believed. By all accounts she had had a miserable life; falling in love with a man and running away with him, only to find out that he cared for her money, not for herself. But at least that other Ursula had had *some* sunshine, she had known what it was to marry the man she loved, there must have been a brief spell of happiness before the awakening, while she—the Ursula of today——

'Good morning, Ursula! I am glad to see you. How are you and how is my naughty girl? Tell her she is to come and see her poor daddy and mummy next weekend.'

'Greta is very well, Mrs Mason,' Ursula replied politely, 'I will give her your message.'

'Do—like a dear girl. Now *you* are a model child compared with her! And how is dear Mrs Weldon?'

Ursula replied suitably, and presently followed the rest of the small and select congregation into church.

Mrs Weldon seemed better at dinner and talked pleasantly to Ursula, but the matter of finance was not again alluded to between them. As Ursula watched the small cameo-like old face across the table, and thought of the grave in Whitechurch, she began to wonder at this great-grandmother of hers. In those far-off days, when she had been a young woman, ruling over the business in the city and the house in the country, with equal exactitude and success—what had she been like? Kate had said that old Mary Molloy had spoken of the lovely girl who had come as a bride to Clodagh; of her tiny feet and hands; her blue eyes and honey-coloured hair; of how beautifully she had dressed, and how her husband and son had adored her. Now that husband was dead, and the son as good as dead to the hard old woman who had never forgiven him for marrying one of whom she did not approve. If only she had guessed about Ursula's visits to the River House! The girl shivered suddenly at the very thought, so that Mrs Weldon remarked, 'I hope you have not caught a chill, Ursula. Perhaps you had better not return to town this evening.'

'Oh, but I must, grandmother! I could not be late for the classes in the morning.'

Ursula went back to the flat that evening and life went on for her in the usual way.

She met Jack Weldon one evening in Grafton Street, and for a moment she thought of asking his advice about Mrs Weldon. But she put the notion aside—it would never do. The mere fact that he was one of the family at the River House seemed to make such a thing impossible. Suppose the old lady ever heard of it?

Meanwhile Jack, all unconscious of her thoughts, was asking if she would come to have tea somewhere? But she refused rather curtly and he did not press the invitation. She liked Jack, but wanted to have nothing to do with any member of that family. They talked for a few moments in an aimless way and she was thinking it was time to move away, when he asked, suddenly: 'I suppose you have not been inside a Catholic church yet?'

She stared at him without replying for a moment. Truth to tell, she had almost forgotten his parting words to her on the evening of the party at his home. Then she remembered, and replied, rather coldly: 'No—I have not.'

He smiled down at her. 'Well, I think that you will often enter a Catholic church in the future,' he said. 'I often see you kneeling in prayer before the Tabernacle.'

'You often see me?'

'Yes—I see you kneeling as I have said. Call it a vision if you like. I have those queer visions sometimes—but they always come true.'

Ursula felt vexed—how ridiculous to talk like that.

'I am afraid that you will be disappointed this time,' she said, coldly. 'And now I must get back to the flat—good-bye!'

Yet, strange to relate, it was on the following afternoon that Ursula happened to be passing the Carmelite church in Whitefriars Street, and moved, partly by curiosity, partly by what Jack Weldon had said, she entered the building.

It was a bright spring day, and the contrast from the daylight without, and the twilight within the church, was the first thing which struck her. Then as her eyes became accustomed to the interior, she noticed with surprise the number of people who were kneeling here and there, some at the side altars, others before the Tabernacle. Ursula felt rather shy and embarrassed, but no one seemed to notice her, not a glance was thrown in her direction. However, she could not stand there, gazing around, so she dropped into a seat facing Our Lady's Altar. There her attention was immediately attracted by the quaint Madonna and Child of the statue erected over the altar. It seemed so old, so strange, that Ursula began to study it.

She did not know its history, nor that it is known far and wide as Our Lady of Dublin—so dear to the heart of every Dubliner. To Ursula it was just an uncommon, rather strange statue. Several people were kneeling before it, their lips moving in prayer. How earnest they seemed. Strange, she thought, to feel like that. She was sure that she could never pray with all her heart like those people. But of course there was a lot of superstition mixed up with their religion—and then all those images. She gazed around her, but always her eyes returned to Our Lady of Dublin and the Child in her arms, with little hands outstretched to all the world.

Ursula had no idea that she was looking upon one of the most interesting statues in all Dublin, and the work most probably of some pupil of Albrecht Durer, if not the master himself. She did not know the history of the statue from the time when it was first set up in St Mary's Abbey, near the present Capel Street, to the present day. At that time it was adorned with a silver crown, and this crown is said by some historians to have been used in the coronation in Dublin of Lambert Simnel, but this is not certain. The Abbey was later transferred by St Malachy to the Cistercians, who occupied it until its suppression by Henry VIII in 1544. The Abbey was then granted to the Earl of Ormonde for the purpose of a stable, and the statue condemned to be burned. The back portion was actually burned, the remaining half being carried by some person, who wished to preserve it, to an inn yard, where it was placed face downwards and the burned half used as a pig trough. It is not known when it was rescued from this position, but it is next heard of in the old church of St Michan's parish, Mary's Lane, in 1749. This chapel was given up, and Petrie tells us that shortly after this time, the ancient silver crown was sold for its intrinsic value to one Mooney, a silversmith, of Capel Street, and the Bishop of Canea says that the statue 'found its way in some unaccountable manner to the ordinary sale shop and was purchased by the late Very Rev Dr Spratt, OCC, who set it up in the Carmelite Church, Whitefriars Street, where it may still be seen.'

In 1915 the Shrine of Our Lady of Dublin was formally erected in the church and the statue re-erected in a prominent position above the altar of Our Lady. The white plaster, with which it had been covered, as far as living memory went, was removed, and the statue shows once more the brown colour of the Irish oak which is the material from which it was first fashioned so many centuries ago.

But Ursula knew nothing of all this as she sat there, gazing at the Madonna and Child. She only knew that she liked it—that it appealed to her in some queer comforting way. As she got up to leave the church she found herself looking back at it, and thinking that she would come again to see it. Her lips seemed to say 'I will come again and see you.'

The next moment she was smiling at herself. 'Why—I was nearly speaking to it,' she thought in amazement. 'I had better mind myself or I will be asking the Madonna to help me.'

Still smiling, she emerged into the busy street once again, taking with her a strange feeling of peace and solace.

CHAPTER XVI

THE SOUL OF URSULA

It was May at last. Winter had fled, and trees and flowers and birds all proclaimed the joy of Our Lady's month. Even in the city one knew it was May. The trees and shrubs showed it in St Stephen's Green, and the baskets of the flower girls piled high with fragrant blossoms.

As the days passed, the pavements grew hot and weary beneath the feet of those forced to tread them, and soon every weekend saw tired workers seeking the country or sea which lies so close to our city.

At the River House, May was a lovely month. The garden with its wealth of flowers and its cobbled path sloping down to the river's bank made a picture for any artist. A peaceful spot indeed on this warm evening when May was nearly gone and the roses were saying to one another: 'Next month is *ours*—June, the month of the roses!'

In the garden were seated Maureen and her uncle. They had been earnestly discussing something which was of great interest to them.

'I can tell you I *was* astonished,' Maureen was saying. 'You know, Uncle Jack, I never dreamt of such a thing. Ursula, of all people. Isn't it strange?'

'I am not surprised at all,' he replied, quietly. 'I have been expecting this for some time now.'

'Expecting it? Expecting that Ursula, of all persons——'

She paused as if the thought was beyond belief, and her Uncle finished the sentence for her.

'That Ursula should become a Catholic? Yes—I have thought that she would. In fact, I knew that she would.'

'But how? What made you think such a thing?'

He smiled. 'Oh, just one of my premonitions. Anyway, it's grand isn't it?'

'Yes, splendid. But, Uncle Jack—she will have a terrible time when the old lady knows.'

His face darkened. 'As if it mattered what that person thinks,' he said.

'You are very hard upon the grandmother,' said his niece. 'How strange to think she has lived so long and that she is your grandmother and my great-grandmother—and also Ursula's. After all, she is only the product of her period and upbringing. She is like one alone in a strange land—because the world of today is a strange and incomprehensible land to her. We should not be too hard upon her.'

'Perhaps so—but I have good reason to remember her.'

'I know that. But don't you think she must have been sorry when she found out who it was that she had handed over to the military?'

'No—I don't believe it would have made any difference. She would have done the very same if she had known who I was all the time.'

'Then she must be hard indeed. I often wonder will she unbend and forgive grandfather before she dies?'

'You may be sure she will *not.*'

'What in the world will she say to Ursula when she tells her?'

'That is just what is worrying me,' replied Jack; 'it will probably mean that the girl will be cast out without a penny to make her own way in the world.'

'Oh, surely not! What would she do? I wonder if——. Why, talk of angels! Here is Ursula herself.'

Maureen ran up the garden path to welcome her cousin and brought her to the river side where there were a few comfortable old chairs. As Jack shook hands and pulled one of the chairs forward, he noticed at once that something had happened, although he said nothing.

But Maureen was not reticent. After one glance at Ursula's face she cried: 'What has happened? Have you told your grandmother?'

Ursula smiled tremulously. 'I have just come from Clodagh.'

'Yes—I guessed that. This is Saturday, and I knew you were to stay there until tomorrow evening. Ursula—*have* you told her?'

'Yes, I thought it best to tell her at once. I would have been wretched—feeling that I was staying there under false pretences as it were. Besides, there would be the question of going to church in the morning and all that. So I told her that I was under instruction and was going to become a Catholic.'

'How did she take it?' It was Jack who asked.

'It was terrible. She rose from her chair, shaking all over, and for the moment I thought she was going to strike me. But then she sat down again—I do not think she was able to keep on her feet—and was quite still and motionless for a few seconds.'

Ursula paused for a moment and the others watched her pitifully. She was so pale and unhappy looking. But she continued her story almost immediately.

'Grandmother spoke then, her voice was dreadful. "Do you mean what you say?" she asked. And I told her yes, that my mind was fully made up. She asked then where I had first got the idea, and she said: "Have you had any intercourse with those people at the River House?" I don't know how she guessed it as I had not mentioned you. She just seemed to sense it in some queer way. So I told her that I had been seeing you here, but that none of you had asked me to become a Catholic. I did not tell her'—smiling wistfully at Jack— 'about your vision. I simply said that I felt God had called me and I must obey.'

'Did she argue much?'

'No—I do not think she would have been able, she was so upset. I feel miserable at the thought of bringing this sorrow upon her, but how could I help it? What else could I have done?'

'You could have done nothing else—taken no other course,' replied Jack; 'you know you did right Ursula. And although it may seem hard that you had to tell her, it was the only thing to do. She would have had to hear it, sooner or later, and it was best that she should hear it from your lips. And now what did she say at the finish? What about your future?'

'She told me to leave Clodagh—and never return, never darken the doors again. I had to leave at once—poor Kate was in a terrible state, I had hardly time to speak to her—and I have come here on my way back to the flat. But of course I cannot stay there now—I have no money. Grandmother said she would not give me another penny. I could do as I liked, she would not support me any longer. I must look for work of some sort, so I came here to see if you could help me to get work—I don't mind what kind it is——'

'Oh, Ursula—don't talk like that—and don't worry! You will stay with us for the present, until we see what is best to be done.'

'No, Maureen—I couldn't do that. I must be independent and earn my own living. I am young and strong, surely there is something I can do——'

Jack interposed, quietly: 'Of course there is Ursula. There will be no difficulty in finding something suitable. But, as Maureen very wisely says, you must stay here for the present—it is your place. Go into the house, Maureen, and tell your mother that Ursula will be staying—she will be so glad.'

Maureen flew off and then Jack spoke very gently and tenderly, yet with a matter-of-fact sincerity all his own, to the girl who was beginning to know a little of what it means to be a convert. He did not refer again to her great-grandmother, but spoke of the goodness and the love of God; of how thankful she must feel for the wonderful grace she had received; of how happy she would be when she was received into the church. There was something about Jack in this mood that reached the hearts of those who listened to him. A different Jack Weldon this, from the dour, rather taciturn one whom so many people knew.

So it was arranged, and Ursula took her place in the family circle at the River House. She found a different life to that lived at Clodagh, or to what she had grown accustomed to at the flat in Elton Street. Maureen was a contrast to Greta Mason and Flower Brown. She went to Mass every morning, came home to breakfast, and then off to the commercial school. Ursula went with her, both to Mass and afterwards to the school. The fees for her present course had already been paid, so that was all to the good, and Mr Weldon and Jack both held out hopes of work for her, so she did not worry unduly. She refused all offer of money from them, a couple of pounds which she had in hand would suffice for her tram fares and other incidentals. Her clothes and other belongings had been sent on from the flat, and she settled down to share Maureen's room.

Of all the family, Ursula liked Jack Weldon the best. He had always shown his best side to her, had been a real friend, never abrupt with her as he was sometimes with the others. He was 'Uncle Jack' to her and she would go to him in any trouble. He liked her, too, especially when she was suffering from the hard-hearted attitude of his grandmother. Never had he forgotten the day in 1916 when she had handed him over to the British. He had been released later on with the other Republican prisoners, but if he had been going to his death that day—as well he might—it would have been all the same to Faith Weldon. 'A bitter, hard old woman with a heart of ice and a will of iron.' Thus he summarised his grandmother.

William Weldon said little about his mother. He had not felt very strong of late, and was glad to take life as easily as he could; attending to his work when the briefs came in, reading in the garden when at leisure.

They were a happy family on the whole at the River House, and Ursula was quick to note the difference that religion makes when it is a reality in the daily lives of those who profess it.

There was, however, one reason why Ursula did not like living there, and that was because she was now compelled to listen to so much talk about Terry Owens. She had tried hard to forget him— never to think about him. Now, she was forced to hear his letters discussed, bits of them read out. It appeared that his father was a little better, but not very strong yet, and still wished his son to remain with him for a while longer. Terry did not expect to be able to cross to Ireland for another month—or more.

None of the family except Maureen and Jack knew that Ursula had cared for Terry and had believed that he cared for her. Had they known this, they would not have talked so freely about the coming marriage. Those who were in Ursula's secret thought it best to say nothing, it might only complicate matters. Yet they hated to see her suffer, as they knew she did at times. To give Ursula credit, she was very brave, her pride prevented her from shirking any allusion to Terry, as she did her best to join in the conversation.

She was really fond of Maureen. She could be nothing else, for the other girl had been so good to her that she must have had a hard heart indeed if she did not love her in return. Any jealousy she might have felt was gone; in its place only a dull ache of pain remained. Sometimes she would think how happy Maureen must be—unimaginable happiness—but if a tiny bit of envy tried to make itself felt, Ursula would at once say to herself, 'She deserves it—deserves every bit of happiness that comes her way.' And as the days went past, and the time drew near for her reception into the Church, Ursula felt a strange peace coming upon her such as she had never experienced before.

It was August before the family at River House heard any definite news about Mrs Weldon—and even then it was not really definite. Kate Doyle had been several times to see them and to have a talk with Miss Ursula. She knew the family well, ever since that night in 1916, when she had hurried along the road from Clodagh to bring the news of Jack Weldon's arrest. It had been midnight when she had slipped out of the house and sped on frightened feet down the lonely road to Rathfarnham, to bring the news to his parents. She had nearly been dismissed that time from Clodagh. She had often wondered how it was that Mrs Weldon allowed her to remain. Not that the mistress ever guessed that she visited the River House—she would have got short notice if that had come to light!

This was her evening off, and as Ursula went to welcome her, she saw at once that Kate was worried.

'What is wrong, Kate?' she asked. And Mr Weldon said quickly, 'Is anything wrong with my mother?'

'The mistress is not sick, sir, but I'm afraid there is cause enough for her to be troubled.'

'In what way?'

'Well, sir, that Mr Clayton hasn't been next or nigh the house for near a fortnight, and she seems terrible worried—not like herself at all. I'm afraid she has lost money in some way or other. I do hear her talkin' to herself at times—a thing I never knew her to do before—and it's about money all the time. Every day she keeps askin' if there's no letter for her—watchin' the postman, she does be, and watchin' the gate for that Mr Clayton. He must have let her down badly some way or other. Is there any means of findin' out about her money affairs? Could you do anything at all, sir?'

'We could see Mr Manton,' interposed Jack, 'he is her solicitor and must know about her business affairs.'

'But the mistress has signed a lot of papers for Mr Clayton lately,' said Kate, 'Delia was asked to witness her signature. I'm afraid that man has cheated the poor lady by some means—and she always so clever!'

'But remember how old she is now, Kate,' said Mr Weldon. 'It would be easy for a man, such as this Clayton must be, to dupe an old lady like my mother. However, I will see Mr Manton first thing tomorrow and see what I can find out.'

The next morning found him in the offices of the legal firm who had acted for the Weldon family for so many years. But when he stated his business, Herbert Manton shook his head.

'I am sorry that I can give you no information,' he said; 'Mrs Weldon took all her business out of our hands some months ago.

I may say that I heard rumours to the discredit of this Clayton of whom you speak, and I did my best to persuade her not to have any dealings with him. I went out myself to Clodagh but she refused to see me. In what state her affairs are now, I cannot tell you.'

'But is there no way in which you could find out? Or can you suggest any step which I could take?'

'We could do nothing, Mr Weldon, we are not private enquiry agents. As a legal man yourself, surely you should know the best steps to take in the matter.'

Herbert Manton was not too cordial to William Weldon. He had heard his father speak of his marriage and the pain it had caused to Mrs Weldon. It was the opinion of Mr Manton that if the man before him had made a suitable marriage, his mother would not now be in the financial plight to which her foolish behaviour had apparently brought her. Had her son remained with her to advise and guide, she would not have been left, in her old age, to the mercy of a sharper, such as he had reason to believe this Clayton to be.

He rose from his seat to show the interview was over, and William Weldon took his departure.

From enquiries which he and Jack made in the city, the reports about George Clayton were far from good; not only that, but it seemed that this man had not been seen about his usual haunts for some weeks now. The general opinion was that he had left the country, taking his ill-gotten gains with him.

William Weldon was much troubled, but he knew that at the moment there was nothing he could do. Kate would inform him at once of any developments.

Maureen wrote and told Terry about it. She knew how interested he was in the old lady of Clodagh. 'She will see no one,' she wrote. 'I wish you were here as you might be admitted—she always liked you so much.'

In his reply, Terry told her to keep an eye upon Clodagh and to let him know how things went on. He was very anxious about his father who had taken a sudden turn for the worse, so that it was impossible for the son to leave him for the present. 'The dear old dad,' Terry wrote, 'he wants me all the time. We have nurses, and everything possible is done for his comfort, but his one cry is for me, and I could not be absent from his side. My darling girl, I wish I were with you again—a thousand times a day I wish it! But good times are coming, please God, and when my old man turns the corner—I shall fly across and be with you once more, as quickly as a plane can bring me.'

In a postscript, scribbled in a hurry, he wrote: 'Your news about Ursula is just *swell*. Give her my congrats.'

Maureen duly gave the message, but did not say it had been added, almost as an afterthought, in a postscript. Not that Ursula would have minded. A short while ago, she would have bitterly resented the fact, but the Ursula of the present was not thinking much about Terry Owens. A greater love was filling her soul—a love before which all earthly affections were as naught, and as if they had never been.

On the 14th August, 1934, Ursula was received into the Catholic Church, making her first Holy Communion on the 15th. It was a beautiful morning, and as Ursula walked to the church with Maureen and Mrs O'Dwyer, she felt like one in a dream. She was very nervous, too, so that Maureen glanced anxiously at her once or twice.

But once Our Lord had come to her, a sense of perfect peace, and happiness beyond all telling, filled her soul.

'Are you happy, Ursula?' asked Maureen softly, as they were walking home.

'Oh, so happy, Maureen!' And she added, in a whisper: 'Thanks be to God for His unspeakable gift!'

In the evening Ursula went by herself to the Carmelite Church in Whitefriars Street, and knelt before the well-known statue, so beloved by thousands.

'Dear Lady of Dublin,' she said, 'I want to thank you. It was you who first brought me comfort and happiness when all the world was dark and empty. And now, dear Lady of Dublin, please pray for me—always!'

CHAPTER XVII

DESOLATION

A September day at Clodagh. In the garden the flowers of late summer and early autumn combine to make a gay show. They are running wild, growing as they like, without the guiding hand of a gardener to control them. Pat Doyle had been dismissed some weeks ago, not through any fault of his own, but simply because there was no money to pay his wages. Only two persons remained now at Clodagh—two old women. The old mistress and the servant.

Kate did her best, but it was as much as she could do to look after Mrs Weldon and keep the house in some order. The garden was left to look after itself.

On this afternoon the mistress of Clodagh was sitting by the window, hoping against hope, that she might see George Clayton's car arrive at the gate. It was now over two months since she had seen or heard from him. In his last interview with her he had been jubilant over certain shares which she had bought—on his recommendation—assuring her that they would soon be very valuable, and that if she liked she would be able to sell at a large profit.

'But I should advise you to keep them,' he had said. 'They are far too good to sell.'

It had been exceedingly difficult to obtain these shares—so he had told her—and she had been obliged to raise a loan on Clodagh, including the furniture. A friend of George Clayton's—to whom Mrs Weldon had taken an instant dislike—had made the advance. The sum agreed upon was seven hundred, to be repaid within three months. Of this sum Mrs Weldon only received six hundred, the other having gone on what Mr Isaacs called 'necessary expenses'. She had signed the documents presented to her, and these were duly witnessed by an oily youth who attended Mr Isaacs, and Pat Doyle, who laboriously and distrustfully signed his name, solely to oblige his mistress.

The loan settled, the old lady felt rather uneasy, remarking to the two men that she hoped it would be all right, and that the shares would really prove good, as she did not at all like the idea of raising a loan on Clodagh.

'If I cannot pay you in three months,' she asked, turning to

Isaacs, 'does it mean you can sell the house and furniture?'

That honest and good man smiled at the very thought.

'My dear madam,' he replied, 'these shares which you are now so fortunate as to possess will soon be able to pay back my tiny loan—and probably long before the three months. Am I not right, Clayton?'

Mr Clayton assured her that this was so, and with many words of congratulation that she had been able to secure such valuable shares, the two gentlemen departed.

She had not seen either of them since, and in another fortnight the three months would be up, and she had not the money to repay the loan. Indeed, she had hardly any money at all. She and Kate were living mostly on the produce of the garden and the poultry.

At the end of the fortnight what would happen? That was now her constant thought—a veritable nightmare.

She knew little about the shares. Silver mines somewhere. In Mexico, she thought, but was not sure. The two men had talked and talked so that she had felt quite confused for the time being. That was over two months ago, and they were to see her again in a week's time. She had certainly thought that George Clayton would have called, but he had not done so. Neither had he written.

Faith Weldon was a very old woman, her brain not what it used to be, otherwise she would never have been duped by these unscrupulous men. But her faculties were not as they had been some years ago, and her anxiety to increase her income so as to be able to keep Clodagh and the gardens as they had been kept in the past, had tempted her too invest all her capital, and then to raise a loan on Clodagh itself. Had Mr Clayton not assured her that she would be repaid a hundredfold in a short time?

But now she was becoming really anxious, as day by day went past. She had written several times to Clayton's address in Rathfarnham, and had received no reply. Still, the letters had not been returned, so evidently he was at that address and not gone away. She had not written now for over a week, and it suddenly occurred to her that she would take the bus and go and see him. She was feeling a little better and it might do her good to go out. There was a bus which came to the end of the road, returning to the city at about twenty minutes to twelve. She would go by that as far as Rathfarnham. Unfortunately there was no bus back until about three o'clock. However, she might happen to meet one of her friends who would give her a lift. If not she must only try and walk home. If she could only see Mr Clayton she would not mind having to walk back.

Kate was uneasy when informed of this resolve.

'Will I come with you, ma'am?' she asked.

'Certainly not, Kate. I am not so feeble as all that.'

She was ready to start when the bus arrived, and in a few moments she was at Rathfarnham. Dismounting, she walked down the new road with the painfully new bungalow type of house which had lately sprung up like mushrooms all over the place. She was looking for 'The Nest' —the name of the house inhabited by Mr Clayton. She found it easily enough, and going up the garden path rang the bell. While waiting she noticed that the tiny garden was neglected and full of weeds—a contrast to 'Mon Repos', next door, where a lady in a smart overall was busily weeding.

There was no reply to her first ring, so Mrs Weldon rang again and again. The lady suspended her weeding operations and leant over the railings dividing the two gardens.

'Excuse me,' she said, 'but did you want to see Mr Clayton?'

'Yes. Could you tell me when he will be in?'

'I am afraid not. He has gone away.'

She was taking rapid stock of Mrs Weldon as she spoke. Such a quaint, old-fashioned person. It made one think of the song, 'The Little Old Lady'.

'Gone away? But not—you do not mean that he has left here?'

There was a tremble in the old voice which touched the heart of Mary Baxter.

'Will you come in for a moment and I will tell you all I know,' she said. So Faith Weldon stepped down one narrow little path and up another, and followed the lady—passing a sleeping infant in a pram—into the usual small room, with folding doors. Mrs Baxter was very proud of her home and kept it in spotless condition, and it was with an air of pride that she drew forward an arm-chair for her visitor. She little guessed that the same visitor was thinking how unpleasant it must be to live in such cramped surroundings. How different from her beloved Clodagh, and how she would hate to live in a house like this. The thought of Clodagh renewed her anxiety to learn what she could about George Clayton.

'Do you know Mr Clayton?' asked Mrs Baxter.

'I have had some business dealings with him,' was the reply, in the thin, well-bred voice, 'and I wished to see him. But I suppose he is absent on business?'

'Well, yes. He may be. But my husband thinks he has just done a bunk!'

'Done a——? I beg your pardon, but I do not understand.'

'He means he has gone off—left the country.'

'But for how long?'

'Oh, Joe thinks he will never return. You see, he was a shady customer mixed up with those bogus companies—getting money from silly people——'

She stopped suddenly as she caught sight of the old lady's face. As Mary Baxter told her husband later, she could have slapped her own face for not being more careful. Of course, this poor old thing was one of Clayton's victims. How dreadful she looked.

'I am so sorry!' she exclaimed, impulsively; 'I never thought—'

Mrs Weldon tried to smile politely, but only succeeded in forcing a twisted grin to her lips.

'It does not matter,' she said; 'I only wanted to see him for a few moments. Can you give me no further information?'

'Only what I have told you. He is supposed to have left the country, but he paid his rent in advance and ᴏo the landlord can do nothing about the house until the next quarter is due. I hope,' timidly—for that this old lady was no ordinary person was plain to be seen—rather like a dethroned queen— 'I hope that you have not allowed him to cheat you of much?'

Mrs Weldon rose.

'You are very kind,' she said, coldly, 'but it is nothing to signify. I merely wished to see Mr Clayton on a matter of business. And it is quite probable that he will return soon.'

'Yes, of course,' agreed Mrs Baxter, but the tone belied the words. 'Will you not stay and rest for a little—let me get you a cup of tea—you look so tired.'

Had she said, 'You look as if you had received your death blow,' it would have been nearer the truth. But there was something so standoffish, so 'touch me not,' about this old lady that she did not like to say too much.

'I am perfectly well, thank you, and as Mr Clayton is not here at the moment, I will go home.'

Mrs Baxter wondered where 'home' might be, and she ventured

to ask:

'Have you far to go?'

'Not very far.'

'Perhaps you will be able to get a bus?'

'Perhaps I may. Thank you for your kindness—now I will say "Good day".'

Not offering to shake hands, the old lady departed, leaving Mrs Baxter staring after her, half vexed at what she considered a snub, half pitiful at the poor broken old woman. She was quick to see that here was one of the victims of that Clayton, who had been their next-door neighbour—always so friendly and nice—and of whom so many people were talking now.

Meanwhile, Mrs Weldon set off to walk home to Clodagh. There would not be a bus until after three and she did not like to wait in Rathfarnham. There was not a shop or house amongst the older residents where she would not have been welcome to sit down and wait as long as she liked. Only the newest of newcomers did not know the mistress of Clodagh. But she felt she could face no one today, especially those who had known her for so many years.

So she walked slowly onwards towards Whitechurch. Just as she was near the Protestant Church, she saw a figure approaching—and it was a figure which, even after many years, seemed very familiar. Strange to relate, Faith Weldon had never come face to face with her son since his reception into the Catholic Church. He had been a fine young man then. He was now an old one, grey-haired, stooped.

Straightening herself to her full height, she was passing on when he stepped in front of her.

'Mother,' he said, 'do you not know me?'

She turned upon him one glance from the keen eyes—faded and dim now, but which he remembered so bright—as she replied, in tones of ice: 'No—I do *not* know you, sir!'

And so she went on, leaving William Weldon staring after the mother who had once loved him so deeply, and whom he had worshipped from afar as a boy and young man. He had been horrified at the change in her. Indeed, had not blood called to blood, he had hardly recognised her. Not that he had not expected a change, remembering her age, but she had been walking along, worn, bent, as one who had been stricken to the heart. And the hopeless look upon her poor face! True, she had straightened herself to reply to him, but that was but for a moment. He knew that she was a broken woman. Immediately he guessed that she must be in financial trouble. That man, Clayton, must have robbed her to a pretty penny. He must ask Kate to find out what she could, and surely there must be some way of helping his mother. It might be done without her knowledge. He must talk to Jack about it.

The fortnight went by and no word of George Clayton. On the morning after the day on which the three months had expired, Faith Weldon was sitting in the garden at the side of the house. Kate had brought out a chair to a sunny spot and settled her as comfortably as possible. Her faithful heart went out to her old mistress, so desolate and lonely, and a prey, as she knew, to terrible fears. The day was lovely, one of those sunny autumn days that are sent to cheer us before the cold blasts of winter come to our land. Faith Weldon's tired old eyes gazed around the garden, where the gay flowers were blooming on every side, and the trees turning to russet and brown. How she had loved her garden! How she still loved it, and how she hated to see it becoming weed-grown and neglected. If only things had turned out as she had hoped and expected, if those shares had materialised as Clayton had promised that they would—how happy she would have been on this fine autumn morning. Those horrid weeds—what progress they were making! She wondered if she could possibly manage a little weeding with Kate's help? But then Kate had more than enough to do as it was; she was not a young woman, she was stout, too, and unwieldy, and gardening always made her back ache. No she would not ask Kate. After her early dinner she would try what she could do herself. Lately she had been so worried over the repayment of the loan that she had been unable to think of much else, and then the weather had been wet and cold. But today was really beautiful, and things might not be so bad after all. Mr Clayton might return at any moment and explain everything. She did not like that Mr Isaacs—an odious man—but it was hardly likely that even he would expect the loan to be repaid on the very day it fell due. Besides, there was surely some means by which she could renew the loan. By paying a fine. She would try and pay the fine somehow. In fact she would *have* to pay it, as of course she could not lose Clodagh. *That* was simply out of the question—not to be even thought of.

At this moment she caught sight of Kate's stout figure coming towards her, and as she drew near, Mrs Weldon noticed that she was looking anxious and worried.

'Well, Kate—what is it?' she asked.

'That Mr Isaacs, ma'am. He's here, askin' for you. I said you were not too well, but he said it was important and that he must see you. He is in the drawing-room now.'

So he had come. That horrid man, whose very name had been a nightmare to her for these weeks past. From her seat she could not see the front of the house or the gate, and she had not noticed the noise of the car, quiet though it was there on the slope of the mountain-side, with no traffic save the rumbling of farm carts and an occasional motor. But he was here. And she must see him. Faith Weldon had never been one to put off the evil day. Marshalling all her courage, she rose from her chair.

'I will see him at once, Kate,' she said.

'Oh, ma'am—will I not tell him you are not well enough? Sure I'll get rid of the old fox someway—lave him to me!'

'No, Kate. It is best that I see him now.'

In the low-ceilinged drawing-room, Mr Isaacs was gazing around him with much satisfaction. Quite a number of nice little objects here. They should fetch a good price at the auction—especially that bureau and those old prints. And then there was the silver. That had been included in the agreement, although he imagined that the old lady was ignorant of the fact, not having read carefully any paper which Clayton produced for her signature. An easy old pigeon to pluck—and no mistake. His cousin Abe—otherwise Mr George Clayton—had done a good bit of business. Yes, the house and furniture—every bit of which was good—and the gardens and field attached should certainly fetch a tidy sum. He should have a fine profit on the six hundred which he had advanced to the old woman.

'You wished to see me?'

The quiet voice made him turn from the scrutiny of a hunting print to meet the level glance of the mistress of Clodagh.

The oily smile appeared at once. 'Why, yes, Mrs Weldon. I just called to collect my little loan. It will not take you a moment, I am sure, to sign a cheque for the amount. I should not wish to detain you from your pleasant rest in the lovely garden.'

Mrs Weldon sat down in her high-backed chair and motioned

her visitor to be seated.

'Mr Isaacs,' she said, 'I am sorry to say that I have not the money to repay your loan.'

He feigned great surprise. 'You have not the money? But, my dear lady, you said that you were sure to have it by now and——'

'Pardon me, Mr Isaacs—you and Mr Clayton said so. You both assured me that the shares which Mr Clayton bought for me would pay such good dividends that I would be able to repay the loan easily.'

'And did they not?'

'No. I have had no dividend at all from Mr Clayton—neither do I know where he is.'

'Not know where he is?' Again the feigned surprise, while he tried to hide a satisfied smile. 'That is really too bad. However, he will no doubt return soon now—business was very pressing, I expect, and called him away suddenly. If it were possible for me to afford to wait for my money, I should have been only too glad to oblige a client of his. But I am in a fix for ready money at the moment and so must ask you to repay the six hundred immediately.'

'But I have not got it, Mr Isaacs, therefore you will have to wait a little for your money. If perhaps you could see to the selling of those shares for me—the Silver Mines in Mexico——'

He laughed callously. '*Those* shares? I am sorry to tell you that they have proved quite useless. Practically all the money invested in them is lost.'

For the moment Mrs Weldon did not comprehend what the words meant. Then, as she realised their import she gave a little cry. 'But you both assured me that they were excellent shares—that is why I invested all my capital and raised the loan. They cannot be *quite* worthless! Surely there will be some means of getting my money back.'

'I am afraid not. Clayton also, as you know, invested a large sum in these mines and no doubt he has lost heavily, too. When he returns he may be able to suggest something to you, but in the meantime I must ask you to let me have my money at once.'

There was a note in his voice which caused Faith Weldon to grow suddenly very cold. In spite of her efforts her voice shook as she repeated: 'I am sorry, Mr Isaacs, but I have not got the money to repay the loan.'

'Then I must only proceed with the sale.'

Proceed with the sale? A great darkness came upon her for a moment and her own voice sounded very far away as she asked 'Just what do you mean?'

'I mean that I will sell this house and land, furniture, silver—everything that is included in the agreement you signed.'

'But not—not at once? Surely you will wait—if only for a little while——'

'I am sorry, madam, but as I have already informed you, I am in temporary need of the money—urgently in need. My solicitor will write to you about the date of the auction. Of course if in the meantime you can pay me the amount due, I shall be very glad. But otherwise, I must stand by our agreement—signed by your own hand.'

What did those words recall to Faith Weldon's mind? A school concert long ago—how long ago!—ending with the Trial Scene from the Merchant of Venice. 'I will have my bond' —those were the words which came to her now, as she listened to Mr Isaacs repeating his ultimatum. Yet his words conveyed little to her confused mind. An auction at Clodagh! Such a thing was simply beyond her comprehension.

Mr Isaacs was standing up. 'I will bid you good day, madam—there is no more to be said.'

He held out his hand but Mrs Weldon took no notice of him, she remained seated in the old-fashioned chair, looking as if she were carved in stone. He shrugged his shoulders and left the room and the house, his eyes noting with satisfaction the gardens and pleasant surroundings of the lovely house of which he—Isaac Isaacs—was now the legal owner.

But Faith Weldon remained motionless in her chair, a small black cocker licking the withered hand that was clenched on the arm of the chair.

CHAPTER XVIII

IN CITY PENT

It was Kate Doyle who brought the news to River House. At first they could hardly believe what she had to tell. The family had seen but little of Kate lately as she was seldom able to leave her mistress, but now she had made a point of coming, leaving her niece to stay with Mrs Weldon.

'Of course the mistress does not know that I am here,' she said: 'she would never let me come. But—oh, Mr Weldon—is there nothing that can be done? We got word today that the auction will be held in a fortnight. It will just kill the mistress—and that's certain!'

'But this must not be!' exclaimed William Weldon. 'Clodagh sold to strangers! My father would turn in his grave. Can you suggest anything, Jack?'

'What can I suggest? We have not got six hundred pounds between us, and if we had, the old lady would not accept it at our hands—of that you may be sure. And don't you know, too, that this Isaacs does not want the loan repaid. What he wants is the proceeds from the sale—why, he is bound to make a huge profit. He will about treble the sum which he advanced. How any woman could be such a fool passes my comprehension!'

'What I want to know, sir,' said Kate, 'is whether there is some way by which we could get the mistress away from the house before the auction? If she stays there for that day—and I'm afeared she'll want to—she would just die, watching her house—her home for all these years—being sold to strangers.'

They talked a long time discussing the matter in all its bearings. Ursula was terribly upset. She felt that she must see her great-grandmother as soon as possible. They had not met since that day in May when Ursula had been told to leave Clodagh and never return. But things were different now, the old woman was in dire trouble, surely she would see her. She would try anyway. Ursula was rather surprised to see that Maureen seemed the least worried of all the family. She could not understand why this should be so, as her cousin was so kind-hearted. But now she appeared not to worry at all. As for Jack, although he had never forgotten his grandmother's behaviour to him, he still felt a kind of pity for her now, in her lonely and desolate old age.

'Of course it is all her own fault,' he said. 'If she had asked for advice in the proper quarter, either from Mr Manton or from her own relations, she would not have been allowed to be so foolish.'

'It is no use saying that now, Jack,' replied his father; 'your grandmother was always very determined and used to having her own way. She forgets her age and failing faculties—of which these scoundrels took full advantage. We must only try to help her in some way now.'

'The first thing is to see her—get her to talk to us,' said Ursula. 'Do you think she would let us in, Kate, if we try?'

'I could not say, Miss Ursula, but sure you can try. When will you come to the house?'

'Tomorrow—and you must do your best to get us admitted.'

It was William Weldon who spoke, and so it was arranged.

Accordingly on the following day, Ursula and Mr Weldon arrived at Clodagh. It had been spring when Ursula had last seen her old home, and now it was autumn. But how beautiful the old place looked to her as they pushed open the gate and walked to the door.

The ring was answered by Kate, who immediately exclaimed—according to plan—'Why, Miss Ursula, is it you!' They stepped into the hall and waited while Kate knocked on a door at the right. A voice said : 'Come in,' and she entered. But she did not close the door after her, and with a whimper of delight, a little black cocker rushed out and straight into Ursula's arms.

'Why, Judy!' she cried, 'dear old girl—how are you at all?'

Judy was not able to talk, but she had no need to do so. She expressed clearly her delirious delight at seeing her young mistress again. And indeed, the little dog was pleased beyond anything—she had been so lonely. It was depressing for a dog—as Judy would have told you—to have to live with just two old women, neither of whom cared for a good walk, or would allow a dog to scamper at their side while they tramped over the hills. What ages it seemed since she and Ursula had gone together up the heather-covered slopes of Tibradden, where all the rabbit holes could be sniffed out. But now the good days would surely come again, and Judy frantically licked Ursula's face, her tail wagging furiously while she tried to say: 'I am so glad you are back—I did miss you so much!'

The sitting-room door had been left ajar and William Weldon heard his mother's cold tones from within. She was speaking quite clearly.

'No—I will not see them, Kate.' she said. 'Please tell them to leave.'

Kate murmured something, but her pleadings were in vain. The old voice only commanded her in sterner tones to deliver her message to those who were waiting in the hall.

But Ursula had heard the words, too, and putting Judy down, she ran past Kate into the room. Her grandmother—as she always called her—was seated as she had so often seen her, in a high-backed chair by the fire—a very small fire.

'Dear grandmother,' she cried, 'don't send us away—please! Uncle William is here—he wants to see you so much. Won't you speak to him?'

Mrs Weldon drew herself upright and her glance fell with cold disapproval on the girl who knelt beside her.

'No,' she replied. 'I will not see him—nor do I wish to see you. You have chosen to join those members of my family who are a disgrace to their name, and therefore you can remain with them. I do not wish to see you again, and must ask you not to repeat your visit.'

She might have been speaking to a complete stranger and the girl was cut to the heart. She did not reply, but William Weldon, who had been standing at the door, came forward.

'Mother,' he said, 'surely you cannot be so hard? We are only come to offer our help—to see if we can be of any use to you in your trouble—'

His mother interrupted quickly. 'Who told you that I was in trouble? How do you know anything about my affairs? And what interest can they have for you?'

'The greatest interest—as you know well. There is nothing we would not do to save you from worry—to save Clodagh for you.'

'For yourself, I suppose, you mean?' was the bitter retort. 'Well, Clodagh is not for you—and never will be, whether it remains my property or whether it has to be—sold. It will be all the same to you. And now will you kindly leave me—I wish to be alone.'

The two listening to her, and, who both in their own way

loved her, realised that there was nothing more to be done—for the moment anyway. Perhaps later on they might be allowed to help her. Not that they thought it likely, knowing, as they did, the iron will of Faith Weldon. They must only see if others could succeed where they had failed. Sadly they turned away to leave the room and the house. At Ursula's heels went the black cocker. Judy was feeling uneasy about the interview at which she had been present, she did not understand what it meant, but her doggy instinct told her that something was wrong. She had made up her mind not to lose sight of Ursula if she could help it. Kate was weeping silently as she opened the door for them and they made their way down the garden path to where Jack was waiting in the little two-seater. He saw at once by their faces that their mission had failed.

'So it was no good?' he asked, adding dryly, 'I expected as much.'

As Ursula stepped into the car, Judy sprang in beside her.

'Oh, Judy, old girl—you must go back,' said Ursula. 'I cannot take you with me.'

The little cocker's tail, which had been wagging overtime, dropped between her legs, and she raised her mournful eyes to the face of her young mistress. Ursula's own eyes were wet as she gave the dog a hug, saying, 'No—it's no use, Judy. You cannot come—you must go back. There's a good dog now—do as you are told.'

At that moment Kate came to the gate calling for Judy.

'She is here, Kate. She wants to follow me.'

'The poor little beast! Come, Judy—come back here! Goodbye, Miss Ursula, and you, sir, and Master Jack. I hope you will be able to do something for the mistress—sure she's not fit to be left alone—and I'm not much good meself—God help me!'

'You are splendid, Kate, and I don't know what we would do without you. Take care of my mother—but I know you will—and let us know at once if anything happens. Goodbye!'

'Goodbye—and God bless you all! Come, Judy!'

Kate returned to the house followed by a dejected dog. An irate old lady was waiting for her.

'How dare you admit those people into my house? You were perfectly well aware that I did not wish to see them. If you behave like that again, I shall have to dispense with your services.'

Kate made some excuse. She did not want to annoy Mrs Weldon more than was necessary. Of course she knew quite well that if she were to leave, no other servant would come in her place. It was several months since she had received any wages, she seldom got a free evening, and there were other disadvantages with which no modern maid would put up for a day. But she kept quiet and she left the room after making her apology.

The old woman glanced at the hearthrug where Judy sat, her sad spaniel eyes one big question mark, as she gazed at her mistress. Faith Weldon reached down and stroked the dog.

'So even you would leave me, Judy? I thought you would be more faithful.'

The tone of voice stirred the doggy heart, and Judy turned and licked the withered hand resting on her black coat.

And so the autumn shadows fell and twilight gathered about the old woman and the little dog, as they sat alone in the old house on the slopes of Tibradden mountain.

But as Faith Weldon sat there she was thinking. Thinking and planning. Her body might be quiet but her mind was active. She knew that unless a miracle happened Clodagh would be sold in less than two weeks. She could not stay to see that take place. Kate's fears that she would wish to do so were unfounded, she could not have borne it. She was all anxiety to get away before the auction. She possessed some jewellery of her own; a few good rings, some old-fashioned ear-rings, bracelets and big brooches. If she could dispose of these, surely the money would suffice to keep her for the short time which she felt she had to live. She had a presentiment that once she left Clodagh, her days on earth would be short indeed. Food—and not much of that—and a lodging would be all she would require.

She must sell the articles as soon as possible and make the necessary arrangements, and this must be done without Kate's knowledge. She felt bitterly the fact that her old servant had been in communication with the River House. Mrs Weldon was too quick not to have guessed that the visit to Clodagh had been pre-arranged. Also, she remembered that Kate had been out for several hours last evening. She would have no more of that sort of thing. For the future, she would look after her own affairs, keeping them from Kate. She was sharp enough, even now, and laid her plans accordingly.

The next day when Kate had gone to see her sister in Rockbrook—who happened to be conveniently ill—the old lady took the bus into the city and went to a well-known firm of jewellers. They were an old Dublin firm of good repute, honest in all their dealings. It was lucky indeed for Mrs Weldon that George Clayton was not at hand to recommend another of his friends. Asking to see the manager, she was shown into his private room, for his father had done business with John Weldon in the past, and the son—now an elderly man—knew Mrs Weldon. He opened his eyes with surprise when she told him the purpose of her visit. Opening her handbag, she produced several pairs of heavy antique ear-rings, bracelets and brooches, and from her thin fingers she took three rings. The rings were really valuable, the stones very fine, far more valuable than the other objects, as Mr Wilson explained to her. The fashion in jewellery—as in all else—had changed, he said, and some of the articles she wished to sell would only be bought for the gold they contained. But the rings were valuable—there was no question of that.

After some discussion he offered the old lady the sum of fifty pounds for the lot.

'And that is really the very most that they are worth,' said Mr Wilson; 'it is a pity that you have to dispose of these articles. Their sentimental value to you must be great.'

He paused a moment. He was a kind-hearted man and guessed that she must be in some difficulty. Perhaps she would confide in him—he might be able to advise her.

But Faith Weldon froze at the first sign of curiosity on his part.

'I wish to sell them, as I have told you,' she said; 'if this is all you can offer—I must accept.'

'That is all. Of course you are at liberty to try elsewhere, but I can assure you that you would get no better offer. Shall I write you a cheque now?'

She cashed the cheque and took the bus home to Tibradden.

Kate was relieved when she saw her return; she had been anxious, not knowing where her mistress had gone.

'Oh, thank God!' she cried; 'I was afeared something had happened to you ma'am. I couldn't for the life of me think where you had gone.'

'I had business in town,' replied Mrs Weldon, stiffly; 'there is no reason for you to be at all anxious about me. I am quite capable of taking care of myself.'

A few days later she went into town again. This time she told Kate that she was going and would return by the afternoon bus. On reaching the city she went to an Apartments' Agency and obtained the addresses of several people with apartments to let. But her quest proved fruitless. She felt tired out after going round a few of them; none was suitable, she was appalled at the rents asked, and many of the places seemed dirty and stuffy.

It was several days before she found anything at all suitable for the rent she could afford. By now she was terribly tired, and often wondered how she managed to keep going back and forth into the city. A false strength upheld her, and she went from place to place until, in a street near St Stephen's Green, she found what she thought would suit. Just one room, and off it a tiny hole—not much bigger than a cupboard—called by the landlady, 'the kitchenette'—and which would hold a small gas stove and a shelf for her crockery and pans. For this accommodation she had to pay seven and six a week, and Mrs O'Grady assured her that she was getting it 'for nothing'.

When all was settled, Faith thought it was time to acquaint Kate with her plans for the future. Besides, she owed her some money; she was not sure how much, but it must be paid. Kate was thunderstruck. That her mistress had 'been up to something', she had guessed and had been anxious and uneasy about her, but that she had actually gone and taken lodgings for herself in town—and in Glen Street, too, which was little better than a slum—was really terrible.

'And there is no use telling the people at River House,' said Mrs Weldon, looking coldly at Kate's amazed face; 'I will not see any of them. I can manage quite well for the short time which I have to spend in this world—it cannot be long. You will please arrange for my clothes and other articles which are my personal property, to be sent on to me at this address—33 Glen Street. Also re-direct any letters that may come—although I expect none.'

Yet it is likely that in her heart, Faith Weldon was hoping against hope that George Clayton might return at the last minute and put things right. But, in the meantime————

'You will stay here until after the—sale?'

Kate nodded, unable to speak, but her mistress went on with Spartan courage 'I am taking Judy with me. When I die you will take her. Try and keep her for the rest of her life. How happy are dogs that they have not to live on for years and years in this weary world! I am tired, Kate, and will go to bed.'

She moved to Glen Street three days later. What bitterness of heart came to Faith Weldon at leaving the house which had been her home for so many years, will never be known. She walked down the garden path, carrying just a handbag and with Judy close at her heels, and never looked behind once; never flung one backward glance at her beloved garden, at the clematis-covered porch, the diamond-paned windows—all that had spelt home for her since she had come there as a girl bride, over sixty years ago. Erect, upright, she walked steadily to the gate, passed through, and so out on the road beyond where the bus for the city was waiting a short distance away.

Kate came with her and saw her settled in her new lodgings. The good soul was horrified at the narrow space, the ugly surroundings—all so different from Clodagh. The mistress would not live long in that place—she was sure of that. She wept bitterly when taking leave of the old lady and Judy, but Mrs Weldon retained a calm attitude all through.

It was only when Kate had gone and she and Judy were really alone in their strange and unfamiliar surroundings that the slow, painful tears of old age—so different from those of youth—trickled down the withered cheek, and fell upon the silky head of the cocker who had jumped on her lap. There was silence in the room while the old woman and the little dog sympathised with one another in their loneliness and poverty.

Outside in the street an organ began to play 'Oft in the Stilly Night.' The old lady knew every word of the song and they found an echo in her heart at that moment :

> 'I feel like one who treads alone
> Some banquet-hall deserted,
> Whose lights are fled, whose garlands dead,
> And all but he departed!'

CHAPTER XIX

THE AUCTION AT CLODAGH

Greta Mason and Flower Brown were still partners in the flat in Elton Street. It was October again—just a year since Ursula had joined them there. They missed her when she left them the following May, both for her own sake and for the money she contributed towards the rent. It was seldom they met her now and had often wondered how she was getting on. Now Greta was telling Flower the news which she had heard about Ursula.

'You have heard me speak about that Mrs Hamilton—she lives out our way, they bought Colonel Grey's place a year ago. Well, she came in today for a face massage—such a face!—and while I was doing her she asked if I knew the people who lived in Clodagh? When I told her that I had known them all my life—that the two families had always been neighbours and friends for umpteen years, she at once thought that I knew all about Ursula's latest stunt. When she saw I did not she was charmed to tell me all about it. What do you think it is?'

'I have no idea—not the foggiest. But that girl might do anything!'

'She has turned Roman Catholic.'

'*What!*'

'Yes—I thought that would make you sit up.'

'It comes of living with her Catholic relations, of course. They have got round her. But what will the great-grandmother say? Isn't she a rather bigoted person?'

'I should say so! But, as it happens, she has enough troubles of her very own just now.'

'Is she ill? I thought she was one of those old ladies who live to a century and over.'

'She has got herself into pretty bad financial trouble. It must be bad, indeed, because there is to be an auction at Clodagh next Wednesday, and I am asking leave to attend it. My esteemed parents will both be there, and I want to see the fun—I love auctions, and this should be a great sight—they have lovely things for sale.'

'It won't be much fun for poor Ursula,' said Flower, who was far more kind-hearted than Greta Mason. 'She must feel it terribly.'

'Oh, she will have the excitement of her new religion to keep up her spirits. It is the old woman who will probably die. I cannot imagine her living through such a disgrace—as she would consider it. Anyway, I want to be there. There is some lovely silver and other things. I believe it is all to go. How on earth could the old lady have got into such a mess? I heard she borrowed money from the Jews.'

'Gosh! The poor old dud! I am sorry for her. I wonder will Ursula have to look after her now?'

'She won't be allowed. Mrs Hamilton said she heard on good authority—she's an awful old gossip—that the family from the River House called there and that Mrs Weldon refused to see them.'

'Well—I call that the frozen limit! To be so hard at her age. When did you say the auction was to be held?'

'Next Wednesday. Will you come?'

'If I can get off I will. I like auctions, but I am sorry about this one—it seems such a pity to break up a home like Clodagh. I wonder will Ursula be there?'

'Can't say, I'm sure. I am wondering if Mrs Weldon will stay for it? It will surely kill her.'

On the following Wednesday, the two girls set off for Clodagh. Special buses were running on account of the auction, and the road outside the gates of Clodagh was crowded with private cars. The auction had caused much interest amongst collectors. There was also a number of the usual type of antique dealers present and it was evident that keen bidding was expected.

The two girls followed the crowd into the house, and as they went from room to room and saw the various articles of furniture marked out as lot this and that, Greta, in spite of her would-be hardness, felt a lump rising in her throat. She remembered the happy hours spent at Clodagh when she was a child—a schoolgirl. The sun was shining quite brightly on the old house, this fine autumn day, and in the garden late roses were growing beside masses of gay autumn flowers.

The crowd walked through the house and around the garden, speculating on the sum which the auction would realise. It should be a good sum.

'I understand that the house is to be sold first,' said a lady standing beside Greta; 'I hear that there are several interested parties here, so the bidding should be keen.'

'I hope it won't take too long to dispose of the house,' remarked a man nearby; 'I am not interested in the property, but I should like some of the silver.'

'Oh, *that!*' I am afraid you will have little chance with all the dealers who are here—they will snap all that up.'

'If they get the chance.'

'Of course they have the chance—they have all the money nowadays.'

The auctioneer, Mr Shandon, took his place on a kitchen table which had been brought out on the porch, and from there he announced the sale of the house and grounds. He made the usual speech about the beauty and value of the place, and finally stated that the sale would now commence and that Clodagh and the lands adjoining would be sold to the highest bidder.

While he was speaking, Greta glanced around and presently noticed Ursula standing somewhat apart, at the side of the house. Mr Weldon, with Jack and Maureen, were with her. It was evident the Ursula was making a great effort to control her feelings, but she was pale and nervous.

The bidding for the house and land started at seven hundred pounds; then a voice cried, 'and fifty,' and the bidding continued until two thousand was reached. There was a pause then, but almost immediately the same voice which had made the first bid and had been bidding ever since, called again, 'And one hundred.' So it went on until the sum of three thousand was reached and Clodagh Cottage fell under the hammer to a young man who was a stranger to all present. Tears were falling now from Ursula's eyes—tears which she could not keep back. So Clodagh was gone—dear old Clodagh. Her home. She thought of the days when she had been so happy there, but with all a girl's impatience had only longed to get away to the city and freedom. She knew better now and would have given the world to have those days back again. She thought of her grandmother, sitting alone in her room in Glen Street, no doubt visualising what was taking place at Clodagh. Glancing round and seeing the crowd of curious people, the eager faces of dealers, the jealous looks which one collector cast at another, the disorder and noise, it seemed to Ursula that she must be in a nightmare—this was never peaceful, serene Clodagh, the lovely old house which for a hundred and fifty years had stood amidst the beauty of the Dublin hills. How humiliated it must feel! The spirit of the house must be weeping in anguish. She roused herself from senseless repinings as she saw the auctioneer advancing towards the young man who had purchased Clodagh. She wondered who he was? Was he buying for himself or for another? She thought it must be for some client of his. He would hardly want a place like Clodagh. But of course one never knew. She said to William Weldon: 'I think he has been bidding for someone else. What do you think, Uncle William?'

'Yes—I think so, too,' replied Mr Weldon.

The young man in question was now in conversation with Mr Shandon, and after a few moments the auctioneer beckoned to Mr Isaacs who had been watching them from a short distance. He now came forward with his usual oily smile.

'This gentleman has bought the house, Mr Isaacs,' said the auctioneer; 'he has produced satisfactory credentials. He is acting on behalf of another party, and he tells me that he has orders not only to secure the house, but also the furniture, silver, pictures—everything which is for sale. He wishes to know if you will name your own price—which will be paid over immediately?'

But this did not suit Mr Isaacs. He shook his head with well-feigned regret.

'It cannot be done. The auction was advertised, advertisements have appeared in all the papers, people have come from far and near' —he waved podgy hands in the air as if to describe a circle round the world—'the furniture and other articles must be sold as advertised. If this gentleman is so keen it is open to him to bid for any article he wishes.'

The young man bowed stiffly.

'As you wish,' he replied. 'I only thought that it might save trouble if you fixed your price and sold all together.'

Mr Isaacs smiled. 'I hope you will be able to secure all you want,' he said, and departed to where a friend of his own was standing. To this person he explained matters, and he promised to put up the bidding of every article as high as possible. Isaacs rubbed his hands. 'He will pay for what he wants—pay a double price. That is good—very good!'

So the auction proceeded, each article being put up for sale and duly bid for. It was soon noticed, however, that the same person who had bought the house itself was evidently keen on securing the furniture also. No matter how high the prices soared—he would bid even higher. Before long there were few to bid against him, and had it not been for Isaac's agent, the stranger would have had it all his own way. But that man kept the bidding high, and Isaacs rubbed his hands together as he murmured: 'Good business—good business!' How George Clayton would enjoy the joke.

At last all the furniture was disposed of to one buyer. The pictures and silver came next. More than one wealthy collector of old silver had come to bid, but no matter how high they went, they were always outbid by the quiet young man, who stood like a sentinel in the one spot, bidding for each article that came under the hammer. A large potato ring of old silver was the object of keen competition, but the highest bidders had to eventually retire and leave the field to the quiet young man.

And so it went on with monotonous sameness until the last article had been sold to this Mr McMahon, of the quiet voice and imperturbable mien.

When all was over, and the crowd moving away, casting glances of curiosity—some of them hostile—towards the young man, Ursula was amazed to see Maureen, who had been standing silently beside her, saying little all the time, go up to him and shake him warmly by the hand. She then brought him over to her family, saying, rather shyly: 'This is Mr McMahon. He has been acting for Terry at this sale. I cabled to him as we had arranged.'

Ursula stared in surprise, as did the others. She felt almost dazed, not for the moment comprehending what it meant.

'*What* did you say?' asked Mr Weldon.

McMahon smiled as he shook hands. 'I hope you will all forgive me for not taking you into my confidence at the start,' he said; 'but I was afraid that old robber, Isaacs, might get suspicious and think it was some kind of put-up job between us. As it was the villain managed to put the prices up to a fearful rate.'

'Do you think that Terry will mind?' asked Maureen, anxiously.

McMahon laughed. 'Not he! He gave me unlimited power. I was to buy the place and all it contained—no matter what it might cost. Terry is a cousin of mine, although I only saw him once for a short time while he was over here. I live in Westmeath and had never seen this place, but now that I have done so, I must say I do not wonder that Terry wished to buy it. Of course'

—with a smile at Maureen—'I understand why he was especially anxious to buy. By the way, I understand that a very old lady lived here? I suppose that she did not stay for the sale?'

'That is my mother,' said Mr Weldon, 'she would not remain, and no wonder. It would have broken her heart.'

'But how pleased she will be now! It will cheer her up to know that the house is still in the family. I suppose you will want to tell her at once.'

There was a rather strained silence. How would the old lady take it? How would she react to this new condition of affairs? They were, one and all, wondering about this. It was Ursula who broke this silence. 'Mrs Weldon is my great-grandmother,' she said, 'and is very proud. I have lived with her all my life so I know her. She must be told, but there is no saying how she will take the news.'

'Well—we must only hope for the best,' said Mr Weldon; 'and now Mr McMahon, you will come back with us for a meal—you must be famished! I am tired and hungry myself—but your throat must be as dry as a herring bone! We live in Rathfarnham and Jack has his car here.'

'That is very good of you, Mr Weldon, and I will be only too glad to come. I want a talk with you all.'

They went off together, Maureen and Ursula passing by Greta and Miss Brown in the crowd without seeing them.

'Well—that beats all!' said Flower. 'That young man must have been bidding for the family all the time. Where on earth did they raise the needful?'

'Don't be a fool,' replied her friend. 'He was bidding for Terence Owens, of course. Isn't he going to marry Maureen? That will keep Clodagh in the family, but I don't know what Ursula will think about it. To say nothing of the old dame herself.'

Needless to remark, Mrs Weldon and her daughter were amazed at the news. The chief question discussed, however, was the attitude which the erstwhile mistress of Clodagh might now adopt. How would she react to the new conditions? And—above all—who would tell her?

'I will,' said Ursula.

'But will she let you in?'

'I think she will. Anyway, I can but try.'

After tea, she and Denis McMahon were in the garden, strolling down the path to the riverside. He was telling her of his home in Westmeath, a pleasant farmhouse standing by the shores of one of those lakes for which that county is famous. He told her that he lived alone with an uncle, a very old man. When he died the farm would come to Denis.

'Not that I want to see Uncle Dan go,' he said. 'He has been very good to me in every way, and I have lived with him since my father and mother were killed accidentally when I was a youngster of ten. The only thing we fight about sometimes'—with a laugh—'is the rather old-fashioned farming methods of the old man. He won't till enough—that's another thing. Using the good soil as cattle ranches to feed John Bull! However, he must have his own way—I would only be talking to deaf ears! But when I think how much better the farm could be run—it makes me furious.'

Ursula glanced at him from time to time as he talked. She saw a tall broad-shouldered young man, who seemed to have about him the very breath of the Irish countryside. His keen grey eyes looked as if they were always scanning the sky for weather signs, his hands were brown and strong. A man—every inch of him.

He saw a slim, dark-haired young girl, rather quiet, one who seemed to have already shaken sorrow by the hand, young as she was. Yet, looking closer at her, he noticed the look of peace and deep-seated happiness which seemed to surround her. It was not until he knew Ursula better that he heard her story—and understood.

It was decided that Ursula should go alone on the following day to Glen Street, and explain matters to her great-grandmother.

'Would you like me to drive you there?' asked Jack. But she said no—she would rather go quite alone.

CHAPTER XX

EXIT

All that day, now drawing to a close, Faith Weldon had sat, motionless, by a tiny fire in her room in Glen Street. Judy sat at her feet, and if ever a dog looked miserable and unhappy—she did. Now and then, her mournful spaniel eyes would seek those of her mistress as if asking, again and again : 'What is the matter? Why are we staying in this horrid place? When are we going home? I cannot live here—I hate it!'

Her mistress took no notice of her. She was conscious of the dog's presence, but felt too ill to trouble about Judy. She had been feeling ill ever since she got out of bed that morning.

When going to bed the previous night, she had been sure that she would not sleep. How could she when the morrow would be the day of the auction at Clodagh? The day upon which Clodagh would be for sale—to be knocked down to the highest bidder.

To her surprise, she had fallen asleep almost at once.

Dreams had come to her in that sleep. So vivid, that when she awoke she still thought they were real. She was taken back to Clodagh, seeing her life there in a series of living pictures, passing, one after another, before her mental vision.

She was with her husband on that first evening when they had returned from their honeymoon. She was pacing by his side along the garden path, one hand on his arm, the other holding up her rich flowing skirts. 'So you like Clodagh?' he was saying. How tall and strong he was—she was only up to his shoulders. How lovely the garden looked that June evening.

Then she was with Willie—her handsome, clever son. He was going to make a great name for himself at the Irish Bar. Ursula was different—a strange girl, sullen, resentful. She must get John to speak to her seriously.

She was kneeling now by the bedside of her dying husband. The memory, fraught with pain, almost awoke her and she stirred uneasily in the bed. But sleep closed in upon her once more, and the dream continued, going on like a serial story, as is the way with some dreams.

She was in her office in Capel Street, engrossed in business, full of energy, directing, controlling. Happy in her work, proud of her business capacity.

And then it was an evening in summer and she was waiting for the daughter who had run away—not to return for seven years; and then only to die.

Another evening and she is listening to her son as he speaks of the girl he is about to marry, shattering her dreams of the future, leaving her to live her lonely life at Clodagh.

Again the old woman stirred. It was cold and she shivered. Some bells were ringing the hour. Of course—it was Christmas Eve. That blessed Christmas Eve which had brought little Faith to her doorstep—the dear child who was to become the apple of her eye, her one comfort through the years that followed—years all too short.

'Faith,' she whispered, 'little Faith—where are you?'

Again the coldness came upon her and she was walking by the seashore at night, lonely, dark, with the dismal murmur of the waves beating—beating. And she remembered that Faith was gone.

And now Ursula was gone, the last to leave her. She was alone at Clodagh, and over her hung some dread premonition. What was it? What was Kate saying? 'Mr Isaacs to see you, ma'am—he says he must see you at once.'

An auction. An auction at Clodagh—everything to be sold.

'Kate? Where are you? Did you hear what that man said? How cold it is! Put some more coal on the fire.'

Shivering, she awoke. Awoke in a dingy room in a narrow street. Judy, who lay across her feet, stretched herself and came and licked the wan old face. She put out her hand and stroked the dog.

'We must get up, Judy,' she said.

But when it came to getting out of bed, she felt suddenly very weak. With trembling hands she dragged on her dressing-gown.

'If I can make myself a cup of tea I will feel better,' she thought.

She went outside her door to fill the kettle from the tap on the landing. A girl who lodged upstairs was doing the same thing, and started when she caught sight of the old lady. She had only seen her once before, as Mrs Weldon had been such a short time there, and kept entirely to herself. 'Poor old thing! How dreadful she looks! She should not be living alone. I wonder has she no friends or relatives?' Thus thought Rose Belton.

She drew aside at once to allow Mrs Weldon to fill her kettle, and then noticing the shaky hands, said impulsively : 'Let me fill your kettle! Can I help you in any way? Make your tea? You look— not very well.'

'I am perfectly well, thank you,' was the cold reply; 'please finish at the tap and then I can fill mine. I do not wish to cause you any delay.'

The girl, thus rebuffed, said no more, but quickly filled her kettle and went back to her own room.

Mrs Weldon, kettle filled, put it on the gas ring and made her tea. She could eat nothing and had not the energy to dress properly.

And so she sat there all day, sometimes dozing over the fire which she had managed to light. She was very cold and kept feebly pulling her dressing-gown more fully around her. Towards evening the fire went out, for there was no more coal in the wooden box which Mrs O'Grady had given her as a coal and wood receptacle.

Poor Judy, whose fare had consisted of a few slices of bread and water, was miserable, but sensing that her mistress was the same, only pressed closer to the old woman, as if to give her sympathy and warmth.

When darkness fell, Faith Weldon got into bed and Judy crept in beside her. After a while she fell into an uneasy slumber, during which she wandered again in the garden at Clodagh, surrounded by her family—of whom not one remained with her now. That this had been partly her own fault, that she had been in any way to blame, the old woman had never admitted—and probably never believed.

But tonight she went back to those happy days of long ago— those days which were now 'as a tale that is told'.

At dawn she awoke in a fever, sick, wretched, her head aching, unable to breathe without pain. Frightfully thirsty, she made an effort to get out of bed and reach the water jug, but fell back again on the pillow.

She lay there, sick, alone, until a little before noon, when, through a haze of pain and weakness, she was conscious of someone knocking at the door. Judy, who was lying at her feet, pricked up her ears and began to bark, but almost immediately she was off the bed and sniffing hysterically at the door, her tail wagging furiously. She had recognised Ursula's voice.

The door was not locked and Ursula entered. She was shocked to see her great-grandmother lying there, evidently so ill, hardly able to speak.

'Grandmother!' she cried. 'What has happened? Are you ill?'

A silly question to ask, as she soon realised. The old woman turned her head feebly in her direction.

'Ursula,' she said, 'where have you been?'

Ursula could barely catch the words.

'I am here, grandmother—I came to see you.'

But the fevered mind was back in the past. 'You stayed late at Stone Lodge. Mary has your supper—'

The voice trailed away, and with a shock the girl understood that the old lady thought she was speaking to the other Ursula— her grandmother. In dismay she went to find Mrs O'Grady and ask where was the nearest telephone?

'At the shop across the street?—thank you. And will you please stay with Mrs Weldon while I am away? She should not have been left alone when she is so ill.'

Mrs O'Grady folded her arms. 'I was not aware,' she announced, 'that I was a hospital nurse engaged to wait upon my lodgers when they fall ill. She was up yesterday—said she had a little chill, that was all. I have not the time, let me tell you, young lady, to be looking after old people. It's the duty of them as belongs to them to do that, and if you are so anxious about the old lady—then why didn't you look after her yourself?'

Ursula fled from the landlady's tongue and rang up the River House and a doctor.

Very shortly the sick woman was surrounded with every comfort. The doctor would not allow her to be moved, so two nurses were engaged, one to come for night, the other for day; medicine, fires, nourishment—everything possible was done for her.

It was all useless. The Angel of Death—so long delayed—had come at last for Faith Weldon. Although she was not conscious of the fact, her son was with her in her dying hour, and his son and daughter, while Ursula, her great-granddaughter, hardly left her side. She did not know her son as he was now, but constantly called for 'Willie', and when she spoke of Ursula, it was the older Ursula—her own daughter—whom she meant.

The doctor diagnosed pneumonia. She had no chance from the first; her age, her worn out heart, the strain of the last months—all were against her in the fight for life. Not that she put up any fight.

They had tried to tell her about Clodagh, thinking that the good news might help her, but she did not understand what they meant. Happily for her she had forgotten the present, and during those last days on earth, Faith Weldon lived in the past. She would talk away in the high monotonous voice of the fever patient, about the garden, her husband, Willie at college—all the pleasant things of her life. The troubles and sorrows of more recent times seemed to have been erased from her memory.

On the fifth day of her illness, she awoke from an uneasy doze and looked around her. It was morning and a gleam of autumn sun gave promise of a fine day.

'A lovely morning,' she whispered, and asked the time.

They told her half-past eight.

'It is time the carriage was round, John,' she said. 'Dan should be here.' Then, after a moment she wandered again. 'Let us walk in the garden, how lovely it is in the spring—the perfume of the lilac—' Her voice sank to a whisper and she was silent for a little time. Then, quite suddenly, she raised herself in the bed and reached out her hand. 'Why—Faith!' she said, loudly. 'Little Faith—at last!'

She did not speak again.

CHAPTER XXI

CLODAGH: 1935

'So there is no hope for me, Ursula?'

The speaker was Denis McMahon. He was walking beside Ursula along the road from Whitechurch to Rathfarnham, on a certain day in the April of the year following Mrs Weldon's death.

Ursula was still at the River House, but no longer penniless. Legal action had been taken—or rather threatened—against the honest Isaac Isaacs, with the result that he had been glad to accept one thousand pounds as full payment of the loan of six hundred. As we know, seven hundred was the amount agreed upon, but of this sum one hundred had been retained by him for 'necessary expenses'. No doubt Isaacs felt most unjustly treated, but he quite realised that if the whole affair were to be made public it would be extremely bad for 'business'—in fact it would practically ruin him. So he agreed to what the lawyers proposed, and tried to pay up and look pleasant.

Mrs Weldon had long ago made her will leaving all she had to Ursula, and strange to say, she had left that will in the possession of Mr Manton, so the girl now found herself with two thousand pounds to her credit. She could not but be thankful. She had sorrowed much for her grandmother—as she still called her—and was inclined to blame herself for not looking after the old woman better. Yet it was hard to know how she could have done this. When the grace of conversion had been sent to her, she could not refuse to accept such an inestimable treasure. If only her grandmother had been less self-willed and determined, if she had allowed herself to move with the times—then things would surely have been different, and the old woman would have had her family around her happily at Clodagh.

However, it was no use thinking about that now. And here was the spring—'the sweet o' the year'—when all nature revives after the winter, and it is good to be alive.

Through the winter, Denis had written to Ursula frequently so that they had become real 'pen-friends'. Then two weeks ago he had come to Dublin for a holiday—and was there still. Mr Weldon had asked him to stay at the River House instead of going to a boarding-house or hotel, and Denis had been only too delighted. All the family liked Denis McMahon, he was so straightforward, so healthy in mind and body. They were hoping that Ursula would marry him as it was plain to see that he meant to ask her to do so. One thing had kept Denis back from doing so—and that was the news of her comfortable little fortune. He did not want to be looked upon as a fortune-hunter, and the knowledge that her money would be extremely useful to the farm only added to his distaste. He knew that Dublin people thought all country marriages were 'arranged', made matches, just as much as those marriages of convenience in higher ranks of society. And he quite realised that the fact that she *had* this money would weigh a great deal in his uncle's eyes. But as for Denis himself—he would have gone on his knees to her if she had not possessed one penny to her name.

The family at the River House watched the little play with amused eyes. All, that is except Jack. He, with his usual uncanny insight, had long ago guessed Ursula's secret.

Maureen was so full of her own plans, her own happiness, that she did not think about anything else. She and Terry were to be married in June; their marriage had been delayed on account of the death of old Mr Owens, Terry having to stay in New York to wind up all business affairs. For Terry did not intend to stay in America now, he meant to settle in Ireland—the land of his forefathers. He and Maureen would live at Clodagh. Terry had fallen in love with the old place the first time he had seen it, and already workmen and gardeners were in occupation so that all might be ready for the June bride.

So Maureen was living in the air, and her happiness blinded her a little to the joys or sorrows of other people. That was not her normal unselfish state, but at the moment it was hardly to be wondered at. 'Love's Young Dream' closes our eyes and ears to all things and people except the one beloved.

Maureen's wedding was to take place early in June and she was busy preparing for the great event, besides she had promised Terry to supervise the work at Clodagh. A new bathroom was being put in, electricity installed with all the labour-saving and modern devices which it brings with it. But these were to be arranged so as to disturb as little as possible the old-world atmosphere of Clodagh.

Today, Denis and Ursula had been to Clodagh to see how things were going on, as Maureen was shopping in town. And now, as they were walking leisurely homewards, Denis had put his courage to the test, and asked Ursula to marry him.

And she had said 'No'. Said it quietly, a little sadly, because she hated to give pain to anyone, and Denis was such a dear friend. 'I am so sorry, Denis,' she had said, 'but I cannot marry you.'

He had paled under his tan and did not speak for a moment. Then, with his eyes following the skirmishings of Judy in the hedge, but not even seeing the dog, he had asked: 'Can you tell me whether there is any particular reason why you cannot marry me?'

There was a slight pause before the reply came.

'Yes,' she said then, 'there is a very particular reason.'

She did not look at him as she spoke, and the lovely colour flooded her face. As he watched her, the heart of Denis sank.

'Is it—is it someone else?' he asked.

She bowed her head without speaking and they continued their way in silence. Suddenly she turned and looked at him.

'Denis,' she said, softly, 'cannot you guess *who* that Someone is?'

He knew then. And as the knowledge flooded his soul, he realised that he had always known that there was something about Ursula which seemed to set her apart from other girls of his acquaintance. He had tried to think that it was just that she was more reserved than the others. But now he understood. He knew Whose Bride she was to be.

'Ursula,' he said, 'you—you are going to enter————?'

'Yes, I am entering the Order of the Poor Clares in July—after Maureen's marriage. I should have told you sooner—I feel that now—but no one knows yet except Uncle Jack—he knows everything.'

She smiled at him now, a very happy smile. 'We must always remember our friendship,' she said, 'and pray for one another.'

She held out her hand as a seal of their friendship and he stopped and lifted it to his lips.

'Good-bye, my dear,' he said. 'And God bless you. You *will* remember me sometimes in your prayers?'

'Always, dear Denis—always.'

They were nearing Rathfarnham now and he said suddenly: 'Would you mind if I went for a bit of a walk by myself? I think that it would do me good.'

He tried to smile and she nodded, the tears in her eyes. Denis turned on his heel and went back the way they had come.

He felt that only a lonely walk could help him now; a walk which would make him so physically tired that he would crave but to lie down and sleep. He wondered if he could tire himself that much. He was strong and so used to walking long distances that it would be hard to get really tired. Then he saw the hills, standing sentinel against the sky. 'I will lift up mine eyes unto the hills,' he murmured, 'from whence cometh my help.' He strode on in their direction. Onwards and upwards he went until the summit of Mont Pelier was reached. There he flung himself down near the ruins of what was supposed to have been the Hell Fire Club. He knew its story and wondered how much of it was true? If there was any truth at all in the tales of the wild orgies held there in the eighteenth century, surely the place should be haunted—as many affirm it is. But Denis felt no sense of evil, was conscious of nothing beyond a feeling of absolute peace.

It was dark when he left the spot and late when he reached the River House, but nothing was said, no remark passed. Ursula had taken the family into her confidence that evening after tea, and told them everything. She had thought it best to do this and so no one was surprised, or made any expostulation, when Denis announced that he found he would have to return to Westmeath the following day.

He did not look at Ursula when he said good-bye, just barely touching her hand in farewell. But she understood.

It was a lovely evening in late June, in the year of Our Lord, 1935. Ten o'clock, summer time, half-past eight by the sun. In the garden of Clodagh, Terence and Maureen are walking arm in arm. They have returned that very day from their honeymoon in Achill, and, much as they had enjoyed their time on the wild western seaboard, they were glad to be home.

'Achill is grand, of course, Terry,' Maureen was saying, 'and it was great to hear the Gaelic all round one. But for me there is no place—no place in the whole world—like dear old Dublin.'

'I agree,' he replied. 'Do you remember that first time you sang Lady Dufferin's 'Bay of Dublin'—on that picnic we had to the Feather Bed Mountain, when the Bay lay down below us in all its beauty? I thought it the most lovely song I had ever heard. Often while I was away in New York, walking perhaps along Broadway, I would find myself whistling:

> '"Oh, Bay of Dublin,
> My heart you're troublin'."'

'Dear Terry!' murmured Maureen, and rubbed her cheek against his coat.

A little black cocker who had been rushing up and down the path in wild excitement, now came up to them, wagging her tail and barking joyously.

'Well, Judy—glad to be home again, old girl?' asked Terry. Judy shook herself as she always did when excited, and started to race up the path. Then, suddenly, without any apparent cause, she stopped dead, stood still for a moment, like a dog who is 'pointing'. Then she turned tail and ran back to Maureen, pressing close against her, shaking all over.

'What is it, Judy? What is the matter?' asked Maureen.

The dog whined a little, but still shook as if with fear.

'Oh Terry—what can be the matter with her?'

'I can't think,' he replied, 'unless she's cold. And now that I notice it, the evening does seem to have turned rather cold. Don't you think so, Maureen?'

There was no reply, but Terry felt the hand on his arm tremble, and glancing at Maureen was surprised to see that she had grown very pale.

'What is it, darling?' he asked. She said nothing, but stood still as if listening. Terry found himself listening also, and as they so stood, with Judy pressed closely to them, they heard, coming down the garden path, the tap-tap of high-heeled shoes. Nearer and nearer they came; there was the *frou-frou* of billowing silken skirts, a tiny tinkle of laughter. So close did it seem that instinctively they drew aside to let it pass. Tap-tap went the shoes along the path, passing close, then away from them, growing fainter each second. Presently they could be heard no more and there came silence.

They stood and looked at each other, pale and startled. Then Terry said: 'We must have fancied it, dearest—we were thinking of her.' No need for him to say who it was he meant. 'There was nothing there—nothing.'

'But there *was*, Terry! It was grandmother as she was that night when she, too, came home a bride.'

'My darling—you must not imagine such things—you will frighten yourself—'

'I am not frightened—oh, not frightened! I am *glad!* Don't you see, Terry, it means that she has forgiven us—that she wants us to be happy—just as she was happy here all those years ago.'

Terry kissed her, and said: 'And please God we will be happy! But come, let us go indoors now—it *has* turned cold—or so I think.'

'It has been a lovely day,' replied Maureen, trying to pull herself together, to talk of ordinary things. 'What a glorious sunset we had.'

'Yes—glorious—and promising a glorious morrow.'

Hand in hand they went towards the house, a little black cocker, still a trifle uneasy, keeping close to their heels.

Looking down upon them, the windows of the old house seemed to smile a welcome.

Clodagh had come into its own again.

THE WALK OF A QUEEN
Annie M.P. Smithson

'. . . Desmond raised his eyes and looked at her. She had let her cloak fall on to the back of her chair, and her beautiful shoulders gleamed like polished ivory above the dead gold of her gown, while her great mass of hair shone like hot ashes when they are stirred. He could only look and look again – all his heart in his eyes, and he, who was always so self-possessed, so perfectly at home when talking to the opposite sex, now felt as tongue-tied and gauche as any schoolboy . . .'

In *The Walk of a Queen* the scene is set in Dublin during the War of Independence and it is a fascinating story of passion and intrigue which holds the reader's interest from start to finish.